James C. Mac Intosh

THE GRAVEYARD GAME
A Tale of Suspense

By
James C. MacIntosh

authorHOUSE™

1663 LIBERTY DRIVE, SUITE 200
BLOOMINGTON, INDIANA 47403
(800) 839-8640
WWW.AUTHORHOUSE.COM

This book is a work of fiction. People, places, events, and situations are the product of the author's imagination. Any resemblance to actual persons, living or dead, or historical events, is purely coincidental.

© 2005 James C. MacIntosh. All Rights Reserved.

No part of this book may be reproduced, stored in a retrieval system, or transmitted by any means without the written permission of the author.

First published by AuthorHouse 07/25/05

ISBN: 1-4208-6051-8 (e)
ISBN: 1-4208-6050-X (sc)

Library of Congress Control Number: 2005904938

Printed in the United States of America
Bloomington, Indiana

This book is printed on acid-free paper.

CHAPTER ONE

Young Paul McCulloch ran through the woods, his heart pounding. Small tree branches poked and tweaked his face, but he kept on running, until finally, after ascending a steep hill, he stopped. Placing his hands on his knees, he bent forward, gasping for breath.

After a moment, he summoned the courage to turn and look back down the hill. Staring into the darkness, his gaze was greeted only by the movement of low-lying bushes gently undulating in the soft nighttime breeze.

His thoughts turned to his three friends, Larch, Ritchie and Larry." *They must have run off in a different direction, but they'll be okay, they're probably all home already*", he thought. "Please, God, help *me* get home….. why did I take this shortcut through the woods? Why didn't I stay on the road? The road….if I run down this hill, I can get back on the road, where it will be safer. That's if nothing gets me before then, something from behind a tree, or a bush. Oh, please, <u>please</u> God, help me make it to the road."

Hearing a slight rattling noise, Paul spun around, but there was nothing there. Then he noticed the stand of poplars about forty feet away and realized it was just the wind moving their leaves, making the same rattling sound as the little poplar tree in his yard, over by the outdoor fireplace his dad built. Oh, how he wished he could be there now, safe at 12 Hillside Road, with his dad beside him. He became aware that he could feel the pulse in his temple beating and reached up to feel the enlarged vein, surprised at how it throbbed under his finger.

Paul turned toward an old animal path that he knew would lead him down to the lower portion of Boundary Road, just below "Crazy Roger's" house.

Roger Carey was a seventeen-year old troublemaker, who liked two things: annoying people and flat-out scaring them half to death. He once described to Paul and his friends how he had hung a stray cat in a tree in the woods, then threw stones at it until it was dead. And he laughingly recounted how he had once tied two cats together by their tails, with jute twine and then had watched them scratch each other's eyes out. Those same friends had all stood together at the top of a ridge, watching Crazy Roger engage in vicious combat with another seventeen-year old on an old, partially grown-over cart path in a long gorge below them. The skirmish was over quickly, with no apparent winner, but Paul and his three friends were frightened by the brutality of the fight. Paul was fearful of "Crazy Roger", but, at this moment, even Roger Carey would be a welcome sight to the terrified twelve-year old.

A sudden chill ran down his spine and he felt his whole body convulse in a shuddery spasm. Turning quickly, Paul broke into a hard run down the animal path, this time knowing he would not stop until he was safely at home, where his Mom and Dad were sure to be settled down by now, Dad in his big easy chair, with the newspaper, Mom in her straight-back rocker, probably knitting. Neither of them would be aware of the danger their son was in. When he scurried out of the house after supper, he said he'd be riding his bike with his friends at the end of the street, near the woods.

As Paul ran, he tried to think comforting thoughts, but the safety of home seemed far distant from the darkness of the woods that never before were so deep or so scary. It was hard for him to believe that earlier this afternoon, he, his three friends, Henry "Larch" Stolarczek, Ritchie Bledsoe and Larry Guernette, had played soldiers in the same spot where he now ran for his life.

Finally, Paul sees a raised section of pavement coming into view and his fear starts to ease slightly. He can also see the roof of Crazy Roger's house.

"NO!" from some inner depth of his subconscious mind, a voice cries out.

"*No, what?*" Paul wondered to himself.

"TURN AWAY!" The voice is adamant.

"*From what? Turn away from WHAT.*"

Ignoring the irritating inner voice, Paul contents himself with the thought that soon he'll be safely walking under the streetlight on Boundary Road, in the section where there are lots of houses. Nothing or no one will get him there, with enough people around. His dad always said there is safety in numbers. Now Paul could appreciate what those words meant.

He knows he is running too fast down the path, but keeps on at full stride.

Now, he hears his mother calling him. "Paul….Paul…. Someone or something is grabbing his arm! A sharp pain cuts into his *ankle*.

Then, there came a blinding flash of light, pain and a sickening thud.

Paul……PAUL, WAKE UP! Gasping, he lurches forward, trying to pull his arm free and opening his eyes, looks into the concerned face of Mary Ellen, his wife of thirty-four years. Looking around, Paul realizes he is sitting in his living room recliner.

The fear he felt moments before melted away in the soft, gentle features of Mary Ellen's face, as the realization that he was dreaming slowly took hold. She rested her left leg on the arm of his recliner, letting her grip on his arm ease and slid her left arm around the back of his head in a single motion, so that her hand caressed his cheek. She pulled his head slowly to her breast and with her right arm, cuddled him closely. He did not resist.

"Sweetheart, you were having another nightmare", she said. "This one was a bad one."

"Oh, God!" Paul said, as he cupped his hands over his face.

"I really wish you would talk to someone about them, Paul. They're occurring more frequently, now and I'm afraid it's starting to affect your health."

"Aw, Mare, what am I supposed to do, go to a shrink and tell him I have a bad dream once in a while? He'll laugh me out of his office……. everybody has nightmares from time to time"…

"They're not 'once in a while', Paul, this is at least the fifth one you've had this week……..and they're getting worse……look at you, you're covered with sweat, you're breathing hard, this is not natural, no these aren't your run-of-the-mill nightmares and I'm getting really worried for you, Honey."

"This is the fifth one that she knows about" he thought.

Paul broke free from his wife's embrace and rose from the chair, reaching into his pocket for his handkerchief. He wiped the sweat from his brow and dragged the cloth down the side of each cheek, finishing with a sweep around the back of his neck. He returned the handkerchief to his pants pocket

"I'm not going to a shrink!"

"Paul, you're being stubborn and foolish. You've got to get rid of this hang-up you have, that it's not 'manly' to see a psychologist. If you would just…"

"Mary Ellen, I'm not going to go see a shrink, period. It has nothing to do with not feeling manly and everything to do with feeling like a jackass, telling a psychologist I'm having 'bad dreams' like a little kid, who's afraid of the dark."

Mary Ellen stood up, faced her husband and reached for his hands, lifting them both slightly in hers. "Paul, listen to me closely; if you were to see someone about these dreams, there's a very good chance they could get to the root of the problem and maybe get them to stop. If, however, you choose to ignore them…..well, you know they're only going to get worse. Not only have they been more frequent, they are getting longer and seem to be more upsetting to you than when they first started. Look at yourself in the mirror and you'll see the effect that the loss of sleep has had on you."

"But I'd feel like a damn fool telling someone about …."

"Honey, do you think you're the only person who has problems that you're reluctant to discuss? A good therapist is going to put you at ease and I promise, will not 'laugh you out of his office'. Will you at least consider it; for me?"

"Mare, you know when you look at me with those beautiful brown eyes, it's pretty much all over for me. Yes, I will think about it, I promise."

She leaned forward, kissed him softly on the lips and touched his cheek.

"Thank you." she said.

"What's for supper?" he asked.

Mary Ellen laughed. "I guess the dreams don't bother your stomach at all."

"Well, I kind of skipped lunch today....I had to run a couple of errands, so right now, I'm really starved.

"Believe it or not, I had just started supper, when I heard you moaning and thrashing about in here, so I'll finish peeling the potatoes and......

"Never mind the potatoes. We're going out to eat tonight. It's the least I can do for all of the aggravation I've put you through this week."

"You don't have to do that, Paul. I can have your meal ready in a short while."

"I insist, besides, we could both use a break from the routine."

Mary Ellen placed her hands on her hips, in a feigned indignant posture. "Oh, so my meals are just 'routine' are they?"

Paul slipped both of his arms around her waist and pulled her to him, looking into her eyes. "You're still so beautiful! How did a schmuck like me ever end up with a gorgeous chick like you?"

She laughed more heartily this time. "I'm afraid my 'chick' days are over, but I'll see what I can do to cover up this old wrinkled face before we go out.'"

"Get outta here," he laughingly said, as she turned to walk away. Paul reached out and gave her butt a light tap, causing his wife to skip playfully on her way to her makeup station on the bedroom dresser.

Fifty-eight year old Paul McCulloch stood there in the living room, thinking how truly lucky he was. He was fairly successful in his career as an electrician, earning enough to live comfortably and also happy in this line of work.

Mary Ellen had given him two great kids, Mike, 33 and Kathy, 30, both on their own now, Mike, himself, married and father of two boys. Kathy hadn't married, but was doing well as a Customs Inspector at Logan Airport. She dated, but was in no hurry to settle down.

His marriage to Mary Ellen had been the end result of a childhood romance. To friends, theirs was the classic love story. Paul never tired of telling folks openly how much he loved his wife, how lost he would be without her.

One thing Paul knew, for sure, was that Mary Ellen was right on the money when she said his nightmares were getting more frequent and were also getting worse. This one was the worst yet and he was still a little shaky. *"What the hell is always chasing me?"* he wondered to himself.

The one thing Paul and Mary Ellen didn't know was that, in the next fifty one hours, this man's perfect life would become no less than a *living* nightmare.

CHAPTER TWO

5:42 p.m., Tuesday, August 17, 2004

The phone rang in Henry Stolarczek's office, just as he was about to close the door on his way out. He paused in the doorway, until the answering machine kicked in. Henry was surprised to hear Paul McCulloch's voice, as it had been a while since they had been in touch.

"Hey Larch", the voice said, "How are things going? In case you don't recognize the voice, this is Paul McCulloch. Hey, buddy, when you get a chance, give me a buzz, maybe we can have a coffee or something. Actually, Hank, can you call me ASAP? There's something I need to ask you.......in private. It's no big deal, but I need to know the answer to a problem that's been bugging me and I think you're the only guy who knows it. Thanks, Larch. Catch ya later."

Henry stood there for a moment wondering what was on Paul's mind. McCulloch wasn't the kind of guy to ask for anyone's advice, or to sit in a coffee shop. *"I should call him right back, but it can wait till morning, I'm really tired and hungry.......but what if it's something important....aw shit!"*

Setting his canvas bag full of blueprints down on the floor, he hurried over to the phone on the desk and thumbed through his beat-up Rolodex for his old friend's number. After locating it, he dialed up Paul's house and then waited as the phone rang several times, then the message, "Hi, you've reached the McCulloch residence; we can't come to ...."

Henry waited for the message to finish, then at the beep, said; "Paul, what's up? I just got your message on the way out of my office. I hope everything's okay. What did you do, hang up the phone and run out of the house? Jeez, I called you right away. Listen, I usually stop at Forbes for coffee in the morning, after I get my crews set up, which is around 8:30 to 8:45. I'm buying, if you want to stop. I'll look for you."

Henry Vincent Stolarczek ran a construction company, which did very well. An honest man, by nature, he was well liked and respected in the community. "Larch", as he was known since childhood, had never married. His best friend since pre-school days had always been Paul McCulloch. They grew up three houses away from each other on the same street in the little town of Sheridan and their childhood days were filled with adventures, from sledding on the big hill in Donovan's field and throwing snowballs at passing cars on the road below, to summertime hikes in the woods, usually to the mud pond a half mile in behind Talbert's house, where they would spend hours catching frogs, turtles, salamanders and anything else that moved in the water, then sneaking into old Mr. Gradowski's apple orchard, stealing the green apples and eating them behind his privet hedge. They almost always ended up with bellyaches.

Henry was two years younger than Paul and had always looked up to him as an older brother. He admired the way Paul was always trying to find something different to do throughout their childhood. Life around McCulloch was interesting and sometimes exciting…..like the time Paul talked him into going into the old abandoned house at the furthest end of their street, only after it got really dark, then telling him once they were inside, how the old hermit who used to live there, had committed suicide by hanging himself…."RIGHT THERE", Paul screamed, his eyes wide with mock horror, as he pretended to see something behind Henry. This action had almost caused Henry to wet his pants, but he soon found himself laughing nervously with Paul, who was bent over, holding his stomach, giggling, until tears came to his eyes.

Despite the fact that Paul McCulloch was the quintessential practical joker, it was almost impossible to get angry with him and if you did, you couldn't stay that way for long. Paul just had this way about him and you knew that whenever someone got him good, he'd laugh the hardest. *"He could pitch, but he could also catch pretty well."* Larch thought to himself.

Setting the phone back on the receiver, Larch sat down in the chair off to the side of his desk, the one that visitors to his office usually sat in and continued in his reverie, remembering how a summer's day just could not be complete for Paul, without some sort of adventure mixed in, at some point. Most of the adventures seemed designed to test your courage. It was as if he was trying to prove to his buddies that he wasn't afraid of anything……..and he pretty much wasn't.

A long distant memory popped up again of the old abandoned house, where Paul had almost scared the life out of his younger friend. This memory was of another night, when Paul came up with the idea of one guy in the group having to enter the house through the front door, climb the stairs to the second floor, wave out the window to the assembled boys below, then descend the stairs and exit the house from the *back* door and calmly walk back to the front yard, where he would receive a few pats on the back from his impressed buddies. For a bunch of pre-teen boys, this was the height of bravery.

Larch, Ritchie and Larry had planned to set up Paul for a really good scare on the night when it would be his turn to go into the house. The boys had cajoled Ritchie's father, [who was only too willing] to help them in their plot. Ritchie Bledsoe's dad had been the recipient of one of Paul's pranks, driving his new Buick down the street two weeks after he'd put it on the road and hearing a loud, steady, clanking sound. Upon investigation, he discovered the source of the noise; stones, in both of his front hubcaps. Later, when Ritchie, Larch and Paul walked through his kitchen, Paul had said: "How's the new car running, Mister B? Nice and quiet, I hope." Then, when Ritchie's dad made eye contact with Paul, he was greeted with a sly wink and that infectious smile.

"When you least expect it, Paulie, it might be tomorrow, or six months from now, but I *will* make you pay. Remember that, boy."

Paul McCulloch giggled and joined his friends in Ritchie's room, where they checked out the latest additions to Ritchie's baseball card collection.

Larch remembered Ritchie's dad as a strange man, thin and small in stature, who walked with a pronounced limp. He recalled him as a smarmy sort of guy who had a kind of edge to him, that Larch now assumed must have been the result of taunting from co-workers. His attitude towards Ritchie's friends was brusque and surly. Larch had thought that maybe Paul made a mistake playing a practical joke on this man. His threat to Paul seemed too childish for a grown man.

But on this night, the plan was for Mr. Bledsoe to sneak into the house through the back door, hide behind a doorway, then jump out and scare Paul as he made his way through the house.

The plan worked perfectly, with the unsuspecting victim entering the house to take his turn with the unseen "spooks" that haunted the old dilapidated house [or at least the minds of the boys] and Ritchie's father patiently waiting in what he perceived to be the best place to leap out and catch the little wise guy by complete surprise and scare the bejabbers out of him.

Everything seemed to be in place for the cunning conspiracy. Paul entered the house through the front door and disappeared into the dark interior. The three boys huddled together across the street, giggling in anticipation of what was to soon transpire. In a moment, their friend would come running out the front door, screaming at the top of his lungs, with a terrified look on his face, for sure. McCulloch was about to get his due. Finally, they'd get him back this one *good* one, for all the times he'd gotten them.

For a long while, no sound emanated from inside the old house. Minutes passed. Then, the stillness of the summer evening was broken by a shrill, piercing, half-scream, followed by the gravelly voice of Mr. Bledsoe unleashing a torrent of obscenities, in a steadily escalating rage.

"GODDAMMIT YOU LITTLE SON OF A BITCH, WHAT THE HELL DID YOU DO TO ME? You DAMN NEAR scared the

LIFE out of me. Get the HELL out of my sight before I put you over my KNEE, YOU LITTLE BASTARD! What the HELL IS WRONG WITH YOU?"

Mr. Bledsoe stomped out the front door, muttering curses loud enough for the boys to realize he was not a happy man, as if they weren't already well aware of that fact.

Pointing his still-shaking finger at his son, he loudly exclaimed; "RICHARD, GET YOUR ASS HOME……NOW! I don't know if I want you playing………COME ON……NOW!

Seconds later, Paul exited the house from the back door, walked calmly around the side of the house, then spotting the huddled boys, broke into a wide grin.

Luckily, for Paul McCulloch, Mr. Bledsoe didn't see him grinning. Still, the enraged man turned back to him, waving his finger inches from Paul's face.

"YOU THINK YOU'RE A REAL SMART-ASS, DON'T YOU?

"Mr. Bledsoe, I'm sorry….I didn't think you'd get mad….. I was just having fun."

"IS THERE SOMETHING WRONG WITH YOU? DO YOU THINK IT'S FUN TO …….never mind."

"I'm really sorry, Mr. Bledsoe. You're a nice guy and I don't want you to …."

Paul was stopped in mid-sentence by the upraised hand of Jeremiah Bledsoe, in a gesture which seemed to indicate an impending truce to the hostilities. It was apparent to Larch and the two boys standing with him on the opposite side of the narrow street that Ritchie's dad now realized he had really lost his temper and felt quite foolish about it.

"Well….maybe I flew off the handle a little bit."

"*A little bit!*" Paul thought. "*You almost slugged me, you old fool!*"

Now, a complete transformation took place, as Bledsoe chuckled, then tousled the boy's hair. "You got me AGAIN, Paulie, you're a sly one. Look, I'm sorry I tried to bite your head off. I didn't mean to say those nasty …"

"That's okay, Mr. Bledsoe. I know you didn't mean what you said. I guess I had it coming, though. Are you going to tell my father?"

"No need for that!" Bledsoe replied. He held out his hand. "No hard feelings?"

"Absolutely not, sir." Paul said as he placed his hand in the calloused hand of his friend's now calm father.

Bledsoe turned to his son, who was nervously shifting from one foot to the other.

"Come on, Richard, it's time to go home."

"Aw, Daddy, can I just stay out a little longer?"

"Fifteen minutes. That's all!"

The still-embarrassed man sheepishly headed back to his house, upset with himself for letting a twelve-year-old get the best of him, but, at the same time glad that he had made things right.

The three boys turned to Paul, all trying to talk at once.

Larch asked the most obvious question. "What did you do to him?"

"Well, to begin with, before we all got here, I saw Ritchie's dad walking through the woods in back of my house and I watched to see where he went. I followed him and saw him sneaking into the back door here"…pointing toward the abandoned building. "I figured that because it was my turn to go in the house, you guys and him must have been planning to get me, so I went back home, then came down the street, so you wouldn't think I knew…"

"Yeah, but what did you do to get him so mad?" asked Larry.

Paul giggled, remembering how he outfoxed Mr. Bledsoe.

"I went in the front door, like you guys saw, then waited for my eyes to adjust to the dark, so I could figure out where he was hiding. I didn't see him anywhere, so I figured he must either be upstairs, or hiding behind the archway between the two back rooms. I didn't want to go upstairs, 'cause I knew if he *was* up there, he'd probably scare me good, so I quietly climbed out the opening where the kitchen window used to be, on the far side of the house, sneaked along the side to the window at the first back room and peeked in. Sure, enough, there he was, behind the archway, leaning forward, waiting to scare me.

Larry was growing impatient. Yeah, but what did you *do* to him?"

Paul calmly continued. "I grabbed a small branch, snuck back to the kitchen window opening, crawled back in and real quietly tiptoed over to the far end of the archway. Then, I went around the left side and came up behind Mr. "B" and slowly brought the stick up to the back of his head, then lowered it, so it touched his neck. You should a seen him jump....gees, he almost came out of his skin."

At this point, Ritchie broke in. "I don't think that was so funny, McCulloch. You're lucky my daddy didn't smack you one."

"*You're lucky my daddy didn't smack you one*" chided Larry. "Why don't you just call him Dada, you little baby.

"Shut up, Guernette!"

"Baby, baby, bay...bee."

"I SAID SHUT UP, GUERNETTE."

"Make me, Lard-o, your 'daddy's a fraidy cat anyhow. He's a baby, just like you!

Ritchie leaped forward, grabbing Larry's shirt with his left hand and swinging a roundhouse right, which Larry was quick enough to duck back from. The combined momentum of Ritchie's advance, however, along with his considerable mass, sent Larry sprawling on his back, with the larger boy on top of him.

Frantically, Larry peppered the left side of Ritchie's head with quick, sharp blows, causing the inexperienced fighter to roll to his right in an attempt to get away from the punches, thereby losing the advantage he had held only seconds before.

This action gave Larry the break he needed, as he quickly slid out from under his adversary and just as quickly swung his right leg over Ritchie's stomach, still pounding away relentlessly at his sweaty head.

Now, simply trying to defend himself against the onslaught, Ritchie put both of his hands over his face, which allowed Larry to mount him fully. From this position, he began to launch a new series of punches, using both hands on the helpless, prone body which lay beneath him.

This was where Larch and Paul stepped in. The winner was clear and letting it go any further was pointless.

There was a code of principles which these boys upheld strongly. If two guys were fighting, it was allowed to continue without interference, as long as it took to determine a clear winner. The only condition which would necessitate stopping a fair fight was when it stopped being fair, when one combatant held such a distinct advantage over the other that serious bodily harm would likely result.

Paul and Larry had witnessed such a battle that past spring, in the schoolyard. Two eighth grade boys, both appearing to be evenly matched, wrestled on the ground, with one boy lying across the head of the other, ignoring the cries from the crowd gathered around that the one on the bottom had stopped moving. Due to the fact that Jeff, the kid on top, was tougher and bigger than anyone watching, no one dared to pull him off.

When the winner finally stood up, a gasp went out from the circle of onlookers. The beaten boy lay lifeless on the asphalt, his face a blotchy red color. Two girls ran for a teacher, but, luckily, by the time she arrived, the boy had come to and was sitting up, dazed and gulping for breaths of air.

Larch remembered Paul telling him about that fight and how it had bothered him that no one, including himself, had been brave enough to stop it. He had vowed to Larch then and there, that he would get their small group to make a pact to never let something like that happen in any scraps they might get into with each other.

"Billy could have been killed, Larch and the worst part was that, I *knew* he could have been killed, but *still* I was afraid to push Jeff off him."

"Hey, NO one would a dared to push Jeff off of him, Paul." Larch had replied, in an effort to cheer up his friend. Then laughing, said; "Unless you wanted to commit suicide."

This fight between Larry and Ritchie was a vivid reminder to Paul of the schoolyard clash that upset him that spring day and he was quick to react. Throwing himself against Larry, he pulled him off Ritchie, yelling "Alright, that's enough!"

Larch helped push Larry away and then leaned over to help Ritchie to his feet, while Larry struggled against Paul's grip. Turning around, he used both hands to push Paul's shoulders hard, causing the mediator to fall backward a couple of steps.

"What's *your* problem, McCulloch?"

"YOU, you jerk! What were you trying to do, kill him?"

"He started it."

"No, he didn't, Larry and you *know* it. You're the one that was calling him and his father names."

By this time, Ritchie was on his feet and yelled to Paul: "I DON'T NEED YOU TO FIGHT MY BATTLES, McCULLOCH!"

This was too much for Larch. "That's right, Rich, you were hitting his fists so many times with your face, I can't believe he didn't cry 'UNCLE'."

"It ain't funny, Stolarczek."

Larry, Paul and Larch burst out laughing, but it only infuriated the beaten fighter.

Now, with tears flowing down his ruddy cheeks, Ritchie launched into a verbal attack on Paul.

"I used to think you were my friend, Paul, but now I'm not so sure. That was a rotten thing you did to my da......my father."

"Hey Ritchie, are you forgetting what he was going to do to me?"

"Yeah, big deal, he was going to scare you. You really made fun of him when you were telling these guys....."

"Hold on a minute, Rich, I never made fun of your dad; I never *would* make fun of him. I think your dad is a pretty brave guy. I think he's a hero."

"Why do you say that?"

"Because my dad told me why your dad walks with a limp,"

"Is this going to be another one of your jokes? 'Cause, if it is........"

Ritchie's shoulders lurched up and down in uncontrollable spasms as the culmination of the evening's events overtook him. He sobbed bitterly in tearful hiccup-like breaths, while his three friends watched somberly, not quite sure what they should do, or say.

It was Paul, who stepped toward the distraught boy and placed his hand on one of the heaving shoulders.

"This isn't a joke, I swear! My father told me that during the war, your dad was fighting in France. His unit got surrounded by Germans and some of the guys panicked, but not your dad. He saw a machine-gunner that was pinning his guys down and ran toward him. He had to take cover behind two dead guys, but from there, he knew he couldn't reach the gunner with a grenade, so he got up and ran closer, but one of the machine-gunner's sidekicks shot him in the leg. Your dad fell down, but managed to throw the grenade and took out the gun with a bull's-eye throw, and then stood up and shot four other Germans. His buddies saw this and over ran the whole bunch!"

Paul slipped his arm around Ritchie's shoulder.

"My dad says he respects your dad, because he's a real man, even though he may not be as big as other men. That's why I said I think your dad's a hero."

Giving his shoulder a squeeze, Paul continued: "I would NEVER make fun of your dad, Rich, ya gotta believe that!"

Wiping his face with the lower part of his tee-shirt, Ritchie sniffled and said: "I'm going home, now."

Then, turning to Paul, he forced a smile, which was interrupted by an involuntary snort. "I never knew that about my daddy. He never, ever talks about the war."

Paul, Larch and Larry stood silently, watching their bedraggled buddy walk out of sight. It was Larry, who spoke first.

"Wow, I didn't know that either." Then, looking toward his house, said: "I guess I'll go home, too."

Once Larry had walked away, Larch stared at Paul, his mouth partly open and moving slightly, as if he were trying to ask a question, but didn't know how.

"WHAT?" asked Paul, slightly exasperated.

"Did his father really do all that stuff?"

"Naw....... my dad said he was just hit by a piece of shrapnel, but I thought Ritchie needed to hear something good about his old man, cause he really looked bad tonight! Plus, Ritchie stood up for him and I thought that was cool.

Larch stood and stared a long while at Paul, who returned his stare with a goofy look, causing both boys to erupt in a burst of laughter.

It was at that moment that Henry "Larch" Stolarczek knew his choice for a 'best' friend had been a good one.

CHAPTER THREE

"Are you coming to bed, now?" Mary Ellen wanted to know. "It's after eleven."

"I think I'll stay up a while. I'm not that tired and if I go in now, I'll just toss and turn." Paul lied, but even though he was tired, the idea of falling asleep to endure the same terrifying dream again, was something he wanted no part of. Maybe if he stayed up until he was exhausted, he'd be less likely to have the nightmare.

If he could stay awake through the eleven o'clock news, then he was sure he'd be able to make it through the late night talk shows, which he enjoyed.

The evening had gone well for Paul and Mary Ellen. They enjoyed their meal at the Red Barn, one of their favorite eating out spots, just outside of Worcester. After, they had driven to a local shopping mall and walked along the concourse, occasionally window shopping, but mostly talking. They talked about the kids, friends, relatives and Paul's work, but did not discuss the nightmares, much to Paul's relief. Mary Ellen was good about things like that. She was not the type of wife who nagged. She spoke her piece, put it out in the open and let it go. But this situation was different and Paul knew his wife would not be satisfied until he agreed to talk to someone about it.

Although the television newscast was on, Paul sat transfixed, staring blankly at the screen. His thoughts were on what his plan of action was going to be. How would he choose a psychologist? How does anyone choose one? Do you ask trusted friends, or just look one up in the phone book? Could someone really help me?

Paul jumped up and walked over to the phone table, scooping the heavy book from the lower shelf, then returned to his recliner and plopped down. Thumbing through the yellow pages, he first looked under "Physicians", but found only a long alphabetical list of medical doctors. Flipping forward a dozen or so pages, he found "Psychologists", but, as he scanned down the listings, what he kept seeing were clinics and large groups, which called themselves "associates". Some of these ads were big boxes, with perhaps as many as a dozen names in them. This was not what he was looking for.

Finally, near the bottom of the second column, one name jumped out at him: "Nathan Feldmar, PhD Licensed Clinical Psychologist, 412 Juniper Parkway." No box with other names, no long listing of precisely what he treated, "*just the facts, ma'am*", Paul thought.

Continuing on down to the end of the listings, Paul noticed three other names of "lone wolves", two women and a man, but he kept going back to Nathan Feldmar, whose location was also appealing, as a visit to his office would not require going into the heart of the city, trying to find a parking space, then worrying in the doctor's office that the time would run out on the meter.

"This is the guy." Paul whispered to himself, then looking toward the bedroom, as if he expected to see Mary Ellen standing there and satisfied that she was sound asleep, he spoke aloud to himself again; "I'll give him a call first thing in the morning."

Morning, however, was still hours away and the realization that sleep, or an attempt to sleep, would soon be necessary, crept up on Paul. Grabbing the remote, he shut the television off, rejuvenated by the hope that calling Nathan Feldmar first thing tomorrow morning would at least get the ball rolling towards a possible end to these wretched dreams.

Paul brushed his teeth, tiptoed into the bedroom, glanced at his sleeping wife and slid out of his slacks and shirt. Easing into bed, he pulled the covers partly up, folding them over just below his armpits. Happy with the relief he now felt as a result of his determination to call Nathan Feldmar, he quickly fell off to sleep.

The path that lay ahead was a familiar one. It was the same path Paul and his friends used on their mostly summertime hikes to the mud pond, where they would wile away many carefree hours. His friends were not with him now, though and it wasn't daytime, but just after dusk. Still, Paul's subconscious mind felt a strange sense of relief, as if his determination to enjoy a good night's sleep had set the tone for a tranquil dream.

There was something else, however, in this dream. Paul *knew* he was dreaming and even though the dream location was in the same vicinity as his ongoing nightmare, he couldn't be sure whether the person in the dream was Paul McCulloch the boy, or Paul McCulloch the man. An awareness of an adult presence startled him. *"No, I'm the grown-up here and you're not going to scare me."* Paul's attempt to reassure himself in his dream state was only partly successful and a worried shiver engulfed his body.

"The adult presence is ME! It MUST be me!"

With lightning-fast speed, Paul is suddenly transported down the pathway, unable to slow himself, passing by bushes and trees at a blurring pace. He kicks his legs, trying to dig them into the ground, but, still he is propelled forward, by some un-see-able dream force, toward the mud pond.

Fear now starts to invade the dream, as the thought of being thrust head first into the mud pond creeps into his subconscious state. This notion, though, was quickly erased, as Paul was swept by the lower end of the pond. Seeing water splashing out from his feet reminded him of a water skier, or, possibly, a car speeding through a puddle in the road.

Paul now realizes that he is heading to the field where his terror dreams have haunted him and there is nothing he seems able to do to stop himself. He is now past the mud pond, moving at blinding speed up the steep hill to the field above. Worse, darkness has now settled in.

Reaching the crest of the hill, his momentum is not slowed in the least and now it relentlessly drives him through the nightmare field to an even worse place......the place he has run from in all of his previous dreams.

The Graveyard Game

Giving in to the unremitting force, Paul's subconscious mind tries a new tact.

"Let it take me where it wants……..it CAN'T hurt me, I'm an adult, a grown man……..a fifty-eight year old GRANDFATHER, for crissakes!"

The worried shiver he felt earlier now became a trembling apprehension. Now, he was into the outer field, near Crater Street, the road to the old graveyard, *"but, no worry, the graveyard was at least a mile and a half up that road. It won't take me that far."*

As if to cruelly mock his thought, the dream force now thrust him even faster, through the outer field, onto the road and at warp speed along the edge of the rural lane, until, to Paul's horror, it deposited him directly in front of the big wrought-iron gates of the old burying ground.

He has stood there many times before, but never has his heart beaten so hard, never has…….."*The BASEBALL, I've gotta get the baseball. No, NO! I can't go in there! It's just me; no one is waiting for me on the road, not Larch, Ritchie, or Larry. I've gotta run home, we'll all come back for the ball tomorrow, when it's light."*

The dream force is slowly pulling…… pulling Paul into the graveyard, past the iron gates……….*"Okay, it's not so bad……..the ball should be behind that stone to the right in the furthest row in back……..don't run now, or it will get me."*

Aware now, that he is walking under his own power, Paul slowly moves toward the rear of the cemetery, head turning from side to side, knowing in his sleep state that there is someone or something here that is going to terrify him, yet not understanding why he continues on…… why not just wake up.

Without warning, Paul is standing face to face with Larry and stumbles backward, falling over a broken headstone.

"Larry! Am I glad to see……

The face is Larry's, but there is no recognition from Larry's eyes. Paul can feel his pulse pounding harder and is aware that he is sweating profusely. Larry stands perfectly still, staring straight ahead.

"Larry, what's wrong? Why won't you say something?"

Paul struggles to get to his feet, but everything is now moving in a slowed motion. His body seems so heavy, almost too heavy to lift off the ground.

Remembering a movie he saw once, where hands came up from a grave and grabbed the unsuspecting hero of the film by the ankle, he wills himself to move faster and finally stands erect.

Turning, he is greeted instantaneously by a horrific, ghastly face and a blinding flash of light, which blocks out the face and causes him to draw in a deep breath, or try to. Panic sets in, as Paul now finds he can't move, can't speak and can't catch his breath. He tries hard to scream, but cannot. Then, summoning all his strength, he forces out a half-scream, but knows no one will hear. Trying again, he is able to scream louder, then bolts upright in his bed, gasping.

Paul turns, sees Mary Ellen still sleeping soundly and is relieved to find that either he didn't scream out loud, or only groaned, not loud enough for her to be disturbed by it. He raises a hand to his forehead and finds it soaked in perspiration. Sitting there in his bed, he waits until his breathing returns to normal, then quietly gets up and heads for the bathroom. After relieving himself, he soaks a wash cloth in cool water and presses it onto his face, rubbing it over his forehead and neck, as well. He walks quietly back to the bedroom, grabs a bathrobe from the closet, then returns to the recliner he vacated only two hours before. Grabbing the remote, Paul turns the television on, lowering the volume to a whisper. Finding an old John Wayne movie, he settles in for a long night, knowing sleep is done for this day.

"What in the hell is going on in my head?" Paul thinks, as the lion roars the start of the film.

CHAPTER FOUR

"Henry, what are you *still* doing here? Don't you have to go and check on your boys? Or are you just feeling lazy today. It's only Wednesday, ya know, much too early in the week for slowing down. I know, you just *can't get enough* of Frank's *delicious* coffee." This last remark was followed by an outbreak of raucous laughter among the seven men sitting at the counter in Forbes Breakfast Nook, along with the dozen or so diners sitting in booths within earshot of Barbara Nolan's sarcastic put-down of owner Frank Denton's well-known inability to brew a decent pot of coffee. Frank had only recently consented to let Barbara make the coffee, after enduring many days of wisecracks.

Before Larch could answer, Frank peeked through the rectangular opening in the wall between the kitchen, where he was working the grill and the counter area, where Barbara was efficiently keeping up with the needs of all her customers and hollered:

"Yer a funny lady.....too bad yer feet don't move as fast as yer mouth, ya might have more'n two bucks in yer tip jar."

"That's my IRS tip jar. I keep the real tip money right here, baby." Barbara said, as she patted the large, jingling pocket on the side of her apron.

"Don't ride her *too* hard, Frank, if she quits and you have to make the coffee, no one's gonna come here." a booth diner yelled out, to the delight of the breakfast crowd.

Frank threw his hands up in the air, in a gesture of resignation and growled "Aaah!", then went quietly about his kitchen business

Bart Johnson, one of the patrons at the counter, looked at Barbara and said: "It's a good thing you're so damn pretty, Babsie, 'cause I sure as hell wouldn't be tipping you on your quick service. Hell, I've been waitin' a good thirty seconds for my refill." He held his coffee cup high, for Barbara to see.

"You *know* that flattery will get you everywhere, Sweetheart." She said, gently patting the side of Bart's bearded face, while filling his cup with hot coffee. "But I *do* think you should get your eyes checked."

Turning to Larch again, Barbara feigns a look of surprise. "Oh, *I* know why you're hanging around, Henry; you're waiting for everyone to clear out so you can finally propose to me. Now, isn't that sweet."

Larch's face turned flush with embarrassment. Completely comfortable around his construction crews, he had always been painfully shy with women, a trait that gregarious ladies such as Barbara loved to tease him for.

Hearing only a few giggles among the scattered guests, Larch determined that Barbara's comment hadn't really gone over as well as she'd expected. True to his gentlemanly nature, he responded with a warm smile "Barbara, if I ever decide to get married, you'd be the number one contender."

Leaning over the counter and squeezing his hand, she whispered "Sweetie, this isn't a prizefighter you'd be looking for, but I *do* appreciate the sentiment."

At that moment, hearing the door squeak open, Barbara glanced over and let out an unladylike howl "Oohh, well I'll be dipped; Paul McCulloch, what in heaven's name brings *you* in here?"

"Your sweet smile, of course! How are you doing, Babs?"

"I *was* doing alright, until *you* came in and spoiled it. Henry was just about to propose to me."

Again, a few chuckles from some of the stragglers.

"Maybe next week" Larch nervously replied.

Barbara tapped the countertop with her hand, winked at Paul and asked; "Coffee?"

"Please."

Taking a few steps to grab the almost empty coffee pot, she managed to pour a full cup for Paul and said "What else can I get you?"

"Just the coffee, is fine."

Barbara shuffled off to check on her other customers, none of which were in immediate need of anything more than a check. She busied herself making a fresh pot of coffee and made out the bills for several diners, who were finished eating.

Paul held out his hand to Larch, waiting for a handshake, which was quickly given by his old friend. "How have you been, buddy? It's been a while."

"Yes, it has. It's hard to believe we live in the same town. I saw you drive by my site on Norwell Street last week. I waved, but I guess you didn't see me."

"Sorry about that, Hank. I've been in kind of a fog lately."

"Paul, I hope you don't mind me saying, but you look like hell."

Ignoring the comment and leaning forward, Paul whispered; "Do you mind if we move over there?" nodding to the corner booth.

"Not at all" Larch said, as he picked up his coffee mug and stood up, then followed Paul to the isolated location.

Once they were seated, Henry could tell by Paul's demeanor that whatever was on his mind was bothering him more than just a little.

"Paul, is everything alright at home?"

"Yeah, everything's fine. It's me, Larch…..I've….I've been having some really weird dreams. We're talking about 'bone-rattling' nightmares, here."

"Bone-rattling, huh? You used to rattle our bones pretty good when we were kids. As I recall, you were real good at it."

"Believe me, this is the real thing. I have these terrible dreams, then wake up soaked in sweat, heart pounding; then, I can't get back to sleep again. I've been walking around like a zombie, just going through the motions at work."

"Well, it's easy to see that you haven't been sleeping. Those bags under your eyes are a dead giveaway. So, how do you figure I can help?"

"Larchie, remember when we were around twelve......well, you were ten or eleven.....we used to go to the old cemetery, off Crater Street, didn't we?"

"REMEMBER?" Larch proclaimed vocally, and then looked around, as if he wanted to apologize to someone who might have been offended by his loud exclamation. Seeing only two or three curious glances in his direction, he leaned toward Paul and said, in an almost whispering voice "Man, you came up with some creepy ideas, but the 'graveyard game' was the absolute scariest experience I *ever* had in my life and that includes front-line combat in 'Nam."

"Tell me about the 'graveyard game', Larch."

"What do you mean?"

"I mean tell me what it was, I.....forgot."

"You're joking, right?"

"No, really, I can't remember a thing about it. Does it have anything to do with the baseball I've been seeing in my dreams? What, did we play ball in the old cemetery, or something?"

"Paul, are you saying you have absolutely *no* memory of what we did there?"

"None, whatsoever. I guess when I fractured my skull that time, the memory went south.......that's what the doctor said at the time. The worst thing was having had to repeat seventh grade, not because of memory loss, but because I lost so much time out of the school year."

Larch drew in a deep breath and leaned back in the booth, then raised his left hand to his forehead, rubbing both temples with his thumb and middle finger.

"Oh, man!"

"Hank, I'm dead serious here. I *need* to know what went on at that cemetery, because I'm pretty sure it's tied in to the nightmares I've been having."

"Paul, *you're* the guy that came up with that game, *now* you're telling me you don't remember anything about it?"

"Larch, I pretty much lost memory from that whole summer prior to fracturing my skull, as near as I can figure. I've tried to match up what memories I *do* have to important dates and events of that time period and find that, roughly, the time between mid-spring of 1957 and when I came home from the hospital in late September, is totally blank."

"If I tell you about the game, will that be enough?"

"Enough for what?"

"Enough to satisfy you."

"I honestly don't know, but it could help me to figure out what's going on. Larch, why are you so hesitant to tell me?"

"Because I don't want to open up a can of worms."

"I don't understand."

Larch squirmed in his seat, raised his hand to his forehead again and massaged his temples. Taking another deep breath, he lowered his hand to the table, looked straight into his friend's eyes and said: "Paul……a long time ago…….actually it was the day before you came home from the hospital after your accident, your mother called all the kids in the neighborhood over to your house, along with some of our parents. She thanked us all for the cards and prayers and said she believed the prayers were responsible for you coming out of your coma."

"Yeah, my mom never told me much about the accident, but my sister told me several years later that I had been in a coma for three and a half weeks."

Then, laughing, Paul said "Mary Ellen says she thinks I occasionally slip back in when she tries to talk to me and I'm watching a ball game."

Larch smiled, then continued: "Your mom also asked all of us to do something for her. She asked us to never discuss anything about the night of your accident with you, *even*, or *especially* if you asked. She knew you had no memory of that night and was afraid it would be too traumatic for you to re-live it. She said that you losing your memory was God's way of protecting you from whatever it was that you saw or ran from and we shouldn't interfere with God. We all promised her right then and there, that we would never say a word about it."

Leaning against the seatback, Larch folded his arms, stared at Paul for a few seconds, then said: "Now you're asking me to break that promise."

"Larch, I hardly think she meant for me *never* to find out."

"I think she did, Paul. What happened that night was pretty horrific and the police thought that you witnessed it."...............

"The *police*! Why were they involved?"

"Why are you doing this to me, man? You're really putting me in a bind, here. I know you want to find out what happened, but I'm afraid that if I tell you, it just might be too much for you to handle."

Paul reached out and placed his hand on top of Larch's folded hands "Old buddy, I'm afraid that if you *don't* tell me, it might be too much for me to handle."

"Okay, Paul ..... I'll tell you......but not here. I don't want you freaking out. Also, there's going to be conditions. How about I come over your house tonight? We'll sit down with Mary Ellen....."

"Oh, no, I don't want her involved."

"Only way we're going to do this, is if she is........*and* only if she consents. Otherwise, it's a no-go.

"You always did drive a hard bargain. You win. I just don't have any choice in the matter. I've *got to find out*."

"Remember, Paul, I'll tell you *only* if Mary Ellen agrees to it."

"I don't think that's going to be a problem. These dreams have had a pretty bad effect on her, too. Why don't you come over for supper? I'll ask Mare to cook up some of that beef stew you love."

"You've got yourself a deal. She makes the best beef stew I've ever tasted."

Paul stood up, took ten dollars out of his pants pocket and dropped it on the table.

"I got your breakfast, Larch."

"Hey, big spender, I only had coffee and an English muffin."

"Ahh, Babsie's a good kid. She can use the tip."

"She may follow you home."

Paul laughed; a laugh that felt good to him, as if he had been relieved of a heavy burden. Talking to his old friend *had* been good for him. He had seen compassion in Larch's eyes and knew that Larch had been sympathetic to whatever it was that he was going through, even though he couldn't possibly understand it.

Saying good-bye to Barbara on their way out, Paul held the door for Larch and when they reached the parking lot, he reached out his open hand and lightly hit Larch's arm. "See you around five-thirty?"

"Ill be there, Paul. What can I bring?"

"Yourself."

They each got into their pickup trucks, waved and drove away.

CHAPTER FIVE

Nathan Feldmar answered his phone on the second ring. The voice on the other end sounded unsure and hesitant.

"Hello, Doctor Feldmar, my name is McCulloch, Paul McCulloch. I.....I'd like to ....I *need* to set up an appointment. I've been having these nightmares........and ....uh......they......they seem to be...... well......they *are* getting worse. I've been losing a lot of sleep and.....

"I have an opening this afternoon, if you'd like, it's a two o'clock cancellation. If that's too soon, I can give you Thursday morning at eleven, or Friday at one p.m."

"This afternoon will be fine."

"I'll see you then, Paul"

Mixed emotions now ran through Paul's mind as he set the phone down. On the one hand, he was glad he had made the call to Nathan Feldmar. On the other, he was kicking himself for coming across like a grade school dropout. In addition, he wasn't quite so sure that this would be the right course of action.

"*I hope this guy doesn't try to hook me into seeing him three or four times a week, or worse, for months or even years...*" Paul thought. "*Maybe he's one of those guys that like to bleed you at seventy-five bucks an hour. I probably shouldn't have called him, or at least I should have checked around a little more......I wonder if he'll really be able to help me.........it sure would be great if he could......how am I going to tell him about the dreams?......where should I start?........I guess he will probably be able to guide me......after all, that's what he does for a living. What does he say when people ask him what he* does? 'Well, I'm a mental technician'…..or,' I'm a nightmare repairman'…..I got it! He tells them 'I'm a bad dream reliever and a homecoming queen'."

This last thought causes Paul to start giggling to himself, then, recognizing the absurdity of the pun, he tries to stifle an all-out eruption of laughter, but instead, involuntarily expels a burst of air through his clamped lips, causing a loud, squeal-like noise.

"Man, I am *so* tired, I'm getting punch-drunk. I gotta try and get some sleep today. I don't really have any jobs that need immediate attention, so maybe I'll take the whole day off and grab a nap. I shouldn't have the dream, at least, I'm much too tired to dream".

Paul checks the kitchen clock, sees that it is now ten fifty-five a.m. and decides that he has just enough time to take a one-hour nap, grab a bite to eat, shower and shave, then meet Nathan Feldmar for his two o'clock appointment.

Debating whether to lay down in the bed, or crash in the recliner, Paul chooses the latter, deciding he'll be less likely to get too comfortable. He kicks off his work boots, sits down and pushes the button on the side of the chair, causing his body to drop into full-recline position.

Lying in this position had a soothing effect on his mind, as well as his tired body and Paul's thoughts turned to Mary Ellen. "*She's probably waiting on some little old lady now, wrapping up some' treasure' she just purchased.*"

Paul's wife worked at Paragon Gift and Card Shoppe, in the city and loved her job. Her hours were 9:00 a.m. to 3:00 p.m. Tuesday through Friday, along with 9:00 a.m. to 1:00 p.m. one or two Saturdays a month. The folks who owned the gift shop [two brothers in their mid-fifties] adored her and weren't at all shy about rewarding her every Christmas with a hefty bonus check.

Mary Ellen McCulloch, in turn was an exemplary employee. Always neatly dressed, she reported to work fifteen minutes early each day, was usually the first one to help a fellow employee when the registers backed up [when she would be working the floor and not required to do so] and went out of her way to please the customers, even the nasty ones. The customers, in turn, often went out of *their* way to tell the owners how nicely they had been treated by Mary Ellen.

"Boy; is <u>she</u> going to be surprised when I tell her Larch is coming for supper tonight. OH, SHIT! I forgot to call her and tell her. She hates it when I spring things on her at the last minute. I gotta call her now."

Jumping out of the chair, Paul picked up the phone and dialed the number for the gift shop. Marilyn, one of the girls on the registers, answered. "Paragon Gift Shoppe."

"Hi....Marilyn?"

"Yes, this is Marilyn."

"Hi, this is Paul McCulloch. How are you?"

"Oh, hello, Paul. I'm fine, thank you. And you?"

"Great!" Paul fibbed. "Is Mary Ellen busy?"

"Actually, Paul she's with a customer right now and she may be tied up a while, would you like for her to call you back?"

"No, that won't be necessary. Would you mind giving her a message?"

"Not at all."

"Would you tell her that I've invited a friend for supper tonight?"

"I'd be happy to, Paul. Is that all?"

"That's it! Thanks, Marilyn, you're a sweetheart!"

"I bet you tell all the girls that." she teased.

"Uh-uh! Just the pretty ones."

"Oh, Paul.....you always knew how to charm a woman."

Laughing, Paul replies "Thanks, again...I appreciate it."

"You're welcome, Paul....anytime. Bye-bye."

Setting the phone back down, Paul hoped that Mary Ellen would not call back to find out the details as to who was coming to supper. *"If she does call back, I'll probably just be dozing off to sleep and that will mess up the nap, but I don't want to take the phone off the hook, or that will send her the wrong message, when and if she calls. Wait a minute......she doesn't know that I decided to stay home, she thinks I'm working, so she'll call my cell phone, then get my voicemail and think I'm too busy to answer. Great! Now, I can lie down and rest."*

Settling back into the recliner, Paul finds that his mind is spinning from the morning's events and starts to sort them out in his head.

"First of all, what the hell did Larch mean when he said the police wanted to talk to me ...because they thought I witnessed it? Witnessed what? He said what happened that night was 'pretty horrific'. The newspaper clipping in my old scrapbook said I fell off a rock wall and landed badly on my head, onto Boundary Road just below Carey's house.......but what was I doing on Boundary Road alone, at that time of night? Never, in my right mind would I be anywhere near' Crazy Roger's' house <u>anytime</u> alone. Jeez, I'm really losing my train of thought, here.......Larch said I looked like hell, he's right. When I looked in the mirror this morning, I couldn't believe how bad I looked..... my eyes seemed sunken in the sockets........no wonder Mary Ellen was so upset.......I actually thought I looked like a deranged lunatic........maybe Larch thought so, too, be sure................."

Paul drifted off in the midst of his thoughts, his tired body longing for some much-needed rest. As sleepy as he was, his mind was about to go into overtime and within a half hour, the latest dream began.

The lower field which was the site of many prior dreams, appeared in his mind's eye once again, only this time, Paul was *walking*, not running. Even more strange was the fact that he was walking in the opposite direction, *toward* Crater Street.

Paul was aware of someone with him and when he turned to his right, was relieved, even happy to see Larch and Ritchie walking alongside. Something else was obvious........Paul was a grown man, while Larch and Ritchie were ten and twelve years old.......but they seemed unconcerned, as if to them, Paul was their age.

"What did his face *look* like, Paul?" asked Ritchie.

"I told you, he just stared straight ahead.......it just looked like he was in some kind of trance, that's all......his face still looked the same."

"Did he say anything?" Larch wondered.

"No, he just stared, then......

The dream starts to become scattered and Paul now finds himself alone, at the entrance to the cemetery, shivering with fear. He is once again the twelve-year old boy. Terrified at the prospect of going into the cemetery, but *needing* to do so, he takes a few tentative steps, then, losing his courage, turns to run, but something is coming straight at him, blocking his escape, a shadowy figure from which he feels a strong sense of evil. Paul peers into the darkness, trying to identify who or what is approaching, then, when his fear starts to overtake him, he turns and runs toward the rear of the cemetery.

Another figure is coming into his sight, this one definitely not evil. Paul runs straight at this new shape, then when he gets close enough, clearly sees the haunting face of his friend, Larry, staring straight ahead, trance-like in his present state.

Paul grabs for Larry's arm, shouting "COME ON, Larry, we gotta get out of here……..he's gonna *kill* us!"

Surprisingly, Larry's body starts to move slowly, with Paul tugging ferociously at his arm. Frustrated, Paul pulls harder, urging his friend to move faster, but Larry can only plod along, like some sort of late-night movie zombie.

Much to Paul's relief, the boys manage to stay ahead of whatever is chasing them, even at the seemingly snail-like pace they are moving. As they reach the rock wall border at the rear of the cemetery, Paul jumps up on top of the wall and helps Larry to climb up, but Larry, after placing one foot on the wall, turns back to the cemetery, shakes his arm free from Paul's grip and starts to walk back……..straight at the 'dream monster', until he is gone from Paul's sight. As Larry plods along, Paul sees a hand emerging from the ground, attempting to grab Larry's ankle, but Larry is unaware. The hand pops up again, a few feet further along, clutching at air and still, Larry does not notice.

Not knowing what to do next, Paul runs along the top of the wall in the direction of the gates at the front part of the cemetery, then sees a horrifying sight……..Larry is in the grip of the shadowy figure…….. still in his trance-like state.

Sensing he is being watched, the shadowy figure, the evil 'dream monster', turns and looks directly at Paul. Raising its arm, the figure points a bony finger directly at Paul, releases the grip on Larry and begins to walk toward Paul, letting Larry's limp body fall to the ground.

The Graveyard Game

Engulfed with terror, Paul is frozen in his position on the rock wall. Wanting to run, his legs are unwilling, but, somehow, they begin to comply with the order his mind screams to them. Aware that he is breathing extremely hard, his ability to run seems to be slowed, not only by his shocked horror, but by the fact that, suddenly, those legs feel as if they are made of iron. He can hear the footsteps of the shadowy figure closing in on him, as he nears the front corner of the rock wall.

Calling upon every ounce of strength in his heretofore un-cooperative legs, Paul is amazed when his leap from the wall, carries him all the way to the dirt road, a` la` superhero, where he lands to the right of the big wrought-iron gates.

Without missing a step, he now runs at blistering speed up the dirt road, leading to Crater Street, pulse pounding once again, but conscious of a sensation that he is not only running very fast, but also very easily. His legs, which felt so heavy before, now carry him along in great strides and when he reaches the top of the dirt road, they turn him smoothly onto Crater Street. Now, he cruises easily along the paved road, daring not to turn his head to look back, still consumed with terror over the fate of his friend.

"Larry must have fainted with fright.......that's what I would have done.........I hope he has enough sense when he wakes up, to get up and run or hide, while this thing is chasing me......unless he's....... God, please don't let him be dead. Help me, God! Don't let this thing get me, too. Please, Jesus, please."

Summoning all his nerve, young Paul turns his head, expecting to see his pursuer hot on his back, but instead sees only the empty street, surprisingly bright, despite the fact there are no streetlights on this section of the road. Fearing the worst, Paul turns around and glances to his side, thinking for sure he will come face to face with his 'dream monster'. Once again, however, he is spared from that dreadfulness.

"He must have cut through the crater and now he's going to jump out somewhere on the road ahead. I'll fool him, I'll cut through the two fields and then when I get to the woods, it's a short run to home."

Paul sees the path which leads to the upper field coming into view on the left side of Crater Street and pushes himself into a hard run, thinking it will be a race to make it to the path and duck into the field before the shadowy dream monster can make it to the roadway.

"Thank God, I made it! I MADE it! Please dear Jesus, help me! Please, help me make it home."

Running past the 'Lover's Lane' where he and his friends would come during the day to look for loose change on the ground, Paul's legs continue to obey his mind's commands to keep on pushing ahead and soon he finds himself running down the muddy, almost vertical path leading out of the upper field to the gorge below, which, in turn, led to the wooded section just before the steep hill to the lower field.

Neither Paul, nor any of his three buddies had ever been able to run down the steep, muddy path before without slipping and falling. It had become one of their summertime games, played on days when they were totally bored and many laughs were shared with some of the hilarious antics trying to maintain their balance and failing, always failing. The path remained muddy, even in the height of each summer's dry spell and the boys could never understand that. Paul's mother could also not understand where her son was playing to get his clothes so mud-covered and usually berated him for 'ruining his clothes'.

In Paul's dream state, there would be no muddy clothes, no flailing arms trying to maintain body balance, just the exhilarating feeling of smoothly gliding down the incline, as if his feet were barely touching the ground beneath.

Now into the wooded section, Paul continues his effortless marathon, hitting the steep hill on the other side of the gorge, leading to the last field before his 'home' woods.

Feeling as though something just bit his face, Paul touched the painful area with his middle and index finger as he ran and felt the unmistakable silky texture which he recognized as blood. The upraised tiny flap of skin told him that a small tree branch was probably responsible.

Fatigue begins to set in as Paul plods up the short, but steep hill to the lower field. When he reached the top of the hill, he stopped to catch his breath. Fearing that the shadowy figure might be catching up to him, Paul turns to look back down the hill, hands on his knees, bent forward. Peering into the night, the only movement he notices is the swaying of some low-lying bushes in the cool evening breeze.

Overcome with the sensation of knowing, in some deep recess of his mind, that he has stood here before, turned the same way to confirm that he was not being followed and would now decide to take the safer route down the animal path to Boundary Road, Paul's mind, in it's dream state, makes a decision to forego that route.

"No dead end this time……..no bright lights……….this time I'm going to do this _my_ way……..I'm going to go home on the path through the woods, leading to _my_ street.

At the point where the two paths met, Paul's decision to alter his own dream leads him to turn slightly left, in order to continue on the shorter path home through the woods. As he does so, an ominous feeling invades his mind, a sensation that if he were to use this route, evil will be waiting.

"No way! I'm _not_ changing my mind. Whatever is waiting _can't_ be worse than the other way. I hate that flash of light……besides, I know……….

Completely without the consent of his subconscious mind, Paul's body inexplicably moves from the wooded path to a point halfway down the animal path. Angered at the blatant dismissal of his route plan, but fearing what he knows inescapably is sure to happen at the bottom of this pathway; Paul reacts by crying out in a loud protest.

In the midst of his shout, a fear-provoking chill begins at the base of his spinal column just above the tailbone and quickly works it's way up Paul's backbone, alerting him to imminent danger. With the hairs on the back of his neck bristling, Paul the man, Paul in the present, _not_ Paul, the twelve-year-old boy, turns to his right and looks directly into the grinning face of the shadowy figure………his dream monster. The face, however, is blank, save for the hideous grin.

Desperate with fear, tempered by the powerful desire to preserve his life, Paul swings hard at the terrifying figure reaching out to him, his preceding shout now turned into a horrific bacchanalian cry, which, in turn sends the chill spiraling up and down his backbone in a hair-raising display of desperation. Intense pain ricochets throughout his right hand, starting at the knuckles and flashing to his elbow like an electric shock and Paul knows he has connected with a punch square on the jaw of the evil figure. At the same time, he feels something grab at his ankle, sees the asphalt of Boundary Road directly in front of him and is powerless to stop his momentum.

A bright flash of light precedes the sickening thud, but Paul can feel no pain. From somewhere in the deepest pit of Paul's inner mind, he can hear the sound of a car engine coming closer, now shutting off. He is aware of no bodily sensation other than a sense of remoteness, as if he were floating in some unreal world, where time would not be rushed about its business, but would pass at an agonizingly feeble pace.

Unaware as to what exactly his situation is, but cognizant of a celestial-like peacefulness overtaking his dream state, Paul hears two voices, not of evil, but gentleness and sympathy, along with familiarity. The lilting brogue in each was instantly recognizable as that of his elderly next-door neighbors, Mr. and Mrs. McQuade.

"Jesus, Mary and Joseph, it's the little McCulloch boy." The gentle voice, filled with concern is unmistakably that of old Philip C. McQuade and Paul wonders in his dream world where he came from……..more so……..where are they?

"Margaret, bring the blanket from the back seat…….and hurry, for the love of Jesus."

Paul clearly hears the sound of shuffling feet approaching, feels the soft puff of air cross his bare arms, senses himself shiver and suddenly, is embellished in warmth.

"Oh dear; Philip, the poor little sweetheart, what do you suppose happened to him?"

"I don't know, Margaret, perhaps he was struck by an automobile."

"*What the hell are they talking about?*" Paul the man wants to know.

"Run up to Moriarty's house, Margaret and tell them to call for an ambulance. Make sure they tell the driver to hurry."

"Oh, Philip, there's so much blood……. will he be all right?"

"Not if we stay here talking, he won't. For the love of God, woman, go *now!*"

Again, the sound of shuffling feet, only this time, they move a little more quickly, until the sound diminishes to silence.

The sound of Mrs. McQuade hurrying away brings forth a memory to Paul of the time he spent almost two hours shoveling her driveway last winter after a snowstorm. She had asked him, because, she said, her husband's 'weak heart wouldn't stand the exertion' and he would be 'too proud of an old fool' to ask for help. Paul's reward for his labor had been seventy-five cents, with an additional fifty cents tacked on for clearing the front walk, but the best part was the overly generous piece of warm apple pie, fresh from the oven that she served him, at her kitchen table, along with a big glass of cold milk.

Now, new sounds approach, gasping and murmuring voices.

"My God, he's gonna bleed to death!" A man's voice proclaims.

"Shush, for goodness sake!" It's the voice of old Mr. McQuade. "He very well may be able to hear you, even though he's unconscious. We *must* keep him calm."

"*Of course, I can hear you! Why can't you hear me! Calm, I'm calm….. I'm fine……nothing hurts……anywhere…….honest to God……..I swear!*"

"What happened……..did you hit him with your car?" A lady's voice demands to know. Paul is not sure, but it sounds very much like Mrs. Carver, who lives diagonally across from 'Crazy Roger' Carey.

"No, we came upon the lad lying in the road." Replied Mr. McQuade to the questioner, then, looking up at her asks: "Do you have a clean towel? My handkerchief is soaked…….it's not doing a bit of good, now."

"I'll get one!"

This time, the sound Paul hears is a slapping sound, the distinctive sound made by the flats that Mrs. Carver always wears.

"*What happened to me? Why can't anyone hear me?*"

The slapping sound returns and draws near.

"I brought two, one wet and one dry."

"Thank you, Elizabeth."

Now the feeling of moist warmth spreads across his forehead, over his eyes and down his face. Then, it is gone and coolness returns to Paul's face, along with an audible gasp from several gathered voices.

"My God, his little face is smashed in…..Oh dear God!" A voice cries out.

"I don't think I've ever seen so much blood" said another.

"Has anyone notified his parents?"

"I don't think he'll make it…..he doesn't look good, at all."

"Shush, all of you! Didn't you hear what Philip just said? You're all making such a fuss…….."

The scolding voice of Mrs. McQuade, who has returned from her assignment, is stopped in mid-sentence by the sound of the ambulance……….but the siren sounds strange…….not like a siren at all…….more like the ambulance siren that Paul heard one time, when his two older sisters took him to a movie. The film was set in France, with a scene where an ambulance roared by the hero and it made a sound that Paul had never heard before…….dee-doo, dee-doo, dee-doo…..similar to the sound he was now hearing…..a sound which was getting louder and closer……..closer, still……….more persistent…….. now just downright annoying…..dee-doo, dee-doo, dee-doo, dee-ring, dee-ring,……….ring…….ring……..

Opening his eyes, Paul is vaguely attentive to the new sound, but unsure, still, as to what the intruding noise is, or where, in the universe, his body is at this particular moment. The only thing of which he is sure, is that he has the power to stop the meddlesome jingle from resonating through his eardrums……..if he could only figure out where it is coming from……

Finally, the cobwebs clear out from his sleep-deprived mind, enough so that Paul now is able to determine that the interruption to his dream-filled state has been caused by the insistent ringing of his telephone.

Lurching forward in an effort to propel himself up and out of the recliner, Paul stumbles forward, in a combination of momentum and grogginess, then, as he reaches for the phone, he hesitates, knowing he is not ready for conversation just yet. Focusing his eyes on the caller I.D. screen, the name "Paragon Gif" appears.

The voice leaving the message sounds distressed; "Paul, where are you? Please call me, honey; to let me know you're okay……..I love you……. Bye."

"Oh, Mary Ellen, sweetheart, I can't talk to you now." Paul says, as if his wife could hear him. "Give me a couple of minutes, okay?"

Ambling back to his recliner, Paul sits down, trying to make sense of the latest episode in his continuing series of weird dreams.

"This is really getting uncanny. It seems as though each dream reveals a little more to me, but what is it that……..my brain, I guess…….is trying to tell me? The part about Mr. and Mrs. McQuade…..they were listed in the newspaper article as the ones who found me lying in the road…….but is the conversation they and those neighbors had in the dream really fact, or just something my fucked-up mind came up with? That <u>had</u> to have been the night I fractured my skull. What……just WHAT the hell is with that shadowy figure? Was something really chasing me that night, or is it just a conjured-up dream horror creature of some kind that I keep seeing in <u>every</u> dream? "

An abrupt urgency prods at Paul, interrupting his dream critique and just as quickly, hits him square in the gut……."FELDMAR!.....Jeez, what the hell time is it?" Paul had long ago stopped wearing a wristwatch, because of his job. Many times, he would be working in an electrical cabinet, in close proximity to live buss work, not particularly the best place to be wearing a metal bracelet or watch. Some of his electrician friends even removed their wedding bands for fear of creating an easy current path, but Paul knew that such an act would not set well with Mary Ellen, so, elected to keep his on his finger.

Leaping out of the chair, Paul scurried out to the kitchen, glancing up at the clock on the wall. He let out a surprised gasp as he saw that the clock read one-forty p.m., which left him twenty minutes to shower, shave, eat and then drive the four miles or so, to Nathan Feldmar's office.

"I've only got time to grab a quick shave, change clothes and get the hell out of here." Paul thought to himself. How the hell could I have slept for so long?"

Pulling his shirt off as he hurried to the bathroom, Paul took his electric razor from the cabinet, ran it over the thickest part of his beard, until he assured himself that he at least looked clean-shaven, then cupping his hands under the running faucet, splashed warm water over his face. His compulsive neatness would not allow him to leave the razor out, despite the fact that every minute counted, so he carefully wrapped the razor cord around the device and replaced it neatly in the medicine cabinet, then hustled into the bedroom, where he removed his work boots, socks and dungarees, reached for the after shave lotion, poured a few drops into his hand and slapped it onto his face. As he set the after shave bottle down on the bureau top, his other hand picked up the deodorant stick in one fluid motion and applied it to his armpits.

Moving to the clothes closet, Paul opened the door, selected a suitable shirt, along with a pair of slacks and put them both on, then slid his feet into a comfortable old pair of boat shoes that still looked fairly new.

Rushing out through the kitchen and taking one last glance at the clock on the wall, Paul sees that it is now one fifty-one p.m.

"Hell of a first impression I'm going to make on this guy." He thought.

CHAPTER SIX

Mary Ellen was starting to become worried. She had been unable to reach her husband for more than two hours now. His cell phone had been set on voicemail during that entire time period, something he never did for more than a half hour, usually when he was in the midst of a critical wiring process that required his complete concentration. She had left three messages, the last one urging him to call her as quickly as he was able, but still had not heard from him. The two calls made to their house had also gone unanswered, as had the messages left there, also.

Normally, this would not have been such a cause for concern, but, because of the problems Paul had been having with his on-going nightmares and resulting lack of sleep, her mind started filling with scenarios in which he had fallen asleep at the wheel and crashed his truck, or some other dreadful thing.

The afternoon had been slow, in the Paragon Gift Shoppe, with only a handful of customers. Marilyn, who was working the cash register, had stepped away several times to help Mary Ellen, who was busy stocking the shelves.

Marilyn Duran had a reputation in the west end of the city as 'man-hungry'. This may or may not have been true, but she was definitely a woman who liked to go out on the town and have fun. If the fun included going home with a good-looking guy, then, so be it. Attractive for her age, which most folks guessed as somewhere in her mid-to-late forties, this twice-divorced brunette never failed to dress in clothes which accentuated her best features, two of them proudly carried on her chest. More than one man had been caught sneaking a peek whenever she bent down to retrieve a bag from under the counter, while wearing a low-cut blouse and some audible sighs could actually be heard when she bent over in her skin-tight pants, while stocking shelves with Mary Ellen, thus displaying her shapely butt.

Almost all of the other girls who worked in the gift shop didn't like Marilyn and some had no problem making it known, through snide comments, but none of it seemed to faze her, or if it did, she failed to show it. The younger girls seemed indifferent, with most of the hostility coming from the older women, who no doubt, were partly motivated by jealousy of their curvaceous counterpart.

The owners of the shop were well aware of both Marilyn's reputation and of the way many of the male customers leered at her, but, Marilyn did what she was hired to do and did it well. She was friendly and pleasant to all the customers, efficient on the register and always clean and neatly dressed. The fact that her clothes were sometimes quite revealing certainly didn't seem to hurt business and with the construction site for a new office building just a block away, the brothers noticed a dramatic increase in the number of work boot and dungaree-clad men who just happened to come in each day around lunchtime, for some frivolous purchase. These men would then stand in line at Marilyn's register, waiting patiently, even refusing offers from one of the other girls, who had opened their register in order to speed things up for the 'customers'.

The one person who displayed no ill feeling whatsoever toward Marilyn was Mary Ellen. From the first day that Marilyn started working in the gift shop Mary Ellen had shown nothing but kindness and heartfelt friendliness to her. That kindness had been gratefully accepted by Marilyn, who had come to look upon Mary Ellen as an older sister. A bond of friendship gradually developed between the two women, much to the dismay of Marilyn's detractors.

It was this bond, this closeness that allowed Marilyn to notice that something was worrying her friend. As they worked together, Mary

Ellen seemed nervous and on the verge of tears, but said nothing. Unable to keep quiet any longer, Marilyn seized the opportunity, when no one was in the store, to ask; "Mary, what's wrong?"

Straightening up, Mary Ellen raised her right hand and shook it in frustration, then said; "It's probably nothing, really..........I've just been unable to get in touch with Paul and I'm a little worried, that's all."

"I'm sure he's all right......have you tried your house?"

"Yes and his cell phone, too......several times."

"Well, he sounded okay when he called before lunch.......maybe he forgot his cell phone in his truck, or something. Men are always doing things like that."

At this point, tears welled up in Mary Ellen's eyes and she fidgeted in the front pocket of her pants, removed a clean tissue and daubed gently under her eyelids, being careful not to smear her makeup.

"Oh, honey!" Marilyn wrapped her arms around Mary Ellen's shoulders. "Why is this upsetting you so much?"

Mary Ellen let out a slight sob and shook her head forcefully from side to side. "I don't *know*! It's.......just a.......completely different problem that's *really* got me upset........this ......I'm just on edge, that's all."

"Would you like to talk about it?"

"No.......thank you, Marilyn......but, no......it's something Paul and I have to work out.......we just *have* to."

The tinkling of the bell at the front door signaled the fact that a customer had just walked in and Marilyn let her arms drop, then squeezed Mary Ellen's hand and said; "If ever you change your mind, I'm here for you; I want you to know that."

Mary Ellen touched the tissue to the corners of her eyes with her free hand, smiled and returned the hand squeeze.

"I *do* know that!"

Marilyn turned and walked back to her register.

Picking up the empty boxes which had accumulated on the floor, in front of the shelves she was stocking, Mary Ellen returned them to the back room, threw them in the big rolling canvas trash receptacle and peeked at her watch. Twenty minutes past two....forty minutes before she could go home and, hopefully, find out where Paul had been and why he hadn't responded to the messages she left on his phone. She thought about calling him one more time and decided against it.

"Something just doesn't feel right. Paul would never intentionally <u>not</u> return my calls........it's just not like him. Lord, I hope he hasn't been involved in an accident........Marilyn is so sweet........but I........I just <u>couldn't</u> tell her about Paul's nightmares.........DAMN those wretched dreams of his.....and what they're doing to his health......God, I love him so much........why is he so stubborn?........why won't he get someone to........

"PENNY FOR YOUR THOUGHTS?" The stentorian voice roared from behind Mary Ellen, startling her so fiercely that she screamed out in fright, jumping and turning in a defensive move, to see who it was. Her surprise was so intense that it caused her to lose her balance as she turned, falling backwards into the side of the trash receptacle, sending it scurrying away and landing her on the floor, where she came down hard. With her hands acting like outriggers, supporting her in a half-sitting position, Mary Ellen looked up at the shocked face of Jack Peyton, one of the owners of the shop.

"OH MY GOD, MARY, I'M SO SORRY!" he boomed. "I THOUGHT YOU KNEW THAT I WAS WORKING BACK HERE. ARE YOU ALL RIGHT?"

"I.......don't think so. My elbow hurts a lot."

"LET ME SEE."

Jack bent down and gently turned Mary's right arm slightly, watching her face for a reaction. She grimaced in pain and he eased off on the twist. He saw a good-sized bruise starting to appear just below her elbow.

"How badly does it hurt?" he quietly asked.

"Pretty bad."

"I think we should get it x-rayed, you may have broken your arm."

"Oh, please don't say that. That would be the worst thing that could happen right now."

"Didn't you know I was here?"

"No, Jack, if I did, I wouldn't have been startled by you." Mary Ellen was clearly exasperated and not in a mood to hide it.

"OH, GOSH........if I even suspected that you didn't know...."

"It's all right, Jack. It wasn't your fault."

"Will you let me drive you to the hospital?"

"Do you really think it's necessary?"

"Mary Ellen, if it *is* broken, you must get it treated. If it isn't, it will only cost you some of your time. Remember, this is an occupational injury and you *will* be compensated for the time you wait at the hospital."

"Jack, for God's sake, I'm not worried about that."

"Let me help you up. I'll go out to the front and let Marilyn know ...."

"What happened in here?" Marilyn, who had just come into the back room, wanted to know. Seeing Mary Ellen on the floor, she gasped; "Oh, my God, Mary Ellen, are you okay? What happened?"

"I'm all right. I didn't realize Jack was working back here and got startled when he spoke to me from behind. I lost my balance and fell, that's all."

Jack' voice, now subdued, chimed in, as he succeeded in helping his injured employee to her feet; "I'm going to take her to the emergency room for X-rays. Stay with her, Marilyn, while I bring my car around."

"Jack, I......I'm not going to the hospital. I'm okay......really!"

"Mary Ellen, I'm afraid I'm going to have to insist......as your employer, I have a responsibility...."

"No, Jack, I'm afraid *I'm* going to have to insist. I'M NOT GOING TO THE HOSPITAL!" Mary Ellen's eyes were flashing with anger.

Taken aback by the hardness in Mary Ellen's usually soft voice, Jack looked at Marilyn with a 'what should I do now?' question written on his face.

Ignoring him completely, Marilyn stepped closer to her friend and quietly asked; "Can I give you a ride home, then"

Without waiting for Mary Ellen to answer, Jack was quick to offer his proposal; "THAT'S A GREAT IDEA; MARILYN, WHY DON'T YOU DRIVE MARY ELLEN HOME IN HER CAR AND I'LL PICK YOU UP IN MINE."

At this point, all Mary Ellen was interested in doing was going home, making herself a nice hot cup of tea and stretching out on the couch, with her aching elbow wrapped in an ice-filled towel. The tension which had built up in her throughout the day, combined with her frightening encounter with Jack and his thunderous voice, had given her a splitting headache. She felt a wide range of emotions running through her, all at the same time; anger, fear, worry, exasperation, aggravation and a growing jitteriness. If she didn't get away from this place, these people, she would not be able to hold it together much longer. If she only knew that Paul was all right, then everything would be okay.

Rubbing her temple with the index and middle finger of her left hand, Mary Ellen drew in a deep breath, in an effort to compose herself.

"That would be fine…….look, guys, I'm sorry…….sorry I snapped at you, Jack, you didn't deserve it….."

"DON'T EVEN THINK ABOUT IT MARY……NOW, LISTEN…..YOU GO HOME WITH MARILYN AND TAKE AS MUCH TIME AS YOU NEED. DON'T WORRY ABOUT ANYTHING…..DO YOU UNDERSTAND?"

Mary Ellen reached out and touched Jack's forearm, squeezing it gently.

"Thanks, Jack…..but I should be back tomorrow morning. It's a little stiff right now, but I'm sure that will go away in a few hours."

"LET'S HOPE SO!" Jack felt differently. He thought that the arm was broken. He was not going to argue with her, however, after seeing her reaction to his insistence that she go to the hospital. "BUT, MY STATEMENT STILL STANDS; YOU TAKE AS MUCH TIME AS YOU FEEL YOU NEED, PERIOD!"

Marilyn, noticing the pained look on Mary Ellen's face each time Jack bellowed and aware that she had been rubbing her temples, decided that it was time to get her out of here, at least away from Jack.

"OKAY, let's get you home, then." She grabbed Mary Ellen's good arm and started leading her to the break room, where she sat Mary Ellen down, then went to her locker for her purse. "Need anything else?"

"Just my purse, that's all."

The two women left through the rear door, leaving Emily, the seventeen year old part-timer, alone to run the store, with much assurance from Jack, that he and Marilyn would be right back.

On the way to her home, Mary Ellen sat quietly in the passenger seat. Marilyn felt it best to give her a few minutes to herself, then, when they were halfway there, decided to try and lighten things up.

"That Jack…..he's something else, isn't he?"

"Oh, Marilyn, you wouldn't *believe* how much he scared me. I was totally unaware that he was back there and when he spoke….in that *voice* of his….I thought I was going to die."

She followed this statement with a teenage-like giggle, which eased the tension and soon both women were laughing at the helplessness that Jack had shown when Mary Ellen blew up at him.

Marilyn, without taking her eyes off the road, said to Mary; "How about this; 'THAT'S A GREAT IDEA, MARILYN…..' Do you think the people in Boston heard him?"

Both women burst out in raucous laughter, until Mary Ellen put her left hand in the air, in a signal to stop.

"Stop it…..please…..my stomach hurts from laughing, but at least it's moving the pain away from my elbow. Oh, God, that felt good!"

Happy that her friend was in a better mood, Marilyn considered asking Mary Ellen once again what had been bothering her, then decided to leave well enough alone. Besides, they were almost to Mary Ellen's house and Jack would be waiting for her to get into his car right away, not wanting to leave young Emily alone for too long.

Soon, they were pulling into Cherry Tree Drive and Marilyn, who had been a guest of the McCullochs on several occasions, drove into the driveway and immediately saw that Paul's truck was not there.

"Well, he's not home…..that explains why he didn't return *those* calls." Mary Ellen said cynically.

Marilyn shut the ignition off, got out of the car and walked around to help Mary Ellen, but, not wanting to be babied, Mary Ellen reached over awkwardly with her left hand and opened the door. She then stepped out and took the keys from Marilyn, thanking her and turning to walk away.

"Mary......." Then, when Mary Ellen turned around, Marilyn continued; "Everything will be okay.....I just *know!*"

Mary Ellen stood and looked into the sincere eyes of her friend and said; "I'm *so* glad I have a friend like you......I love you, Marilyn."

Then, with tears once again welling in her eyes, she waved to Jack, patiently waiting at the end of the driveway in his car, blew a kiss to Marilyn and hurried into the house.

As Mary Ellen walked away, Marilyn, her own face wet from a single rivulet running over her cheek, softly said; "Right back at you, honey.......right back at you." She turned, walked down to Jack's car, got in and rode away.

CHAPTER SEVEN

Paul considered giving Nathan Feldmar a call to let him know he was running a little late, but decided that would probably waste even more precious time. His best course of action, it seemed, was to just get in his truck and go!

Exiting the house from the kitchen into the sunroom, Paul flipped the lock on the sliding door, slid it shut behind him and walked to his truck, jumped in and fired up the engine. Backing out of his driveway, he glanced at the digital dash clock and was surprised and relieved to see that it read '1:37 p.m.' He remembered Mary Ellen mentioning a couple of days ago, that she was going to set the kitchen clock fifteen minutes ahead, so she would be sure to leave on time for work.

Now, able to relax a little, Paul drove down Cherry Tree Drive, past all the modest homes in the subdivision that he and Mary Ellen had called home for the past eight years. His thoughts turned once again to his latest dream, still fresh in his mind.

"*Why am I dreaming about the same thing over and over? At least it seems to be progressing.........slowly.........<u>really</u> slow..........but why old Mr. McQuade......... and Mrs. McQuade? God, I wish they were still alive, so I could ask them what exactly happened that night.........what the circumstances were, all that stuff........WAIT A MINUTE.......Mrs. Carver........she was there, at least in my dream........or at least I heard her <u>voice</u> in my dream........ I <u>know</u> she's still alive, because I talked to Steve last month and he said his mom was in a nursing home, but was adjusting well and seemed to really enjoy* it there. Maybe I could look her up and see if she remembers anything......... it's worth a try anyway."

When he reached the intersection of Main Street, Paul turned and drove south for two miles to the traffic signals. Turning left onto Route 14, his stomach began to let him know that it was long past feeding time. Remembering that he had bought one of those fund-raising chocolate bars for a buck, off the son of one of his customers a couple of weeks ago, Paul opened the cover to the console box and rummaged through it, hoping that the candy bar was still there. Then, he felt the smooth outer wrapper, lifted it out and tore it open with his teeth, holding it in his free right hand. He devoured the sweet treat in two large bites, savoring the scrumptious taste of the nuts and chocolate mixed together.

Coming up was the junction of Route 14 and Juniper Parkway and Paul meandered into the left-turn lane, then catching the green arrow, made his turn onto the final segment of his ride. Glancing at the first mailbox to come into view, he saw the number '586' and was mildly relieved to know that he was on the right side of the street and wouldn't have to cut across traffic to enter Nathan's driveway, if he had one.

Paul slowed his speed considerably when he saw a post with house number '462' painted on it, a move which irritated more than a few of the drivers, whose cars were beginning to back up behind him. The next number he saw was '420' and then he noticed the simple wooden sign, light brown, with faded red lettering, between two posts, neatly lettered with the words....."Nathan Feldmar".

Paul put his directional signal on, then, as he turned into the driveway, smiled and thought; *"Just the facts, ma'am, no frills, no title to alert anyone who recognizes your truck in the driveway that you're seeing a......... <u>freaking shrink</u>! Nope, just the <u>facts</u>, ma'am.........I think I'm going to like this guy."*

At the end of Nathan Feldmar's driveway was a small parking area, which held three, maybe four, cars. Two spaces were filled and Paul pulled into the one on the end of the lot, nearest the fence at the rear of Feldmar's property. The other cars would at least hide the lettering on the door of his truck, which read; "Paul McCulloch, Licensed Electrician, Phone

[718] 215-8876". He really didn't want or need anyone asking questions about what he was doing at a shrink's office, although he could always say he was just checking out a job. Before shutting the engine off, Paul checked the dash clock one last time. It was only showing; '1:55 p.m.

"Time to spare!" he gloated out loud.

When he got out of his truck, Paul looked around, saw an entrance sign on the side wall with one of those hands that had a pointing finger, which was aimed at a small alcove. Stepping into the recessed area, he climbed two cement steps to an old-fashioned aluminum combination door and couldn't help but notice how neatly the entire area around the entrance was kept. The walkway and steps were swept clean, the cement had recently been pointed up and the glass on the door was spotless.... not a streak in it.

"Maybe business isn't so good, if he has this much time on his hands, or maybe business *is* that good and he's hired someone to keep this place looking so nice."

Opening the door, Paul stepped inside and looked around. The waiting area was about the size of a small bedroom, perhaps twelve feet wide and fourteen or fifteen feet in length. A large couch dominated the right wall, with a good-sized easy chair to the left of the couch and two straight-back chairs to the right. In front of the couch was a sturdy glass-topped coffee table, with at least two dozen magazines neatly laid out in four rows.

"This is probably some sort of test" thought Paul. "If I sit on the couch, it might mean that I'm whacky for some reason and if I choose the big chair, that might mean something else, but if I take one of the straight-backs, then I must be a complete nut case, because they don't look at all comfortable."

Paul chose the straight-back chair closest to him and once seated, was surprised at how comfortable it was, especially for his lower back, which had been bothering him a little lately.

There were four small rectangular windows in the waiting room, two on the wall next to the driveway/parking area and two on the wall facing the rear of the property. The windows were all set high up on the wall, so as to let in sunlight, but too high to see in or out.

On the wall opposite the couch, was a clock, but not an ordinary one. This clock was part of a city skyline scene, which looked similar to New York City. The clock was built into a clock tower in the foreground of the picture. In addition, five of the buildings had a single light lit from a tiny bulb in back of the picture and a bridge, which spanned a river in the lower front of the scene, had three lights lit. Paul's first thought was that this must have been a gift from a child or some other family member, who obviously thought this gift was the cat's ass.

For some reason, his thought of a family member triggered the image of Mary Ellen and Paul's heart sank, as he realized he had completely forgotten to return her call.

"Oh, man..........how could I have forgotten to call her, the poor kid sounded so worried..........here I was, so wrapped up in my own little troubles that I........Aw, sonuvabitch..........I could call her now..........yeah, then the door would open and old' Nate would pop out..........I'll just go straight home when I get done here..........she'll understand..........I hope!"

The time on the tacky clock was two minutes past two. No sound could be heard beyond the only door leading out of the waiting room into what Paul knew must be Feldmar's office.

"Probably some guy pouring his guts out in there."

Leaning forward to scan the magazine titles, Paul was again surprised to see several sports magazines, including golf and auto racing. There were the most recent issues of two popular women's magazines, as well as the two weekly national news editions.

Once again, Paul found himself looking up at the clock, which now read five minute past two.

"And *I* was worried about being late. This guy is in no hurry. What the hell am I doing here anyway? Do I *really* think this guy can help me? I don't see how he possibly could. Maybe I'll just leave......yeah, that's it.....he's tied up with somebody anyway......or he's in there cuffing his carrot. I'll wait until ten past two, if he doesn't come out by then, I'm outta here. Besides, Mary Ellen will be glad to see me..........maybe, but she'll also be pissed if she finds out I walked out on a shrink..........if she finds out."

Paul reached for one of the golf magazines, thumbed through the pages without really reading, or caring, what was on them and then threw the magazine back down on the table. He got up, walked over to the tacky clock/picture/scene, stared closely at it and then walked around the coffee table, trying to decide if he should stay, or leave.

One more glance at the cheap clock revealed that it was now ten minutes past two and still, there was no sign of Nathan Feldmar.

"That's it! I'm leaving!" Paul pronounced to himself, as he hurried to the door.

Just as his hand started to turn the knob, Paul heard a soft voice from behind him.

"Paul?"

Turning quickly, Paul felt his face flush with embarrassment and surprise.

"Oh! Hi.......I, uh......thought maybe I......had the wrong time......so I was going to leave......"

Standing in the open doorway to his office, Nathan Feldmar motioned for Paul to step forward. "I'm sorry to have kept you waiting...... my last patient ran over a few minutes."

To Paul, the man standing in the open doorway appeared to be a gentle soul, not only because of the softness in his voice, but also by his very appearance. Standing a couple of inches shy of six feet, he sported a full beard, which was neatly trimmed. The clothing he wore was rather drab in color, a pair of faded olive chinos, which matched the dark green shirt. His shoes were also well-worn, a pair of dark brown oxfords. Judging by the receding hairline and streaks of gray, Paul guessed his age to be late forties, maybe fifty.

Holding out his hand as Paul approached him, he smiled and said; "Hello, Paul, I'm Nathan Feldmar."

Paul, who was still rattled from being caught, trying to bail out, humbly shook Nathan's hand, forcing a half-smile as he did so. "Paul McCulloch; nice to meet you."

Looking around as he entered the office, Paul looked puzzled and asked; "How did your last patient.......leave?"

"I have a privacy exit for all my patients, to remove any anxiety that they might have, of running into someone they know, in the waiting room, on their way out."

As he said this, Nathan pointed toward a door at the rear of the office.

Paul nodded his head, as a sign that he understood, thinking at the same time how thoughtful that was.

Nathan Feldmar's office had an immediate soothing effect on Paul's psyche. It was much bigger than the waiting room, a good twenty four feet wide and roughly the same in length. The immaculately shined hardwood floors were partly covered by a large Persian carpet, which Paul wished Mary Ellen, who loved them, could see.

At the far wall, in front of a rather large window, which looked out on a beautiful garden terrace, stood an antique oak roll top desk, highly polished, opened to reveal a legal pad, two pens and several papers neatly stacked, to the side of the pad. A single chair sat next to the desk, along with the one behind it.

The wall to the right was one large bookcase, from top to bottom, filled with volumes, neatly arranged, with no clutter on any of the shelves, save for a half-dozen or so small carved wooden sculptures, stylishly placed in various spots. In front of this wall, about five feet out, were two large planters, each containing beautifully manicured and flowing plants.

In the middle of the room were three chairs, one, a wingback, which faced the other two, was turned away from the desk in back of it. The other chairs were each large and comfortable looking, although the one nearest to Paul was the larger of the two. Between these last two chairs stood a small round table, with an old-fashioned lace doily on top, upon which sat a box of tissues. Paul couldn't help but let his mind wander to the thought of some stressed-out yuppie bawling his eyes out into a handful of tissues, because he had bought a ten-room colonial in a wealthy sub-division, to go with his new beamer, when times were good and now didn't know where he was going to come up with the next mortgage payment.

The room conveyed a warmth which was irresistible to Paul and his first impulse was to sit in the big soft chair closest to him, which seemed to be calling out to him in some seductive siren manner.

The quiet voice of Nathan Feldmar brought him back to reality.

"Please, have a seat." Nathan gracefully swept his left arm towards the small chair beside the desk, as an invitation for Paul to be seated.

"We have some paperwork to take care of before we get started."

Paul seated himself, as requested, then suddenly realized that he hadn't given a single thought to the method of payment, or what the hourly rate would be.

As if he had read his mind, Nathan Feldmar folded his hands on the desk and said; "First of all, I should tell you that my fee is one hundred and fifteen dollars per session. A session usually lasts about an hour, though, as you have seen, they do tend to run over occasionally. Do you carry health insurance?"

"Yes, I do."

"Which provider, Paul?"

"Xenon....Ultra medical."

"Excellent. That plan will cover up to ten sessions annually. Any sessions that would be needed beyond that would be your responsibility."

"Jeez, how long is this guy planning to keep this going........I knew it! I knew he'd want to milk this for all he can."

"Paul.....did you have a question?"

"Well.....I was hoping it wouldn't take that long."

"Searching for the cause of emotional distress can be a deliberate and slow process, Paul."

"I don't think you really understand, Doc......this problem I have is starting to affect my health.......I don't want to.......I *can't* ....take it much longer without developing a serious medical problem."

"Paul, please feel free to call me 'Nathan'.......I *do* understand the urgency that you are experiencing and I want to assure you, this will not take any longer than is necessary to get to the root cause of your suffering. That having been said, I now need you to fill out a couple of forms and sign them, if you would.

Paul looked over the paperwork, filled in the necessary spaces and signed where needed, then handed it back to Nathan, who checked to see that everything was in order, and then placed it in a folder, which he deposited in his lower right desk drawer, in a hanging file rack. Paul noted that there appeared to be about three dozen files in the rack and wondered if those were the only patients that Nathan had ever seen, or if they were just the current ones. He dismissed the former thought, as obviously, this man had been in business for quite some time.

Nathan closed the desk drawer, stood up and said to Paul; "Let's move over to the comfortable chairs, shall we?" as he grabbed a clipboard with a pad of paper clipped to it.

Paul got up and headed directly to the large chair, which looked so promising, in terms of comfort and settled down, luxuriating in the soft, but firm support the chair delivered to both his butt and his back. Nathan sat in the wingback across from him, about eight feet away.

"Paul, tell me about these nightmares."

"Well……they began about three weeks……. three weeks ago today, to be exact. I dreamt I was in this field I used to play in, when I was a kid……I was running, because…..someone, or something….. I'm not sure which, was chasing me. That first dream only lasted a short while….maybe a couple of minutes."

"And when did you have the next one?"

"The same night. I woke up from the first one, went and took a leak and went back to bed, figuring it must have been something I ate. I tossed and turned a while…..I was sort of upset by the dream…….it was as if I knew it wasn't over……that something wanted me…….but I don't know and didn't then, if it was good or evil, just that it was scary."

Paul was somewhat surprised at the level of interest with which Nathan was watching him. His brow was furled in deep concentration on every word. This was reassuring to Paul and served to remove his pre-stated [to Mary Ellen] fear, that the 'shrink would laugh me out of his office'.

"Do you remember doing anything out of the ordinary, or any strange or bizarre events which might have occurred during that day, or even a day or two before your first dream?"

"No, I don't recall anything like that. As a matter of fact, it was a fairly ordinary day. I had no problems at work, or home, everything went routinely."

Nathan paused to write on the pad of paper and then looked up; he seemed a bit surprised that Paul had stopped talking.

"Please, go on, Paul."

Paul, not familiar with the habit of most therapists to take notes while their patients spoke, resumed his narrative.

"I finally fell back to sleep and during the course of the night, I began to have the *same* dream.......that's never happened to me before....... only this time the dream started on a street before the field, where I was again running from something.....but whenever I looked back, there was nothing there, but I felt as if I *knew* there was something there...... somewhere......... and it was very terrifying.......to know something is close by, yet you can't see it.......but, still, you *know*, you just *know* it's there."

"But you *did* eventually end up in the same field as your first dream."

"Yes, I ran into that field, with the thought that something was chasing me.......I also had these.......I don't know what to call them.......these flashes......of a face....... the face of a friend of mine in childhood."

"And what was your friend's name?"

"Larry.......Larry Guernette."

"Had you recently seen Larry?"

"No, he moved away around the same time I had my accident, back in 1957......I've never seen him since, nor do I know where he moved to."

"Paul, tell me about your accident."

"There's not much to tell, because I lost all memory of that particular night, along with much of the time before that. All I know is that I was found in the middle of Boundary Road, which runs below the street I grew up on. I had a fractured skull and spent three weeks in a coma."

Nathan's face contorted in an indication of sympathy, then said; "I'm sorry to hear that. Maybe we can retrieve those lost memories, but, for now, tell me were there any other faces in these 'flashes'?"

"No.......well, not in *that* dream. I began to see other things........other.....flashes in the dreams I had during the next three weeks.

At this point, Paul stopped talking, distracted by seeing that Nathan was writing on the clipboard paper and Paul wasn't sure if he was still paying attention to what he was saying.

"Please, continue, Paul. I make notes to myself of items I feel are of importance, but I *am* listening, so feel free to continue. I apologize for not informing you of that earlier."

Paul nodded, in understanding, but was a little irritated; wanting to be sure that Nathan was listening closely.

"When I saw Larry's face, I was in the old cemetery off Crater Street, which is......almost a mile away from the field, maybe more. *That's* when I saw it!"

"Saw what?"

"This figure......a shadowy figure. It ....there was no question about this....it....whatever it was......it was pure evil, I could feel it. I get goose bumps just thinking about it and I've got to tell you Doc, uh....Nathan......I'm not the type of guy that scares easily."

"And what did this 'shadowy figure' do?"

"It started to move toward me, pointing it's finger at me......a bony finger."

"Excellent, Paul......... your attention to detail is going to be a big help. Were there any other characteristics about this figure?"

"It was dressed in black......and it had a hood covering its head and face. I saw this figure in *every single dream* after that, but I never saw its *face*."

"Paul, you describe this 'shadowy figure' as 'pure evil'. What made you feel that way?"

"I don't......uh.......I don't think I can really be sure, but I had the sense that it had done something that *was* evil.......something really horrible. I think Larry had seen it do whatever it did........he just looked so terrified"

Suddenly, Paul's head was thrown back into the headrest of the big chair by some unseen force, in a spasmodic movement that went un-noticed by Nathan, who was busy taking notes. Mary Ellen's face flashed onto his thought screen and Paul was consumed with a desire to hold her in his arms, to comfort her. She needed help. *'Mary Ellen, are you all right?'*

"But you have no idea as to what this figure may have done, is that right?"

Paul's heart was now racing from this sudden un-nerving thought of his wife possibly needing his help and when he went to speak, he could only utter a small gasp.

"Paul, are you all right?"

"May I have some water?"

"Certainly!"

Nathan got up, walked over to the bookcase and opened a wood-paneled door in the lower section to reveal a small refrigerator, which contained a dozen or so bottles of spring water. He then opened another door to the left of the first one and pulled out a medium-sized paper cup, which he carried back and handed to Paul, along with the bottle of water. His eyes stayed riveted on Paul.

Paul opened the bottle, poured a half-cup of water and took a sip, then looking at Nathan, thanked him.

"I'm sorry, Nathan, I don't know what came over me."

"Describe to me what you just experienced."

"I'm not really sure *what* happened. It was like something pulled my head back, then......almost simultaneously......I ....an image of Mary Ellen, my wife, flashed in front of me.......but, she.......she appeared to be suffering in some way. Is that weird, or what?"

Paul glanced at Nathan, who continued his riveting stare.

"No, Paul, that is not weird. I want you to think and tell me if you've ever had such an episode before, at any time in your life."

Noting that Nathan had begun writing again, Paul answered quickly and firmly.

"Never!"

"Would you like to phone your wife to make sure that she is all right?"

"I don't think that will be necessary. For whatever reason, there didn't seem to be a sense of urgency in the flash……..it seemed more like…….. there *could* have been, but…..I don't know……..it just seems as if she needs me to ……..tell her everything's okay, or something like that. Maybe it's just my imagination. We've both been under a lot of strain these past three weeks and she has been getting more and more worried about me and these damn dreams. I think my conscience is telling me to go home and give her a big hug, when I'm done here."

Nathan drew himself up in his chair, crossed his right leg over his left knee and set the clipboard in his lap.

"Paul……what you have just described to me is symptomatic of someone who displays perception outside of the normal range of sense perception. You've probably heard it called 'ESP', or extra-sensory perception. If you are in possession of this ability, it may, or may not be tied into your dreams. This is something we will explore in future sessions, but for now, I'd like for you to continue telling me about your dreams, remembering what I said to you about including every detail."

Paul, who had been listening intently to Nathan's words, shifted in his chair.

"Okay……..where was I?"

Nathan lifted his clipboard, scanned it and said; "You were explaining to me why you thought the shadowy figure was evil."

"Oh, yeah……..well, the feeling I was getting was that it had done something bad. I also got the distinct feeling that Larry was tied in somehow……..maybe he had witnessed it……..but there was definitely a connection between Larry and the shadowy figure."

"Go on, Paul."

"The next thing, I was back in the field, the lower field. You see, there are two fields in those woods, the upper field, which runs from Crater Street to the……..what we, as kids, called the gorge and the lower field, which ran from the opposite side of the gorge to Boundary Road on one side and the woods facing Hillside Road on the other. I was afraid that whatever was chasing me was going to get me in the woods if I took that path to my home on Hillside Road, so I chose to run down an animal path to Boundary Road, which was a lot closer and had lots of houses, all close together. The only problem, was when I got real close to Boundary Road, I saw a bright flash of light, then I felt this thud, like something hit me, but I didn't feel any pain. Then I woke up……actually, my wife woke me up, because I was thrashing around and making weird noises…..I guess she was pretty scared, herself."

Paul fixed his eyes on Nathan, as an indication that he was finished. Nathan, who had again set the clipboard in his lap, folded his right arm across his stomach, with the hand tucked under his armpit. His left hand rose to his cheek, where the thumb went beneath his jaw, the index finger touched his cheekbone and the last three fingers curled over in front of his lips. He held this position for what seemed to be too long a time and Paul began to fidget uncomfortably. Finally, without changing the placement of his hands or arms, Nathan spoke.

"Paul, I want you to think hard…….are there any details you might have omitted?"

Unconsciously, Paul imitates the exact posture of Nathan, except that his left thumb rested on his left cheek, while he slowly stroked his right cheek with his index finger, in a contemplative mood. Then, uttering a small gasp, his eyes fix on Nathan's as he points for emphasis, with the cheek-stroking finger.

"OH, yes…….there *was* something else…….as I was running down the animal path……..a voice…….this is really strange……..a 'voice'… that seemed to be coming from way deep inside of me……kind of like in some deep part of my brain…….but it was a……knowing……an authoritative type of voice…….and it really creeped me out. Well, this voice told me…..just before I got to Boundary Road…….it told me to turn away."

"Do you recall anything else…….any fragment, whatsoever, is important, Paul."

"Only that I remember seeing the roof of 'Crazy Roger's house. 'Crazy Roger' was this older kid, kind of like the neighborhood bully. We all thought he was nuts. He did some pretty nasty things."

"Did this 'voice' speak to you before or after you saw the roof of Roger's house?"

"It spoke to me right after I saw it."

"Tell me all you know about Roger."

"There's not a lot to tell, really, except that he was about five years older than me and everyone in the neighborhood had no use for him. The kids were all afraid of him and the parents told their kids to stay the hell away from him."

"What had he done to deserve such loathing?"

"He…..was just plain mean. If a group of younger kids was playing ball in the street, he'd start riding his bicycle around in the same spot they were playing, making it impossible to continue the game. He'd defy anyone to challenge him……he was just always looking to pick a fight, but of course, no one ever took him up on his challenge…….he was just too much bigger and older than the rest of us.

Paul sat up straight in the chair, becoming more animated as he spoke.

"Even when other kids were around, you still weren't safe around that wacky bastard. I remember the night we were all playing in the street in front of his house and he comes out and says to me 'come here for a minute' and leads me into his house. I told him I wasn't supposed to go into neighbor's houses, but that wasn't quite the truth. Actually, my mom had told me never to go in <u>Roger Carey's</u> house. But he was talking really nice to me, like he was my good friend, or something and he said he was going to give me a chance to make some easy money. Yeah, I remember…… he led me upstairs to his bedroom, made me sit on his bed, then, standing in front of me, reached into his pocket and pulled out a five-dollar bill and said it was mine if I'd blow him. I was really scared and said 'No' Then, he unzipped his fly and pulled out his penis and said 'come on, it won't bite you' but I just shook my head, because my throat was so dry I couldn't talk; *man*, I was petrified. 'Okay' he said

'You want more?' then picks up the five and puts down a ten dollar bill and steps closer to my face, as if I'd suddenly change my mind. I was only nine-years old at the time and I started crying uncontrollably. By this time, he was getting pretty angry with me and I thought he was going to kill me. I remember just wanting to jump up and run out of the room and out of the house, but he would have easily stopped me. I tried to scream so my friends in the street would either come and help me, or at least get an adult, but nothing would come out. I just sat on that bed and sobbed, pleading with him to let me go home. Finally, to my relief, he put his dick back in his pants, picked up the ten and said in a really pissed-off voice 'get out of my sight you little crybaby' then as I walked real fast down his stairs, I heard him behind me, saying 'don't think you're gonna hang around here anymore, 'cause if I see you near my house, I'm gonna kick your little ass, YOU GOT THAT?' I didn't answer him, *couldn't* answer him and I felt so humiliated walking past my friends in the street, with tears streaming down my face; then, when I got far enough past them, I broke into a run and didn't stop until I was at my back door. I remember wiping my face with my arm, then going in the house and straight to my room. I never told my mother or father about what happened that night, but throughout most of my twenties and thirties I secretly hoped I might run into him somewhere, so I could KICK HIS FUCKIN ASS!"

Then, in an apologetic tone, Paul said; "Sorry, Nathan, I didn't mean to...."

"Paul, there's no need for you to apologize. I'm glad that you feel comfortable enough to express yourself. Please........ continue."

I guess it's just as well I never did find him, because I either would have killed him, or he would have killed me.

"And you're saying you no longer feel animosity toward Roger?"

"Oh, I feel plenty of animosity toward that piece of shit, I'm just too old, or I guess the proper word would be 'mature'..... enough to know I shouldn't be duking it out with anyone, that's all. I guess I realize that my life now, is too good to throw away by having a heart attack because of a stupid fight......and what if I were to cause him to have a heart attack......or severely injure him......or worse.......that would be just as bad........no, I hardly ever think about him anymore........that is...... until I started having these nightmares."

"Why do you suppose that is?"

"What? That I've started thinking about him again?"

"Yes."

"I'm not sure.......I was hoping *you* could help me with that one."

Nathan shifted in his seat, raising himself up, slightly.

"You obviously still harbor a good deal of bitterness.......*and* some anger too, toward Roger. That bitterness and anger stems from the ordeal that he put you through. As far as the fear you've described in your dreams, of this 'shadowy figure', whose face you haven't seen clearly, I wonder.....if the figure could be the manifestation of the fear you had of Roger, as a child. The unseen face would then be your inability to 'see' where Roger is now. I believe, Paul, that *Roger* is your shadowy figure. We're out of time, now, but I'd like you to hold this theory in your mind. Think about it, whenever you can. Think about what your reaction would be if you were to come face to face with Roger on the street. Be honest with yourself. You did very well in today's session........ the outburst which you felt you needed to apologize for, was an excellent example of your true feelings. This is how we will make progress. I'm very happy with the results of today's discussion, Paul. I would also add that you seem to have excellent recall, regarding your dreams, which is a big plus. Remember, *every single detail*, no matter how miniscule, when we dream, is, in some way, a message from our brain. Sometimes that message is subliminal and sometimes it is strong. Your memory of these details is crucial to understanding just what it is that your brain is trying to tell you.".......

Paul held his hand up, to signal to Nathan that he wanted to ask a question.

"When will these dreams stop?"

"They will continue until we are able to discover what it is that's causing them and take appropriate action to correct the problem. Don't despair, however.......you will find that, even though the dreams may be as intense, or more so, as they have been, the mere fact that you have discussed them with me will bring you a level of comfort that should allow you to sleep better."

Shaking his head in a symbol of resignation, Paul said; "I'm not so sure about that, Doc.......uh, Nathan."

"Paul, perhaps we need to change your mindset. Here's what I suggest you do: when you are ready to go to bed tonight, prepare yourself as you normally would, then go into your bedroom and just before you retire, sit on the edge of the bed, making sure that you will have no distractions. What you then need to do is to plant, in your subconscious mind, the idea that the dreams you will experience are a learning tool and thus are to be encouraged as so, not as something of which you are frightened. To convey this idea, you must sit quietly for at least fifteen minutes, with your eyes closed to avoid distractions and tell yourself over and over that the dream is a positive instrument, not a negative one. Doing this *will help*, I can assure you.

Rising from his chair, Nathan strode over to his desk, where he retrieved his appointment book. Placing it on the desk and leaning over it, he said, without looking at Paul; "Is this time of day good for you........ or would you prefer some other time?"

"This is a good time."

"Let's see......this is Wednesday, I'm going to schedule you for two-o'clock Friday afternoon, which should give you the occasion to experience another dream or two, unless you would prefer to come in tomorrow?"

"Actually, Nathan, I *would* prefer tomorrow."

"Very well, then. I can see you tomorrow at eleven a.m., if that's all right."

"That will be fine."

Turning to Paul, Nathan said; "Remember, Paul........details." Then he held out his hand and said, while shaking Paul's; "If anything else should occur outside of your sleep state, such as the 'flash' you had in our conversation, make note of those details, as well."

Then, leading Paul to the private exit, he opened the door, paused and said; "Paul, would you mind telling me who recommended me to you?"

Paul, looking puzzled, responded; "No one did. I picked your name out of the book. Why?"

"Because, Paul, out of all the psychologists in the city, I'm the only one who specializes in dream analysis. That was meant to be stated in the advertisement I placed in the phone directory, but the printer somehow omitted it."

"Well, I guess that was a lucky coincidence for me, then."

"Perhaps……..I'll see you tomorrow."

As Paul walked to his truck, he became attentive to the thought that Nathan seemed to really know what he was doing and he felt a little twinge of guilt for the irreverent way in which he had earlier perceived him. He also felt a little bounce in his step, then remembered his flash of Mary Ellen and hurried to his truck.

CHAPTER EIGHT

Marilyn slid into the passenger seat of Jack's car and as she did so, her short, pleated skirt rose up past her mid-thigh. Once seated, she glanced over at Jack, who was sporting a grin which Marilyn was quite familiar with.

"EVERYTHING OKAY?" asked Jack, the grin still present.

"She's a little upset, that's all, she'll be fine, I'm sure." Marilyn responded to Jack's grin with a nervous smile.

"DID YOU KNOW YOU HAVE A GREAT SET OF LEGS?" The clumsiness of the question caused Marilyn to emit a small laugh, followed by her incredulous query; "What did you say?"

"I SAID, YOU HAVE A GREAT PAIR OF LEGS, ACTUALLY, I'VE ADMIRED YOUR ENTIRE BODY FOR SOME TIME NOW, MARILYN."

"Jack, are you *serious?*"

As he neared the corner of the street, Jack reached over with his right hand and placed it on Marilyn's left knee, then ran it smoothly along her thigh, letting his fingers caress the warm inner section.

"Whoa, big boy, let's not get carried away, here." Marilyn spoke, as she firmly pushed Jack's roaming hand off the invaded area.

Jack was committed, however and a little rebuff wasn't about to stop him.

"MARILYN, I'VE REALLY ADMIRED YOUR BEAUTIFUL BODY FOR SO LONG, NOW........I'VE REALLY GOT THE HOTS FOR YOU."

"Jack……WHAT IS WRONG WITH YOU?"

"COME ON, MARILYN, HAVEN'T YOU FELT SOMETHING FOR ME? I'VE NOTICED THE WAY YOU LOOK AT ME WITH THAT 'COME HITHER' LOOK."

"Yeah? IN YOUR DREAMS, JACK!"

Jack had turned his car onto Main Street, but after driving a short way, he abruptly turned onto a broken-up asphalt entrance road, which led into an abandoned shoe factory complex, pulling up directly in front of the main office door.

Marilyn knew this didn't look good and braced to defend herself against what she expected to be an awkward attempt to seduce her.

"Jack, why are we going in here?"

"I JUST WANT TO TALK TO YOU; THAT'S ALL."

"Don't waste your time. I'm not interested."

Jack shut the engine off and turned sideways in his seat, facing Marilyn. For a good thirty seconds, he said nothing, satisfying himself with a long, lustful stare, which started at her partly revealed upper leg area and rose slowly to her breasts, pausing there, until Marilyn's irritation became audible; "For Christ's sake, Jack, why don't you take a god dam picture."

Jack made an effort to reply, but was only able to choke out an incoherent response. He suddenly found his throat to be dry and was rapidly becoming aware that his heart was beating very fast. Clearing his throat a couple of times, he took a deep breath, in an attempt to settle his nerves, but each time his eyes caught a glimpse of Marilyn's ample breasts, which were now rising and falling in anger, all his previous symptoms would flare up again. Regardless, he cleared his throat one more time, took another deep breath and concentrated on speaking softly, in his most seductive voice.

"Marilyn………I *want* you *so* badly……..I've been watching you at work for some time now and I find myself thinking about you all the time…….even when I'm out shopping, or when I'm watching television at home. I want to make love to you…….I don't know if I can take this much longer……..you're in my thoughts constantly……..I wonder what your body looks like when you………when you take your clothes off…….when you come out of the shower. I think about what it must be like to lay beside you in bed……..I want to touch you all over……I want to kiss your beautiful lips….. I love the way they always look so shiny…….sometimes when you walk in front of me, I catch the scent of your perfume and I'll try to move a little closer. Once, you bent over next to where I was kneeling on the floor arranging a display case and your hair brushed against my face……..I almost shot a load right then and there….."

"Wow, you really have a way with words."

"Do you think so?"

"Jack, I'm only kidding, for God sakes."

"WELL, I'M NOT! Marilyn……I've just got to kiss you."

As he said these words, Jack leaned over, put his right arm around Marilyn's neck and pulled her toward him, at the same time planting a firm kiss on her lips, while reaching out with his left hand and roughly grabbing her right breast. Her reaction was to push away from him, which she tried to do by pushing on his stomach with her left hand, just as he was lifting himself in his seat to gain more leverage. Doing this caused her hand to slip down to his groin, which further inflamed his passion. Emboldened, Jack seized the opportunity to run his left hand straight up under Marilyn's skirt to her most private area. His grip on her tightened and Marilyn found herself struggling fiercely to release herself from Jack's powerful embrace.

For the first time, Marilyn started to fear that Jack was about to, or had already reached the point of no return. He was intent on having his way with her and she began to wonder if she would be strong enough to break free of the vice-like grip his right arm had on her neck, which was hurting badly. She felt something smooth sliding partly down her back and knew that her gold rose necklace, the same one her mother had given her two months before she died, had broken.

Summoning every ounce of strength she could muster, Marilyn bent her head down while pushing against Jack, but his right arm dropped down to wrap itself around her upper back, where he slid it under her right armpit and, in one swift motion, lifted and turned her, so her back was facing him. He then drew her to him, so that she ended up sitting on his lap. Now, his left arm pinned both of Marilyn's arms, while his right hand reached down and pulled her skirt up high, revealing her panties. He quickly slid his thumb into the waist band and tugged, trying to pull them down. She could hear his raspy breathing in her right ear and knew that unless she stopped him *now*, she was going to be raped.

In one last-ditch effort to get out of Jack's clutch, Marilyn lifted her pinned arms so that her wrists were under his left arm. She then lowered her mouth to his forearm and bit down as hard as she could, holding the arm in place with her hands curled over it, so he was unable to pull it away.

Jack screamed loudly, as the pain from the bite burned into his arm. He had Marilyn's panties partly pulled down and, despite the pain, was reluctant to give up the treasure he held in his right hand, which was now plunged into her pubic area. Marilyn, in turn, bit down harder and then lifted her butt off Jack's lap. She lowered her left hand and grabbed his testicles, digging her fingers and nails into them ferociously, twisting hard at the same time. Still, Jack would not release his grip on her, nor remove his right hand from between her legs. In a lightning-fast move, Marilyn planted her feet against the passenger door and threw her head back as hard as she could. The sickening crack preceded the blood-curdling scream that Jack emitted, as blood flowed from both sides of his nose. He immediately released both his grip and his exploring hand. Marilyn felt him go soft under her bottom, as his entire body went quickly limp. Jack brought both of his hands to his nose and wailed in agony.

Marilyn scrambled out of his car, screaming obscenities as she did so. She picked up one of her shoes, which had fallen off in the car and threw it at Jack, hitting him in the forehead and bouncing back across the seat to her. She grabbed the shoe again and hammered his right leg, then took a final swing at his crotch, connecting solidly with the tip of his now-soft penis. Jack vaulted forward, trying to protect his vital privates with his right hand, while his left hand was fighting a losing battle with the blood spurting from his broken nose.

"YOU SON OF A BITCH, IF YOU EVER TOUCH ME AGAIN, I'LL KILL YOU.......I SHOULD CALL THE COPS AND HAVE THEM LOCK YOUR SORRY ASS UP........AS A MATTER OF FACT, I JUST MIGHT DO THAT........ IF YOU KNOW WHAT'S GOOD FOR YOU, YOU'LL STAY THE HELL AWAY FROM ME.....YOU GOT THAT, YOU SICK FUCK?"

Jack could only sit in his car, whimpering in anguish.

Marilyn put her other shoe back on her foot and quickly walked out to Main Street, mumbling to herself as she walked. She hiked the mile and a half to the parking lot at Paragon Gift Shop, got in her car and drove away.

CHAPTER NINE

As soon as Mary Ellen entered her home, she hurried to the bathroom, where she stood in front of the mirror and removed her blouse to get a good look at her arm, which Jack had told her was most likely broken. Although it was badly bruised, she was able to turn it, without excruciating pain and also able to bend it back and forth at the elbow, where the bruising was centered about two inches below. There was a sizable lump forming and she began to wonder if Jack had been correct in his diagnosis.

"What could have possessed Jack to come up behind me, that way? He <u>must</u> have known that I'd be startled..........unless he intended...........NO, Mary Ellen, you've been watching too many detective shows..........but why was he so quiet, when he said he was working? Was he.........watching me? Don't be silly, he was probably just deep in thought..........Paul gets that way sometimes, when he's trying to figure something out in his head. But why was Jack so damned insistent on getting me to the hospital? Oh, Mary, Mary, you're reading too much into this..........Jack was sincerely concerned for your well-being. Besides, <u>you</u> were the one who was deep in thought..........maybe if you hadn't been daydreaming, you might have heard him back there. Now, lady..........it's time for you to get your little butt in gear and start preparing something for this mystery guest your husband has invited. It's strange, but I'm not at all worried about Paul anymore..........I <u>know</u> he's all right and that he'll walk through that door at four-forty five, when he finishes work. He's always on time."

Mary Ellen started to put her blouse back on, and then noticed a slight tear in the right sleeve, just below the elbow, along with a tiny blood stain.

"Oh, darn, this was one of my favorite blouses, too."

Quickly slapping a bandage over the scraped area of the bruise, Mary Ellen hurried into the bedroom, where she discarded the ruined blouse in the waste basket, pulled off her pants, found a pair of sweatpants and one of Paul's old long-sleeve shirts and put them on, intending to get supper started, then take a shower and dress properly in time for the dinner guest. Ignoring the throbbing pain in her right arm, she rushed out to the kitchen, pausing to think what would be quick to prepare. She narrowed the choice down to steak, chicken or beef stew in the pressure cooker, deciding on the last item.

Once everything was started, Mary Ellen jumped in the shower and a half-hour later, her hair was dried, she was dressed and ready to greet Paul and whoever he was bringing with him. The familiar sound of Paul's truck pulling into the driveway caused Mary Ellen's heart to jump and she ran to the window to confirm what her ears had heard. She glanced at her watch, which read three twenty five and wondered why he was home so early. Mary Ellen also noticed that Paul was alone, in his truck and no other car had pulled into the driveway.

When Paul opened the door and stepped into the sunroom, Mary Ellen was there waiting. She smiled warmly, her eyes brimming with tears, walked to him and hugged him tightly, once again ignoring the pain in her right arm.

"I'm so glad that you're all right.........I was so worried about you....... where have you been? I've been trying to get in touch with you all day."

"Oh, sweetheart, I'm sorry. I met Larch at Forbes Coffee Shop this morning and asked him to come for supper. Then I was really tired, so I decided to take the day off and try to get some sleep. I *did* call you, but you were busy, so I left a message with Marilyn. Didn't she tell you I called?"

Mary Ellen released her embrace, stepped back, but still held her husband's hands in hers.

"Yes, she did, but I wanted to find out who was coming for supper and you didn't answer your cell phone.......all I kept getting was your voice mail, which, by the way, you also didn't answer....."

Paul held his right hand with the fingers pointing straight up and his left hand horizontally over the fingers in the almost universal 'time-out' indication.

"I was so tired that I didn't want any interruptions to my sleep, so I put my cell phone on voice mail and crashed in the recliner. I fell into a pretty deep sleep and almost missed my appointment.........oh, yeah, I never got a chance to tell you that I had an appointment today with a psychologist........."

Mary Ellen let out a relieved gasp and said; "Oh, Paul, that's wonderful! How did it go?"

"Actually, it went well......really well. I like the guy. He seems to....... I don't know exactly how to say it, but he seems to......understand what I'm going through with these dreams........ and something else......I picked the guy at random out of the phone book and he tells me that out of all the ones in the book, he's the only psychologist in the entire *city* who specializes in dream analysis........it wasn't in his ad, because the printer made a mistake. Strange, huh?"

"Yes, it is, but how did you schedule an appointment so quickly? I thought you'd have to wait at least a week or two."

"He had a cancellation. It was for two o'clock today, so I figured, 'what the hell', why not take it and get the ball rolling on ending these crazy nightmares."

"Honey, I'm so happy that you did this........there are so many questions I want to ask you, but the first one is; what time is Henry supposed to be here?"

"Relax; he's not coming until five thirty. Uh, I hope you don't mind, but I told him you'd make beef stew."

"Oh, you did, did you? Well, it's too late, because I've already got supper going."

Seeing the disappointment in Paul's face and his valiant attempt to conceal it, Mary Ellen was unable to keep up the ruse any longer.

"YOU relax, the beef stew is cooking........can't you smell it?"

"Mary Ellen, how did you know?"

"Just a lucky guess, I suppose."

"Uh.......there's something else....."

"Well, you're just full of surprises, aren't you?"

"Mare, I'm serious.......I asked Larch to come here for a reason. He's going to tell me about the 'graveyard game'."

"The graveyard game. What the heck is that?"

"Not 'is'..........'was'.........it was some kind of creepy game that I supposedly came up with. The only trouble is, I don't remember a damn thing about it. I'm pretty sure it's tied into my dreams, though, because I've seen these flashes of things in them, that ....well, why don't we wait until Larchie fills me in. Oh, and another thing.......I also asked him to tell me what happened on the night I fractured my skull....... with your okay, that is."

"I'm not so sure that's a good idea, Paul. Henry should know better than to...."

"He had no intention of telling me anything. He only agreed after I hounded him about it. Mare, whatever is causing my nightmares is somehow connected to the night of my accident; I *know* that, for sure."

"But, Paul.......it's going to be hard for you to deal with."

Paul placed both of his hands on Mary Ellen's shoulders and looked her straight in the eyes; "In my dreams for the past three weeks, I've seen a grotesque shadowy figure, which chased me out of a cemetery, one of my childhood friends turned into a zombie and I've run through the same field about two dozen times, with God knows what chasing me. I've lost over one hundred hours of sleep and twelve pounds. If that isn't enough, when I looked in the mirror yesterday, Count Dracula was looking back at me. I've dealt with that, Mare........I've dealt with *all* of that."

"I know you have, Paul......we *both* have. I just hope that this is the right decision."

The worried look in Mary Ellen's eyes convinced Paul that whatever secret his mother had sworn all of his childhood friends to so many years ago must have been a doozie.

"So.....you won't object to Larch telling me what I need to know?"

"Honey, I want to see these terrible dreams you've been having come to an end. If you think learning about that silly game and what happened on the night you got hurt so badly will help somehow, then how can I object?"

"Trust me, Mare.......I *know* it will."

Mary Ellen looked into her husband's eyes and smiled. "The last time you told me to trust you, I ended up pregnant."

Laughing, Paul replied; "Yeah, but that was over thirty years ago. I'm much more mature now."

Then he hugged her hard and Mary Ellen cried out in pain.

"What's wrong?" Paul asked, confused as to what he might have done to hurt her.

"Oh, I fell at work this afternoon. Will you look at my arm and tell me if you think it's broken?" Mary Ellen rolled up the sleeve on her arm and pulled back the bandage to reveal the wound.

"Wow, you've got yourself a badly bruised arm, but I don't think it's broken. Try bending it."

Mary Ellen complied with her husband's request, letting him gently turn and pull on the arm.

"Nope, not broken. If it was, you'd be passed out on the floor by now. Larch can confirm it later, if you want. He was a medic in the service and saw his share of breaks, I'm sure."

"I'll take your word for it, Paul."

"So, tell me, Mare.......how did you fall? You were standing on one of those chairs that I've warned you to stay off, weren't you?"

"No, I was in the back room and Jack startled me. I lost my balance and fell, that's all."

"How did he startle you? Didn't you know he was there?"

"It was probably my own fault. I was sort of zoning out and he snuck.......*came* up.....behind me; then, in that *voice* of his, he said

'PENNY FOR YOUR THOUGHTS!' My God, Paul, he scared me half to death. Anyway, I spun around fast and just lost my balance and fell backward, right on my fanny. I was so embarrassed, I felt like a fool, sitting there on the floor with Jack looking down at me."

"You started to say he snuck up on you. He probably did. I never trusted that guy. He always seemed like a creep to me. Do you think he was trying to make you jump, as his idea of a joke?"

"I don't know what to think, honey. I used to think he was a nice guy, but Marilyn told me he has been making some suggestive remarks to her. Now, I wonder if it's possible that he was watching me. Then he kept insisting that he take me to the hospital, but something about the way he was behaving just didn't feel right to me. Marilyn asked if she could give me a ride home and Jack practically knocked the door down, knowing he'd be giving her a ride back to the gift shop."

"Are you uncomfortable working there?"

"I never was, until today. Now I'm not so sure. Paul, I love that job so much. The girls I work with are all nice to me and Jack and his brother, Ralph, have always treated me well. The hours are good and I enjoy meeting and talking with the customers. Now, I feel differently about Jack.......he's starting to make me nervous."

"You might want to run all of this by Ralph. He seems to be a fairly solid guy. He always struck me as the type of guy who wouldn't put up with any bullshit from anyone, not even his little brother. And he thinks the world of you."

"But what if I'm wrong?"

"Bring Marilyn along to verify the suggestive remarks. I'm telling you Mare, if *I* saw 'creep' written all over Jack, I'm sure Ralph has wondered about it. He's not a stupid guy."

"I don't know, Paul……..maybe I should just wait a while and see what happens."

"That's your call, sweetheart. Just be careful around that guy, okay?"

"I will be."

"Now……are you going to be able to get supper going, or do you want me to help?"

"I'll be fine, Paul. Actually, the beef stew should be ready in ten minutes, or so. It *would* be a big help if you lifted the pressure cooker off the stove for me, when it's ready."

"I think I can handle that." Paul sensed that Mary Ellen was either holding back on something that was bothering her, or was just frazzled from the day's activities, but she wasn't her usual upbeat self. "Mare…….have you got something else you want to say?"

"Yes…….I have." Mary Ellen fiddled with the plates and silverware, not making eye contact with Paul. Finally, she glanced up and said; "Paul, I don't know anything about this 'cemetery game' that you spoke about…"

"Graveyard game" Paul corrected her.

"Whatever……..the thing is……..I *do* know what happened to Larry Guernette at the cemetery and I think…….you should hear it from me. Henry can fill you in on the details. Come and sit with me in the living room." Mary Ellen held out her hand for Paul to take and led him into the living room, where she sat on the couch and patted the cushion beside her, inviting him to sit there. Paul sat down slowly, and then turned toward Mary Ellen, lifting his left leg and tucking it under his right one, his left arm draped over the back of the sofa.

"This sounds ominous."

"Well, Paul, I'm curious…….didn't you ever wonder what happened to Larry that night?"

"Yes, I did, but no one ever wanted to talk about it. All I know is that whatever *did* happen that night must have scared him pretty badly, because he and his family had moved away by the time I got home from the hospital.

"Paul………they didn't move away because they were scared. They moved because……..they wanted to get away from this area." Squeezing his left hand, Mary Ellen spoke tenderly; "Honey…..Larry was brutally murdered at the cemetery……..and everyone seems to think you may have witnessed it. On top of that, the police believed that the murderer chased you."

Upon hearing these words, a sudden, horrific flash blazes before Paul's eyes, an image of Larry lying on the ground, the shadowy figure standing over him, turning toward Paul........pointing it's finger......... saying something, but saying what? Paul concentrates hard, oblivious to the woman sitting next to him. He peers at the shadowy figure........ it is angry with him........but now, for the first time, Paul is able to see it's eyes and it isn't anger he sees in them, but fear......FEAR! *This thing is afraid of <u>me</u>! But, I didn't know that, then.......is that right? So that's why I was running through the woods........ I ran, because I was a twelve-year-old kid who just saw his friend murdered by this.....this..... monster......this monster who is pointing it's finger at me and yelling at me........'YOU'RE DEAD!"*

"Paul.....Paul, honey....talk to me. Are you all right?"

Mary Ellen's voice, distant at first, is now close and Paul shakes his head, blinking his eyes at the same time. He feels Mary Ellen shaking his left arm, then turns to her, tears forming in his eyes. With a choking voice, he begins to speak; "It's all starting to make some sense, Mare. These dreams I've been having.......Larry is usually in them........Oh, man! I was so close, just then, to seeing its face."

"Who's face? Paul, what are you talking about? You're starting to scare me."

The look of apprehension on Mary Ellen's face begged for an explanation.

"I'm talking about the face of that shadowy figure that has chased me in most of those dreams. I saw something, just then.......a sort of recognition.......in it's eyes. It *knew* me......and I *know* I've seen those eyes before........at some time in my life. You know, in the back of my mind I always wondered.........maybe suspected........that Larry was dead, but I guess........I don't even know why I felt that way, I just did, Mare. Whatever is making me have these dreams........it's like I'm being teased........it shows me a glimpse of something, then a flash of something else.......but it seems to reveal a little bit more with every dream I have. Now, it's showing me stuff when I'm wide awake. I just had a flash of some sort that clearly showed Larry lying on the ground, next to a stone, or maybe a gravestone, with this monster standing over him. Damn it, I almost had the face in the flash……..but I know it's going to come to me, sooner or later."

Mary Ellen leaned over and kissed Paul softly on the side of his mouth and gently rubbed the back of his neck with her left hand.

"Honey, you've been through so much in your lifetime. I don't know what you saw, but my heart breaks every time I think of how a twelve-year-old boy could have been terrorized so much that he lost his memory. And now, you've got to endure these awful nightmares……..I've been praying so hard that these will end soon. I just hope this man can help you do whatever needs to be done to stop them……..for good."

"I'm not sure whether the loss of memory was caused by the skull fracture or what I saw……..if I really did see something bad. By the way, the guy's name is Nathan Feldmar. He has a practice set up on Juniper Parkway, in the city. I'm going back for another session tomorrow morning, at eleven o'clock. Oh, that reminds me………"

Paul jumped up from the couch and went into the kitchen, where he retrieved a pencil and piece of paper. Mary Ellen, curious, followed.

"What are you doing?"

"Nathan wanted me to keep track of any flashes I might have and what they were about. He said they would be helpful."

Unable to determine whether Paul had fully absorbed the news of Larry's murder and was blocking it out, or if it just hadn't hit him yet, she asked; "Paul, are you *sure* you're all right? I'm worried about you."

Turning away from what he was writing on the paper, Paul set the pencil down, walked to her and slid his arms around her waist.

"I'm okay, Mare……really, I am. Yeah, I'm a little shocked to hear that Larry was murdered, but, you have to remember, it was almost fifty years ago. It's not like I just saw him yesterday. Do you know how he died?"

"The paper said he had severe head injuries."

"Who found him?" Paul removed his arms from his wife's midsection.

"He was found by a young couple from the city. They had parked their car and were out for a walk, because the man wanted to show his girlfriend this beautiful old cemetery and when they walked in to the graveyard, Larry's body was draped over the base of a............ broken headstone."

"What did I just say, Mare? You see, these flashes are real......they're trying to tell me something. I *saw* Larry's limp body next to a stone. This is incredible."

"Paul, I've been uneasy about your nightmares, but now you say you're getting 'flashes' and it's starting to scare me. What does the psychologist say about them?"

"He didn't say much, only that they weren't that unusual. He was very interested in the one I had in his office. It was strange. I had only been there about fifteen minutes and was telling him about the first couple of dreams I'd had, when, BAM!......I get hit with this image of you.......looking like you ....I'm not sure whether you needed help or had gotten hurt, but I felt like I wanted to hold you and tell you everything was okay."

Mary Ellen perked up upon hearing this. She gazed intently at Paul and asked; "Paul, do you remember what time you had that flash at the psychologist's office?"

"Yeah, I looked at Nathan's watch when he handed me a bottle of water. It read twenty past two."

The gasp that Mary Ellen uttered caught Paul by surprise, then, putting two and two together, he knew the reason for it.

"Don't tell me......that was the time when you fell, wasn't it?"

Mary Ellen answered the question with a somber nod of her head.

"Mare, now *I'm* starting to get wigged out by all of this. Wait until I tell Nathan about this. He seems to think I might have ESP." Paul was unable to control his laughter at this thought. Mary Ellen, embracing the release of tension, laughed with him.

"Well, Paul, I've suspected that for years. You always know the precise time that supper is ready and I've often wondered how you never failed to find your Christmas presents, no matter how well I hid them."

They both laughed heartily, not so much that their words were funny, more that it was one of the few times they had been able to laugh in the past couple of weeks. It was Paul, who spoke next.

"Speaking of supper……shouldn't that beef stew be done by now?"

Reaching up with her left hand and patting Paul's cheek tenderly, Mary Ellen replied; "You *do* have a one-track mind, don't you? Yes, love, it should be ready now."

"Mare, are you sure your arm is okay? I'll be glad to help you with anything you need done."

"Honey, I *told* you, I'm fine. All I need you to do is lift that heavy pressure cooker and release it for me, then pour the stew into the big bowl on the counter."

Paul complied with his wife's request and then announced he was going to take a shower before Larch arrived. Mary Ellen busied herself with the meal preparation, happy that her husband was home safe and sound, totally unconcerned about the throbbing pain in her right arm, but *deeply* troubled by his account of those 'flashes', believing their very presence to be a menacing sign.

Silently, she prayed that someone would be able to help Paul find an end to his nightmares and that Nathan Feldmar would be the man for the job.

CHAPTER TEN

Larch was beginning to worry that he might not be able to keep his dinner appointment with his old friends, Paul and Mary Ellen McCulloch. Things had not gone right on this particular site all day. Now, it was three o'clock, the time when his crew normally started to wind down and start putting away all the equipment and a problem had developed. One of his backhoes had broken a hydraulic line and spilled about fifteen gallons of oil onto the soil, where it was quickly being absorbed. He had called the environmental people immediately and they had dispatched an agent to assess the damage. The only problem was that the agent had a forty mile drive and hadn't arrived yet. When he did arrive, it would take him at least a half hour to do the damage assessment, then a clean-up crew would be called and it would take the better part of an hour before they arrived. Finally, the clean-up process itself, would take well over an hour. Larch knew he was looking at a minimum of three hours, more like four, as the environmental boys loved to suck up the overtime. As the owner of the offending piece of equipment, he was required to stay until the agent finished his report, then he would sign it and, at that point, would be allowed to leave, putting his foreman in charge of finishing up after the clean-up was completed. He hesitated to call and say he'd be late, because there was still a chance that he'd be able to make it on time. It all depended on what time the agent arrived.

Pacing the construction site, which was located on Main Street, bordering the old shoe factory complex, Larch meandered over to the edge of that property, thinking to himself what a waste of a good sturdy building, to let it just sit idle. His mind began conjuring up different ways that the complex could be re-vitalized, somehow, making good use, not only of a fine old brick building, but of prime land, as well. Standing about three hundred feet from the building, Larch had a good overall view of the right side of the complex. He slowly walked deeper into his site to gain a better view of the rear portion of the shoe factory building, noting the condition of the loading dock, which, despite its age, was in remarkably good condition. As he stood there, pondering the costs involved in cosmetic work to make the property rentable, in the event he were to purchase it, the air was broken by the sound of a woman screaming, not far away.

Larch turned instinctively back toward the construction site, only to see his crew busy greasing the machinery, biding their time until the agent arrived, far enough away, apparently, that they did not hear the scream. Trying to ascertain exactly in which direction the sound came from, he listened again, for perhaps another scream, but only a soft late-summer breeze wafted by his ear. Just as he decided to enter the complex property and walk around to the front of the building, in an attempt to locate the source of the scream, Larch heard his foreman calling out to him that the environmental agent had arrived. As he walked back to the oil spill, he turned and saw a dark sedan moving quickly out of the complex entrance drive, spewing up pieces of the broken asphalt. But the car was too far away to either read the license plate, or even see how many people were inside. Larch strained his eyes and was pretty sure the driver was the only occupant of the vehicle. He watched, until the car disappeared behind the overgrown brush along the entrance drive.

Then, as he neared the spill location, he caught a good side view of the suspect car speeding up Main Street toward Sheridan, his home town. It appeared that the driver was distracted by something or someone lower down on the passenger seat, or perhaps on the floor of the car, as he seemed to be struggling to hold it in place.

'It's probably just a couple of kids screwing around' he thought. Still, Larch felt it best to remember the car and the time he heard the scream, just in case.

The environmental agent was friendly and efficient, introducing himself, them quietly going about his work. In less than half an hour, he had completed his assessment and called in the necessary people for clean-up. As he presented a relieved Larch the completed report at four fifteen, it was quickly signed and Larch was on his way home, leaving his foreman in charge.

On his way home, Larch thought about the upcoming evening and what Paul's reaction might be to hearing that their friend, Larry, had been killed the night Paul nearly split his skull in two. He was beginning to have second thoughts about agreeing to let Paul in on the events of that night and secretly hoped that Mary Ellen would decide that it would be best not to tell her husband anything. He had given his word to Paul, however and would proceed, if Mary Ellen approved, to tell him everything he knew about that night. Larch smiled at the irony of how an event that took place nearly fifty years earlier, could be so fresh and vivid in his memory, but indeed, it was. It was also the most terrifying night he had ever experienced.

Larch arrived at his home by four thirty. 'Home' was a renovated farm house located in the north end of town. The house had been built in 1860 and had once been the centerpiece of a thriving dairy farm, Jensen's Dairy, which prospered for more than one hundred years, before being driven out of business by the big 'super farms', whose sheer volume allowed them to price their milk products low enough to lure even Jensen's most loyal customers away. The three Jensen boys had all chosen to work outside the farm, so when their father died, they convinced their mother to sell the property and buy herself a small modern ranch, which she reluctantly did. The man who bought the farm in 1974 had grandiose plans, but did little or no upkeep and, consequently, the house, barn and outbuildings all fell into disrepair. The new owner's financial problems eventually led to a foreclosure in 1980 and the property being put up for auction by the bank less than a year later.

It was at this auction where Larch, being the high bidder, became the newest owner of the one hundred and ten acre farm, which little resembled the fine condition that farmer Jensen had left it in, just eight years earlier.

Larch, whose construction business had finally gotten off the ground as his reputation as a man of his word had spread, was facing a fairly hefty expense to bring the buildings back to good condition. He formed a plan to prioritize the repairs, starting with new roofs on both the house and barn, followed the next year by a new heating system in the house, shoring up the sills on the barn foundation and replacing several hundred feet of rotted barn board. All cracked and broken window panes in all buildings were replaced and every window in the house went from wood to vinyl. Little by little, Henry V. Stolarczek accomplished his goal of once again making the old farm house a comfortable home. It took him twelve years, but he now had a place to which he was happy to return at the end of the day. He had expanded his garden each summer, until it now comprised nearly an acre of plantings. Summer evenings found Larch happily working in that garden, his favorite hobby.

To visitors and anyone who drove by Larch's 'gentleman's farm', the first impression was one of neatness, almost to a fault. The rock wall, which ran along his border, parallel with the road, had been neatly rebuilt, all sixteen hundred feet of it; in addition, every tree and shrub was perfectly trimmed, causing one to believe the owner must employ a gardener to maintain them. Summertime visitors entering the long driveway were treated to a six hundred foot-long border of colorful annual flowers on each side of the driveway, from the entrance, all the way to the front porch of the main house. The driveway culminated in a cul-de-sac directly in front of the porch. The island in the middle of the circle of asphalt featured a lush display of perennials, mixed with enough annuals to provide a dazzling greeting to visitors. In the center of the island stood a thirty five-foot tall flag pole and leading up to it, was a pathway, made from flat stones. The garden was, of course, weed free and covered with a generous layer of dark mulch, against which the flowers stood out all the more vibrantly.

Having never married, Larch had grown accustomed to coming and going whenever he pleased, so when he found himself obligated to be at a particular place at a certain time, it tended to be a big deal for him. For that reason, as he walked from his truck to the front porch, his mind raced with thoughts of how he should dress and what should he bring. Despite the fact that Paul had told him earlier this morning all he needed was to bring himself, Larch decided to stop and buy a good quality bottle of wine. He also thought it would be a nice gesture to bring flowers for Mary Ellen and wondered if she would be offended should he put together a bouquet from his own garden, rather than from a commercial flower store. His mind also wandered back to the reason for his invitation to the McCulloch home, which, of course, was to inform Paul not only of what happened to their friend Larry, on the night Paul fractured his skull, but to also explain the strange game they had been playing that day and night, to the same man who invented it, in the first place.

'I wonder why Paul started having these nightmares all of a sudden. How can you live almost your entire life, after recovering from such a serious injury, without any apparent problems and then suddenly start having nightmares about something that you don't even remember? He said he has a six-month blank period. That has to be tough; I can't imagine what it would be like to go through life missing an entire summer of your childhood. He didn't mention whether he's seeing anyone about these dreams; I sure hope he is.

As he entered the house, Larch set the mail that he had collected from the box near the road, on the kitchen table, checked his watch, which read four thirty-two, then went into the bathroom, took a shower and shaved.

When he emerged from the shower, he went and dressed, then headed out to his large mixed-variety garden, where he carefully selected a generous bouquet and brought it into the kitchen. He wrapped it in newspaper, ran the lower part under cool water and finally put the homemade arrangement into a plastic grocery bag.

Larch left his home at ten minutes past five, drove to the package store in the center of town and chose a good quality merlot to bring to his hosts. Leaving the package store, he checked his watch one more time and then drove to the west end of town, to the McCulloch's home, ringing the front doorbell at precisely five thirty p.m.

CHAPTER ELEVEN

Despite the nagging pain in her arm, Mary Ellen had set a table that was fit to welcome a celebrity, right down to linen napkins and tall candles. In a way, Larch *would* be treated like a V.I.P., as it had been years since the three of them had gotten together. Paul and Mary Ellen had, on occasion, run into Larch, but only for a friendly 'hello, how are you?' type of conversation. Mary Ellen remembered how it was just a month or so ago that Paul had suggested inviting Henry over for dinner and a night of cribbage, which he loved to play, but then came the nightmares and everything seemed to change after that. Paul had become jittery and irritable, mostly, she hoped, only because of a lack of sleep, but she feared there was more involved than sleep deprivation. His personality had started to change, just a little. The fun-loving guy she had been married to for these thirty four years was becoming preoccupied with his dreams and less able to laugh easily, as had always been the case. The dreams seemed to be controlling his mood and she was relieved that he had taken her advice and gone to see a psychologist.

Pausing as she set the last piece of silverware down on the table, Mary Ellen said a silent prayer that her husband would soon be his normal self and his nightmare world would be gone forever.

Then, the front doorbell rang.

"I GOT IT!" Paul cried out, as he went to answer the door.

Mary Ellen walked to the living room to watch as Larch walked into the house and shook hands with Paul.

"I see you're still 'old reliable', always on time. Paul welcomed Larch.

Henry, smiling, handed Paul the bottle of wine. "Here, I thought we might enjoy this with our meal."

"WOW! This is top-shelf stuff." Then, in a contrite tone, Paul said; "You didn't have to do that, Hank."

"I know I didn't *have* to, but I *wanted* to." Larch replied. Then, as he stepped from behind the front door, he produced an enormous bouquet of flowers and held them out for Mary Ellen.

"And these are for you, Mary."

The audible sigh that escaped from Mary Ellen gave away her delight with the gift. "Henry…….these are absolutely beautiful! Oh, look at all the pretty colors…….did you arrange these yourself?"

"Yes, they're from my garden. I hope you don't mind."

"Henry, I think this is the most beautiful bouquet of flowers I have ever seen. I can't believe you went to all that trouble…."

"No trouble at all, Mary."

Paul, looking on with interest, patted Larch on the back of his shoulder and said; "Why, you old smoothie, I didn't know you were so debonair with the women."

At this comment, Larch blushed slightly, which did not go unnoticed by Mary Ellen.

"Paul, don't embarrass him" Mary Ellen said, as she set the flowers down on the little foyer table, then stood on her tiptoes and gave Larch a kiss on the cheek, along with a hug. "Thank you Henry, that was *so* thoughtful of you! Don't pay any attention to him. He's just jealous because he didn't think of it."

Larch, uncomfortable with the display of affection from Mary Ellen, now turned a brighter shade of crimson and Mary Ellen, recognizing his discomfort, spoke; "Let me go and put these in a vase, right away. Henry, please sit down; I'm sure you and Paul have some catching up to do." She motioned toward the two reclining chairs, as she spoke, and then went about her business, leaving the two men alone in the room.

"Can I get you a drink, old buddy?" Paul asked. "Beer, soda, coffee?"

"I'll take a soda, Paul, diet, if you have it."

"Good; make yourself comfortable. I'll be right back. Do you want ice?"

"No thanks. I'll drink it from the can."

Paul returned with two diet sodas, handed one to Larch and sat down in the other recliner. He cracked the can of soda, took a sip, then bypassing any small talk, turned to Larch and said; "Mary Ellen told me about Larry."

Larch, who hadn't opened his soda yet, sat with the can in his hand and looked at Paul, then spoke; "Oh……..how much did she tell you?"

"Everything, I guess. She said he was found dead in the old cemetery off Crater Street, by a young couple from the city. She also said he was 'brutally' murdered. When I pushed her for more info, she said he had severe head injuries. Hank……you're going to think this is weird, but I think I might be seeing some sort of re-enactment of his murder in the dreams I've been having for the past few weeks. If I *did* witness the killing, as I'm told, was the belief at the time, then it must have been stored away in some remote part of my brain. Now, it is slowly revealing little bits and pieces to me. All I've got to do is put things together and……..maybe, *just maybe*, I might see who the murderer is. I'm pretty sure this one character, a shadowy figure that keeps appearing in the dreams, is the murderer, but I can never see his face clearly."

Paul paused, looking at his friend and smiled, continuing; "Have I managed to convince you that I'm a certifiable candidate for the Looney bin?"

"That's some pretty heavy stuff you just laid out there, but no, I don't think you're going crazy. What you need to do, though, is talk to a professional about your dreams, otherwise they *will* drive you nuts. Actually, Paul, I had some experience with guys in Nam who had similar cases like yours. These were guys who had witnessed some pretty horrific deaths, usually to their buddies and usually at close proximity. Some of them had memory loss, like you, while others tried to block it out of their minds and refused to get counseling. These are the guys you see today, in the cities, walking along the street talking to imaginary people and always looking over their shoulder, for who knows what. People laugh at them, but no one can ever know the horrors those poor guys went through, over there. The sad thing is that they didn't have to end up like this."

"Larchie, you don't have to convince me to get help. Mary Ellen already did that and I just started seeing this psychologist over on the west side of the city. I've only had one session and already feel like a big weight has been lifted off my chest."

"That's great, Paul. Do you mind if I ask who it is, you're seeing?"

"His name is Feldmar…….. Nathan Feldmar and he seems to have a nice way about him, you know……sort of laid back, slow and easy type."

Larch became somewhat elated upon hearing Paul say this.

"Paul, I've heard about him. He's treated some of the guys I was just telling you about…….and he's good, *really* good. You couldn't have picked a better man to see than Nathan."

"That's good to know. I've got a good feeling about him, myself. It's obvious that he knows what he's doing."

The conversation is abruptly ended by the sound of Mary Ellen's call from the doorway of the living room to 'come and get it.'

Paul got up from his chair and held out his arm in the direction of the kitchen, saying to Larch; "After you, buddy."

They sat down at the kitchen table and all enjoyed the hearty stew, engaging mostly in talk of the weather, sports, work and anything but the topic of the evening, which would follow the meal. When the meal was over, Larch insisted on helping Mary Ellen clean up the dishes and the three childhood friends laughed and joked their way through the clean-up process, leaving the kitchen spotless. Mary Ellen made a fresh pot of coffee and they all sat down again, at the kitchen table, where the talk became serious. Larch began the conversation, looking directly at Mary Ellen.

"Judging by what Paul told me before our meal, I guess that you don't have a problem with me filling him in on some of the things he's forgotten."

"I had my reservations, Henry, but after giving it some thought, I realize that this could help him put an end to these.......horrible...... nightmares he's been having and anything that will speed that along has my blessing.........so, please tell him whatever it is he wants to know."

Turning to Paul, Larch pushed his cup a little toward the center of the table, folded his hands in front of him and said; "Paul, you asked me this morning to tell you about the graveyard game we used to play. At first, I thought you were pulling my leg; you *do* have a reputation for that."

All three of them laughed easily, breaking any tension that might have started to build. Larch continued; "But the more I thought about it, the more I realized how tough it must have been for you to go through your whole life, knowing you had no memory of a part of your childhood. So, let me get this straight........you remember everything before and after the summer of 1957, but the summer itself, right?"

"That's about right, except for the fact that I've been getting these little tidbits thrown at me in the dreams, which, along with the flashbacks, have awakened part of my memory, just not enough of it, that's all."

"Well, sometime in July, I think it was near the end of the month, you came up with this crazy idea that you thought was just the *greatest* thing to do. I remember the night you told us about it. We were all sitting on the stone wall in front of Talbert's house, bored out of our minds. It was one of those hot, sultry nights, when you'd sweat without doing anything. All of a sudden, you jumped up and said you had a great idea for a new game and we could play it tomorrow. You said it would be a neat way to test our courage, not that we needed it tested........do you remember another game that you came up with, where we all took turns going into that old haunted house at the end of the street?"

Paul laughed; "Oh, yeah.......the one where Ritchie's father almost killed me. That was great, but man, he really lost it that night."

Larch turned to Mary Ellen and, bending his thumb in Paul's direction, said; "*He* had fun, but *we* usually ended up getting the wits scared out of us."

Mary Ellen was quick to concur with Larch; "I always knew he was a practical joker and it's just as well I never knew some of the silly things he did to you boys. I'm sure there were days when you wanted to get him back."

"We tried to do just that at the haunted house......."

Paul interrupted his friend at this point.

"Larch, it wasn't really haunted, I just made that up to scare you guys a little more. Do you remember the night I got you with the 'hanging' story?"

Larch threw his arms up for emphasis; "Oh, man that scared the heck out of me. I never wanted to go in that house after that."

Paul laughed once more, then said to Larch; "Hey, we're starting to lose our focus, here. Go on about the graveyard game, old buddy, I'm anxious to hear about that."

"Well, like I was saying, we weren't particularly interested in having our courage tested, but, at the same time we were sort of intrigued, because you did invent some good games." Then, turning to Mary Ellen again, Larch told her; "By the middle of summer, we were usually pretty tired of baseball all day and hide and seek at night, so whenever Paul came up with a different game, no matter how scary it sounded, we welcomed the break in the monotony."

Shifting to face Paul, he continued "I remember looking at your face, man and seeing how excited you were when you started to explain the new game to us. You picked up the baseball we had used all day and said we would all ride our bicycles up to the old cemetery off Crater Street tomorrow afternoon. You held up the baseball and said each one of us would either put a special mark on it or sign it and then we would all walk into the cemetery and place the ball behind a gravestone, near the back. Then, we would go home for the rest of the afternoon and come back to the cemetery after dark. Three of the guys would wait up on Crater Street, while the fourth guy had to leave his bike and *walk* down to the cemetery all alone, go in, retrieve the ball, then walk back to where the other guys were waiting for him. Then, he would produce the ball and the three guys would check it out to make sure it had their marks on it. If you were brave enough to do it, you passed the test; if not, you knew the taunting and teasing would never end."

Paul had a puzzled look, as he asked Larch; "Sounds pretty neat, but wouldn't it have been easy for someone to sneak back up there before dark and either bring the ball back with him, or hide it closer to where the guys would be waiting, so he wouldn't have to go in the cemetery at night."

"You had that covered. You said that after we placed the ball, we would all come back to Hillside Street and stay together for the rest of the day, only being out of each other's sight while we ate supper. That way, it would be impossible for anyone to sneak back and do that."

"Larchie, I can't believe Ritchie's dad, or yours, for that matter, would let you go there once it got dark."

"They wouldn't. There was no way my dad would let me go that far that late at night. We all agreed to tell our parents we were going to be riding our bikes down at the end of Hillside Street. We knew no one would come looking for us, because that was a fairly safe place to play. Anyway, the next day it was really hot, but we didn't care. We were all psyched up about playing this new game. We made our marks on the ball with an old red crayon, I remember you made a Kilroy face and we all laughed, because it was so funny looking, with the little guy peeking over the fence. Ritchie's bike was the only one with a saddlebag, so we put the ball in there, along with four peanut butter sandwiches crammed in and rode up to the cemetery. It was nice and cool in there, with no sun getting through the trees, so we sat down on the soft moss in back and ate our sandwiches. Then we realized that no one thought to bring any water and our mouths were all dry and sticky from the peanut butter, so we put the ball in back of the gravestone furthest to the rear of the cemetery and took off for home. We were hurting badly by the time we got back, it was so hot and our mouths were so dry that we all went into your house and we each drank about six glasses of water. Your mom couldn't understand why we were so thirsty."

Paul's interest was piqued and he asked Larch; "So, who was the first guy to go and get the ball?"

"You were. You always wanted to be the first to do the scary things you came up with. You used to say it would be really embarrassing if you were too afraid to take the challenge."

"Was that when Larry got murdered?"

"No, that happened a week or so later."

"Well, was I too scared to do it?"

"Heck, no! You walked down to the cemetery, real cool-like and you were down there for what seemed like forever to us, although it was probably only fifteen or twenty minutes. We were really starting to think something must have happened to you and then we saw you jogging up the dirt road, with the baseball in your hand. When you got closer to us, I could see your face was flushed and you were sweating pretty good and I figured you must have been really scared when you were down there, but I knew you'd never admit it. I had to ask you anyway, if you had been scared and you put your hand over your heart and patted your chest, saying it was the scariest thing you had ever done. I looked at Ritchie and Larry and almost burst out laughing. Ritchie swallowed hard and Larry's eyes got really big, it was a funny sight. This seemed like the perfect opportunity to make those guys sweat it out, so I volunteered to go first the next night. I even did 'black, black, no takesies back' on my belt, so they couldn't pull rank on me."

The little group laughed again, giving Mary Ellen a chance to jump in and announce that she would make another pot of coffee, if anyone wanted more. Both men voiced their approval and she quietly set about brewing the coffee, and then returned to the table with a plate full of homemade chocolate chip cookies, which she had made the day before. Paul and Larch dug in to them like a couple of school kids whose mother had just baked them. She then sat down, causing Paul to ask "How did you get that coffee going so fast?"

"I had it all set in the coffeemaker. All I had to do was hit the switch. It should be ready in a few minutes."

Paul turned to Larch, nodding his head in feigned pride. "That's why I married her, she's so efficient."

Laughter filled the room again. Then, Paul pressed Larch for more. "So, did anything eventful happen when you went down to get the ball the next night? You *did* go the next night, didn't you?"

"Yeah, I went the next night.......and outside of being terrified down there all alone in that cemetery, nothing bad happened. I ran all the way down there, went in and grabbed the ball and flew out of that cemetery as fast as I could run. I must have set a record for getting back to where you guys were waiting. Up to that point in my life, I had never been so scared and thought I could *never be* more scared. A week later, I was."

"Well, what took so long for those other two guys to have their turn?"

"Paul, you know how Ritchie was. He kept making excuses for why he couldn't do it on this night or that. Finally, we told him, 'either you do it or we tell everyone in school you're gutless'. He finally went down one night and got the ball. You and I laughed hysterically when we saw him running back, yelling to someone or something 'Don't get me, please'. But, he did it! Then, the next day, he was bragging to everyone in school about how he went to the old cemetery all alone at night and how he wasn't scared, not even a little bit. Some of the older kids came over to listen and Ritchie juiced it up really good to try and impress them, saying stuff like he heard moaning coming from one of the graves. The down side to all of this was that Larry was listening too and he was working himself up into a real state, knowing his turn was coming up next."

"So, when did Larry get his turn?"

"The next night, I'm pretty sure. He said he was tired of putting it off and just wanted to get it over with. It was near the end of the week, Wednesday or Thursday, when he went down."

"You say he was pretty nervous, huh?"

"Oh, he was a wreck, man. The poor kid was trembling, just thinking about it."

"It sounds almost like he expected to die."

"You know, Paul, I never looked at it that way. Do you think someone threatened him?"

"I don't know, but with Ritchie shooting his mouth off all day at school, it's possible someone……..oh, listen to me, 'Joe Detective', out to solve the crime of the century."

"No, Paul, you might be on to something. Ritchie did tell a lot of people and the older kids were especially interested. They might have gone there to try and scare Larry, as a prank. Maybe things got out of hand and ……..."

"And some eighth grader smashed his head in with a rock. I don't think so."

"Yeah, I guess you're right"

Paul folded his arms across his chest and said "I'm confused. Mary Ellen told me that Larry was found by a couple from the city the next day, but if he came out of the cemetery, why didn't he go home with us?"

"Well, that's the point, Paul; Larry *didn't* come out of the cemetery. He walked down the dirt road and we watched him until he was out of sight. He was just so scared, that we all agreed maybe we shouldn't have let him go. You even told him he didn't have to do it if he was really that scared, but he insisted on taking his turn. We waited and waited. It must have been close to half an hour. I knew something was wrong, because it only took me about eight or ten minutes the night I went. That's when you said 'we have to go get him.' We all left our bikes up near the road, because there were some big rocks on the dirt road and it was too dark to see them in time to avoid hitting one and ruining your wheel. The three of us ran down to the cemetery and Larry was no where in sight. You led the way in, Ritchie and I following you and then we saw him. It was awful. He was just standing there, like he was frozen. He had the baseball in his hand and he was staring straight ahead. You asked him what happened and he just whimpered. His face was all tear-stained and he had wet his pants, *man*, he had a strong urine smell to him.

"Larch, *something* must have scared him, maybe an animal?"

"It wasn't an animal, Paul. While you were trying to get Larry to talk to you, this guy came out of nowhere, it seemed. He must have been hiding behind the stone wall in back of the cemetery."

"Was he wearing a black shadowy cape, with a hood?"

"Yes, he was. You can remember that?"

"Only in my dreams. The thing that chases me is a shadowy figure, with bony fingers and a face that I haven't seen clearly."

"That's the same guy, Paul. He came charging at us, growling really low, like some kind of wild animal. I know now, that it was just a guy dressed up like that, but at the time, all I could think was, 'this thing is going to kill us all'. I screamed and started running. I could hear you guys screaming, but I didn't look to see who was running with me. It was every man for him self; you know, the self-preservation thing. About half-way up the dirt road, I turned to look back and was a little relieved to find Ritchie and you right behind me, without anyone chasing us. You said to stop running and we did. Then you said we had to go back and get Larry. Ritchie was bawling his eyes out, begging us to keep moving……..there was no way he was going to go back and if he did, he would have been useless, he was just so scared. That's when you said you had an idea. You told me to take Ritchie home, that you were going to sneak back to the cemetery, grab a couple of stones and peg them at the thing that had Larry."

"I said that? What was I thinking?" Paul shook his head in disbelief.

"You know, Paul, you sounded so sure of yourself, that I didn't even question your plan. I was just hoping that Ritchie and I would make it home safely. I figured you'd take care of things with Larry and bring him home. We just thought you could handle *anything*."

"Yeah, well, you were wrong about that."

Larch sat up straight, miffed at the off-hand comment.

"I don't deserve that, Paul."

"No, you don't, Hank. I'm sorry, buddy. I guess I'm just realizing that one of my good friends died because of some stupid game that I made up. That pretty much means that I'm responsible for his death."

"Paul, we were *kids*, for crying out loud. You can't blame yourself for Larry's death. *You* were the one who tried to talk him out of going down to the cemetery. He went on his own free will. What about me? I could have told Ritchie I was going back with you. He would have had to come, because he would have been too scared to stay by himself. If I had done that, maybe Larry would still be alive. But I didn't, Paul. I took the easy way out, by taking Ritchie home. Do you see what I'm saying? We can't beat ourselves up over this. Larry died because he was too stubborn to listen to reason. He knew he shouldn't go down there, but he did anyway. His death is no more your fault than it is mine, or Ritchie's, for that matter."

Larch settled against the back of the kitchen chair and kept his gaze on Paul, waiting to see if a rebuttal would be forthcoming. None came; instead, Paul put his head down, staring into his lap for a few moments and then slowly raised it up, turning to his friend. Slowly and deliberately, he began to speak.

"From what I've been able to piece together out of my dreams, I went back to the cemetery, got Larry to move a little…….. then it got fuzzy……and the next part I remember is the shadowy figure pointing at me and yelling to me, then……..I was running, always running…….. with apparently nothing chasing me. It always ends the same way. I'm running down the path in the lower field, heading toward Boundary Road, when WHAM! I get hit with this blinding flash………except for the last dream…….that one went beyond the blinding flash…….. I heard these voices……..old Mr. McQuade and his wife, then Mrs. Carver…….."

Mary Ellen interjected; "Paul, Mr. and Mrs. McQuade were the people who found you lying in the street the night you fractured your skull."

Paul nodded in agreement; "Yeah, I thought they must have been the ones. I don't understand why my folks never told me anything about the accident. My mom's standard reply, anytime I asked about it, was; 'if you don't ask, I promise not to tell'. It got so I stopped asking, only because I hated hearing that stupid phrase. I just wish she had given me at least *some* details."

"Honey, she did what she thought was right. She was only trying to protect you. There's something else you should know. Shortly after we were married, your mother and I were having a conversation and she brought this subject up. She told me that it was hard for her not to tell you about the accident, or Larry's murder, but she was going on the advice of your doctor, who felt it best that you not be told. According to her, he seemed to think you would be better off never knowing what took place."

"She sure did a good job of doing just that."

Mary Ellen, who had gotten up to pour more coffee, set the carafe down on the coffeemaker plate, then stood next to her husband and touched his arm. "Paul, please don't hold that against your mother……. she loved you *so* much. Honey, if it were me in her position, I think I would have done the same thing. A mother will do whatever she feels is necessary to protect her children."

"No, I don't really hold it against her. I just think it would have been nice if she had at least told me when I grew up."

Larch, whose voice had been quiet, not wanting to comment on the wisdom of Mrs. McCulloch's decision, now spoke up; "Well, Paul, you're grown up now and we're telling you now."

The little group laughed, once again breaking the tension that had started forming. Paul turned to Larch, took a deep breath and said; "What happened next? I'm assuming I must have gone back down the dirt road to the cemetery, right?"

"Yes, you did. There wasn't any doubt in my mind that you could handle it by yourself. It seemed to me that you weren't afraid of anything. Ritchie and I got on our bikes and rode home. I didn't say anything to my parents, but the next morning, my dad took me aside and told me that you had been badly hurt on Boundary Road the night before and that you might not make it. He asked me if I knew anything about what happened to you and I said 'no', but he must have sensed I knew something, so he kept at me, until I broke down and told him how we had been at the cemetery and someone had scared us. Man, he was mad at me! He told me I could plan on not leaving my yard for the rest of the summer. Later in the day, Ritchie came over to my house and we talked about what happened to you. He was lucky, because his father didn't ask him if he was with you, so he got off without being punished."

"When did they find Larry?"

"Not until the next night. It most likely would have been a longer time, had it not been for that guy wanting to show his girlfriend the cemetery.......you know how hardly anyone ever goes there."

"Did the police question you guys right away?"

"No, my father was the one who called and said his son had some information about what happened at the cemetery that night. They came to my house and asked me a lot of questions and then they went to see Ritchie. After they left his house, Ritchie said his dad went ballistic. He smacked him around pretty good, because Ritchie still had a black eye on Monday, when I saw him in school."

"What did the police ask you?"

"They wanted the names of everyone that was there. Then, they wanted to know what we were doing there. I told them we were just playing, but they weren't buying that. This one cop.......Jensen was his name; I remember, because his great grandfather built the farm I own now........he got in my face and kept saying 'we're going to sit here until you tell me the truth. One of your friends is dead and another one may die, so you better start talking.' He got away with that until I started crying, that's when my dad told him to take his notebook and himself out of our house and not to come back until he learned how to treat people better. The cop that was with him told Jensen to wait in the cruiser, which he did, but not without being visibly ticked off about it. This other cop was a lot more polished. He spoke calmly to me, telling me he knew how sad I was about losing my friend and how he was going to try to find the person responsible and bring him to justice, but he really needed me to tell him anything and everything I could remember. I told him everything.........how we had been playing this game, where we tested our courage, for almost two weeks........ about the guy wearing a dark, hooded cape, who scared us........I told him how you went back alone, while I took Ritchie home, but he was mostly interested in the guy who scared us. I had to describe, in detail, every feature I could remember about him, which wasn't much. The chief came back about a week later, with the nice guy, to verify my story and ask me if there was anything I could add to it, then they never came back after that."

"I wonder what they said to my mom and dad."

"I don't know, Paul, but I know that poor old Mr. McQuade was really shook up about it. He suffered a heart attack the day after finding you in the road and he was hospitalized for two weeks."

"Oh, that's terrible. He came over to my house to see me once or twice, after I got home from the hospital, but he never said a word about having a heart attack."

Larch glanced up at the clock and said; "Look at that. It's almost ten o'clock and it seems as though we've only been sitting here for a half-hour or so." He then stood up, in a sign that he was ready to leave.

Paul smiled and said; "Yeah, time flies when you're having fun." Reaching out, he shook his friend's hand and warmly said; "Thanks, Larch. This meant a lot to me, finally knowing what happened, at least up to a certain point. Now, hopefully, Nathan can help me put the rest of the pieces together."

Larch shook Paul's hand firmly, holding on for a few seconds and replied; "If anyone can help you, Paul, he's the one. Keep me informed, okay?"

"I will, you can count on that. We're not going to let this much time go by again, without getting together, Hank."

"I'm glad to hear that." Larch then turned to Mary Ellen and gave her a hug, thanking her for the meal and 'great cookies'. He left his friends at ten o'clock and headed home.

CHAPTER TWELVE

Once Larch had left, Paul turned to Mary Ellen and expressed to her his satisfaction with the way the evening went, starting with the good meal and then progressing to a highly informative conversation, for him, at least, over coffee and home-made chocolate chip cookies. As he helped her put the last of the coffee cups into the dishwasher, he offhandedly remarked; "Gee, Mare, I hope all those cookies I ate don't upset my stomach. I'd hate to end up having nightmares because of them."

Mary Ellen threw a quick glance at her husband, as if to say 'I don't believe you said that', then seeing him standing there with a wide grin on his face, she burst out laughing. "You're a fool!" she said, shaking her head in mock disgust. "You seem to be in better spirits tonight."

"I am. You know, Nathan was right. He told me that just the act of discussing the dreams with him would make me more relaxed………. I believe 'comfortable' was the word he used. But, talking with you and Larch tonight made me even more relaxed. It also made me a little bit…….. anxious……..to get to sleep, so I can go on to the next level in the dream sequence."

"Paul, are you saying you can control what you dream about?"

"No, I'm not saying that at all, Mare. I'm saying that they seem to progress as I gain more knowledge. Up to now, the dreams themselves, have been supplying the knowledge, so I'm looking forward to seeing what happens tonight, now that I've learned a lot more about that awful night. The key part, for me, is to be able to see the face of that shadowy figure. Nathan gave me some psycho-babble about the face representing Roger Carey and the fact that I don't know where he lives now is the reason why I can't see the face of the figure in my dream."

Mary Ellen drew in her breath, successfully stifling a gasp.

"Paul," she said, her voice trembling slightly. "I had a friend, back in the sixth grade. Her name was Karen Jensen and her father was the police officer that Henry was talking about, tonight. About a week after they found Larry, she overheard her father telling her mother that he and the other investigating officers were positive that Roger Carey was the person who murdered Larry, but they had been unable to come up with any solid proof to back up that conclusion, so they never arrested him. She said her father wanted to take care of things 'the old-fashioned way', but her mother got very angry with him, telling him that, if he got caught, he would lose everything, including his family."

"This Jensen guy sounds like he must have been some sort of loose cannon."

"Karen was afraid of him. She said he had a violent temper."

"I don't know, Mare. I just don't know what to make of all of this. In my first few dreams, I dreamt that maybe Crazy Roger would help me……..or save me……..from whatever was chasing me. But, when I ran closer to his house, a voice way deep inside of me said, very distinctly, 'turn away'. Now, I'm not sure if I imagined it in my dreams, or if something really was trying to warn me, or……..tell me……..that Roger had something to do with Larry's death."

"Well, maybe it will all come together for you one of these nights."

"I can only hope, Mare. I was happy to hear what Larch had to say about Nathan being the best in the business. I just hope he's good enough to help *me*."

Paul, yawning and tired from the day's events, looked to see that the time was ten thirty and readied himself for bed, while Mary Ellen curled up on the sofa, with a murder mystery. Kissing her good-night, Paul warned her not to stay up too late, then went into the bedroom and performed the fifteen-minute meditation ritual that Nathan had suggested, before laying down to sleep.

Sleep came quickly, as Paul's tired body luxuriated in the warmth and comfort of the bed. After two hours, Paul woke up, needing to relieve himself. He heard Mary Ellen breathing next to him, got up and went into the bathroom. Feeling wide awake, he silently cursed himself for drinking so much coffee. He thought it seemed strange that he hadn't had his nightly dream by now, but decided that the coffee must have had something to do with it. Grabbing yesterday morning's paper, which he had never gotten around to reading, off the coffee table in the living room, he sat in his recliner and began reading the sports section. After only a few minutes, a strong feeling of sleepiness overcame him and he put his head back on the headrest, falling fast asleep in a short while. This time, he would not be deprived of his nightmare.

Crater Street was quiet as young Paul McCulloch walked along, heading for the dirt road, which led to the old cemetery. He was alone and the sun had just set for the evening. Something, somewhere in his mind, was impelling him toward the cemetery, with a sense of urgency that demanded attention.

When Paul reached the dirt road, he turned to head down to the old graveyard, noting that now, it had gotten completely dark. Something else became apparent. He was no longer twelve year-old Paul, but his older counterpart. Paul walked cautiously down the dirt road, being careful not to trip over the large stones he remembered were usually lying about on the road. He thought about how they had come to be there and chalked it up to either kids throwing them, or passing cars tearing them loose from the gravel bed. His thoughts were also on the ever-present shadowy figure, which could be lying in wait, ready to spring out at him anytime. He could feel his pulse rising.

Paul now stood facing the entrance gate to the cemetery. "GO INSIDE!" the voice from his inner mind commanded him. He stepped forward, glancing from side to side, knowing the shadowy figure would soon make an appearance. As he neared the middle of the enclosure, Paul's eyes could make out a dark object on the ground, near the stone wall in back. With his eyes riveted on this object, he continued walking forward, until he got close enough to see that it was the lifeless figure of a boy, perhaps twelve or thirteen years old.

The body lay partially draped over a broken headstone, with the lower torso on the base and the right side of the chest resting on the left side of the once-upright stone, which now lay at a familiar angle to anyone who has witnessed the end result of cemetery vandalism.

Both legs were on the front side of the base, while the right arm was settled on top of the stone, partially covering the lettering, which now faced the sky. The left arm was twisted at a grotesque angle, as if it had separated from the shoulder and was turned almost completely around. The head was face down in the mossy grass, the left side illuminated by a shaft of moonlight filtering through the trees.

Paul knelt down beside the body, tilting his head to get a better look at the blood-covered face, but, unable, as yet, to determine whether or not the body is that of his friend, Larry. Reaching out with his right hand, he pushes the left shoulder of the lifeless form, but his hand recoils in terror, as it starts to sink into the flesh. Paul turns his hand to look at what might be on it, but it is clean. Reaching out once more, this time his hand grabs a fistful of hair, in an attempt to turn the head, but as Paul raises the head slightly, he hears the sickening sound of bones breaking, but continues to turn and raise the head, until he is able to peek under and look at the face. As he does so, his eyes notice movement from the lips and it is clear that this is, indeed, the face of his childhood friend, who is STILL ALIVE! Paul leans closer, to within an inch of Larry's face, softly saying; "Larry, don't try to talk, I'll call for help."

The mouth continues to move and Paul stares hard, trying to decipher what Larry is saying. All he hears is a soft, low murmur, barely audible. Frustrated, Paul gently shakes the head of his friend and as he does so, is greeted by the nauseating sight of maggots falling from Larry's mouth. Paul screams in revulsion, instantly releasing his grip on the tuft of hair and jumps to his feet. Feeling a tickle on his right forearm, he looks down to see a half dozen of the white creatures crawling up his arm, some already past the elbow. The scream he emitted at the first sight of the stomach-turning parasites carries into a long, deep-throated wail and Paul flails at his arm with his left hand, in an attempt to remove the invaders.

Struck with the desire to run and get as far away from this disgusting place as is possible, Paul turns and comes face to face with a tall, rawboned man, grinning, as if he were insane. The first thought to enter Paul's mind is that this is *not* the shadowy figure of his earlier dreams. The next thought amazes him. He can clearly see, in detail, every facial feature, from the piercing hazel eyes, with crow's feet in the outer corners, to the leathery sun-tanned face, wrinkled before its time.

The new face sits atop a six foot plus frame, lean and wiry. Not one word came forth from the mouth of this new intruder to Paul's dream world, just the insidious smirk and those eyes………eyes which nearly blazed in the intensity of their stare.

As Paul stood looking up at the trespasser to his dream, he could feel something touching his ankle, but dared not turn his eyes away from the sinister-looking visage that held him transfixed, in its fiendish stare It was not until whatever was at his ankle locked onto him in a tight grip, that he was finally able to turn his eyes downward to discover a most revolting sight. A hand protruding from the ground had secured a firm hold on his lower leg and was pulling hard, trying, it seemed, to pull him into the earth.

In the split second it took for Paul's thoughts to register, the wail he had uttered before had now become a loud, terrified howl, loud enough to awaken him, mercifully, from this latest episode of his own personal dream theater.

Paul sat up straight in the recliner, giving his head a quick shake to clear the fuzziness and then began to take stock of the latest installment of his dream series. 'Who in the hell *was* that guy? What happened to my shadowy figure? And why was *I* the one who found Larry's body?'

Paul got up and headed for the bathroom. He splashed cool water on his face and then dried off. He then walked to the kitchen, where he located the scratch pad and pencil and wrote down the points of the dream that he hoped Nathan would be able to explain to him, in the morning.

As he was bending over the kitchen table writing, an awareness that someone else was in the room sent a small chill up his spine, turning into a full-body spasm, as he simultaneously heard the voice of Mary Ellen say; "Paul, I heard you yell……..is everything all right?"

"Everything's fine Mare. I just had the latest up-date on my continuing dream saga, that's all."

"Tell me about it."

"I don't think that's such a good idea, trust me. You should go back to bed, there's no use in both of us losing sleep."

"Aren't you coming?"

Paul moved toward Mary Ellen and wrapped his arms around her. "I've got the feeling that the nightmares aren't over for tonight, so I'm going to sleep in my truck. That way, I'll be sure not to wake you again. I feel bad about waking you up so many times.

"Paul, you don't have to do that. I'd rather have you safe in the house, than in your truck."

"Mary Ellen, it's not like some boogey monster is going to get me." Paul laughed as he said this, which irritated his wife slightly.

With a bit of a pouting face, Mary Ellen replied; "Do what you think you need to do, Paul. I just don't feel right about you sleeping in your truck, that's all."

"And I don't feel right about always waking you up, so it's settled. If it makes you feel any better, I promise I'll lock both doors."

"I won't feel better until you stop having these dreadful dreams altogether. Until then……..I'm…….." Mary Ellen faltered, then the tears came and she buried her face in her husband's chest. Paul hugged her tightly, then said; "It shouldn't be much longer, Mare……..not much longer."

Mary Ellen sobbed; "You don't know how hard I've prayed for an end to this mess. Paul, I can't take too much more of this. Night after night, you wake up screaming, yelling. You've lost weight, you're taking time off from work and you look like hell……..I just want it to end!"

Paul thought hard, trying to think of something reassuring to say, but the words weren't there. Instead, he pulled Mary Ellen closer, stroking the hair in back of her head. After a few moments, he lifted her chin with the index finger of his right hand and said to her; "I know how hard this has been for you, but you've been there for me, right along. Now I'm asking you to try and hold on a little longer. I *know* this is almost over. We can get through this, Mare, I *know* we can."

Then, hugging her hard, Paul said: "I love you so much, little lady, so much."

"I love you too, Paul" Mary Ellen responded, with a squeeze of her own.

Paul escorted his wife into the bedroom, settled her in bed and then kissed her tenderly, before walking out to his truck. Mary Ellen tossed in the bed, wondering why her husband had let a romantic moment go by the boards.

Once inside the truck, Paul reached behind the seat, pulling out the sleeping bag he always kept there. Pushing the seat as far back as it would go, he spread the bag out and climbed in, fully clothed, minus his shoes, which he kicked off. Grasping the steering wheel, he pulled himself up to where he was in a relaxed position and then draped his hand over the lower portion of the wheel. The big bench seat of the pickup proved to be more comfortable than Paul imagined and it wasn't long before sleep came. Almost as quickly, the dream also came.

Incredibly, Paul found himself back at the cemetery, only this time, as he walked into the graveyard, he heard the sound of a car approaching. "HIDE, NOW!" the inner voice urged. Spotting a tree in the enclosure, which he had not noticed before, Paul tried to hide behind it, but the tree was only five or six inches in diameter, not nearly enough for a man to be hidden. Even so, he stood very still, behind the small tree and watched with relief as the car sped by, a dark sedan, kicking up rocks, some very large, onto the dirt road. The driver, incredibly, appeared to be unaware of Paul's presence behind the tree. As Paul peered into the car, his heart skipped when he saw the face of his new tormenter, the grinning man with the leathery face.

Paul sensed another presence in the cemetery and fearfully, he turned to see the familiar shape of the shadowy figure, standing with its back to Paul, about fifty feet away, near the back of the property. His old aggressor was also unaware that Paul was behind him and seemed to be preoccupied with something on the ground. The conscious part of Paul's mind found his next action hard to believe. Instead of leaving the graveyard, Paul advanced toward the shadowy figure, covering the fifty feet in three or four long only-in-a-dream-type steps. Encouraged by the flash he remembered from earlier, when he saw fear in the eyes of the shadowy figure, Paul reached out with his right hand and gripped its right shoulder. As he did so, a cold chill again penetrated his spinal column and the figure turned, growling. Paul searched the area where its face should be, but saw only darkness. Then, a faint image of two dull eyes slowly emerged.

Despite the terror he had expressed in his previous dreams whenever he encountered this frightening figure, Paul's grasp on its shoulder, grew tighter, buoyed not only by the memory of the fear he had seen in its eyes during his flash episode, but also by Nathan's reassuring words as they parted company, words which had sunk themselves into some area of Paul's subconscious mind and now presented themselves as reinforcements.

Paul could feel, even in his dream state, the hairs on his neck bristling and fresh goose bumps rising on his arms, as his anger at this heretofore terrifying bully boiled over into pure rage, textured with an awareness that he was about to take on the scariest entity he had ever encountered in his lifetime.

"YOU'RE TELLING ME I'M A DEAD MAN? WHO IN THE HELL DO YOU THINK YOU ARE?"

The figure recoiled slightly under Paul's firm hold, trying to squirm loose, but not succeeding. Paul was able, once again, to see a trace of fear in the smoky eyes, further supporting his new-found bravado.

"WHAT DID YOU DO TO LARRY, YOU SON-OF-A-BITCH?"

The voice that answered was so completely different from the ferocious, threatening tone aimed at Paul in preceding encounters, that

Paul knew he now had the upper hand. He felt his adversary slump as it answered, in almost a whimper; "I didn't mean to kill him........ he wouldn't do what I wanted........he fought me........I didn't mean to kill him."

Paul's fury could not be contained any longer and he still was able to see only darkness where the face of the creature should be. He let loose with a roundhouse right, which landed square on the shadowy jaw. The punch, however, instead of connecting solidly, seemed to lose most of its power at contact and now, Paul could hear the maniacal laugh slowly start, then build to a crescendo, as the shadowy antagonist straightened up and slipped free of Paul's grip.

"YOU WANT TO KNOW WHO I AM, DO YOU?" Paul's opponent reaches out with one hand, lifting and shoving him in one motion, sending Paul sprawling on the ground. "I'M THE SON-OF-A-BITCH THAT'S GOING TO KILL YOU, THAT'S WHO I AM"

In a move only possible in a dream, for a fifty-eight year old man, Paul, from a horizontal position on his back, leaps to his feet in one easy movement, facing his foe again.

"That might have worked before, but not now. What you don't realize, you ugly bastard, is that I'M NOT AFRAID OF YOU ANYMORE"

Paul charged head-on directly at his enemy, burying his shoulder in its midsection, the momentum causing the figure to fall backwards to the ground, where it landed hard on its back. Paul could smell the stale breath forced from its lungs by the impact and instinctively turned his head to the right, to avoid the odor. The sight which greeted his eyes immediately turned his concentration away from the battle with his dream monster, who obligingly, failed to take advantage of his opponent's lack of attention. There, in the grass, only two feet away, lay the baseball the boys had used in their graveyard game of courage. Paul clearly saw the familiar marks each of them had made on the ball back in the summer of 1957, all except for his Kilroy face. He reached out with his right hand, to turn the ball around and as his fingers wrapped themselves around the ball, the earth beside the sphere trembled somewhat, then a small fissure opened, through which a hand poked, clamping down firmly around Paul's wrist. His first reaction was to try and pull away, but doing so only made the hand grip his wrist all the more tightly, seeming as if it wanted to pull him into its own abode, deep in the ground. Paul fought hard, pulling with all the strength his dream-state could muster, but the hand held on even more tenaciously and now, a bigger problem emerged, as the shadowy figure now mounted Paul's back and swiftly placed its right forearm under Paul's chin, securing his neck in a stranglehold, while pinning his left arm to the ground.

Suddenly, the realization struck Paul that his aggressor had become aroused, as he felt the undulating movement of the shadowy figure against his backside. With his right hand in the grasp of the hand from the ground and his left hand pinned by his tormenter, Paul twisted and writhed, desperately trying to free himself from the clutches of the now heavily-breathing creature mounted on his back. Its hold on Paul's neck grew tighter and he now found it increasingly difficult to breathe. His right wrist ached in pain, as the hand from the ground gripped him fiercely. With one violent heave, Paul was finally able to break free, just as his eyes opened to witness his aching right hand sliding out from the small circle between the lower portion of the steering wheel and the horizontal center piece which ran through the wheel.

Slowly coming to his senses, Paul felt something around his neck and instinctively reached for it, discovering that, somehow, his head had slid behind the seat belt. The firmness he had felt in the crack of his butt, which he had mistaken for an aroused dream monster, was the passenger-side seat belt connection in between the seat cushions. He tried, in his mind, to make sense of what transpired in this latest dream, but had no answers for the questions in his thoughts

"What in the hell made me have a dream like that? Why would a scary dream monster that said it wanted to kill me, then when it got the chance, decided instead, to try and get its rocks off on me? Oh well, that's two more questions for Nathan."

Paul struggled to raise himself up to a half-sitting position, reached into his pants pocket for his keys and turned the ignition to the 'accessory' position, which illuminated the numbers on the dash clock to reveal the time as four twenty-five a.m. He put his shoes on, after climbing out of the sleeping bag and slid over behind the wheel, started the truck and backed out of the driveway.

"I'll swing down to the donut shop and pick up some coffee and a couple of muffins. By the time I get back, Mary Ellen should be just about ready to get up."

As Paul drove down Cherry Tree Drive he was stunned to hear the nearly audible voice from his inner mind say; "GO THERE TODAY!"

His reaction was to jump slightly, as he thought; "*Go where?*" Despite his silent question, Paul knew where the voice wanted him to go, he just wasn't sure why.

CHAPTER THIRTEEN

Mary Ellen heard the truck start up and back out of the driveway. She hadn't slept well, concerned, not only for her husband's safety, but for his mental well-being as well. Making the sign of the cross, she again prayed silently for an end to Paul's nightmares, then got up and went into the bathroom, where she showered.

Paul returned as she was getting out of the shower and announced that he had brought coffee and fresh muffins with him. His voice sounded up-beat, even exuberant and she wondered what could have happened to cause the change in his attitude.

Once she emerged from the bathroom, clad in her robe, she kissed Paul and asked if he had managed to get any sleep His answer helped to explain his mood change.

"Mare, something is happening with these dreams……..something that leads me to believe they're almost over. Don't ask me to explain it, I can just sense……..you're going to think I'm nuts, but…….. along with the flashes I've been getting, there's this voice……..it comes from deep inside, somewhere."

Tears again welled up in Mary Ellen's eyes as she lamentably said; "Oh, Paul, please don't tell me you're hearing voices. Honey, I won't be able to take that."

Paul gently caressed both of his wife's arms, as he tried to reassure her; "No, No, Mare, please try to understand. It isn't an evil voice…….. not at all. It warned me not to go near 'Crazy Roger's' house and it told me to hide when one of the more frightening characters was about to make an appearance in my latest dream. It also told me to go to the cemetery today."

Paul neglected to tell his wife that the last thing the voice said to him was while he was awake, fearing that might not help to convince her of his sanity. Mary Ellen, however, was becoming more distressed as she listened to her husband. Pulling free from his embrace, she replied; "IT TOLD YOU TO GO TO THE CEMETERY? Paul, I don't want to hear anymore of this talk about voices." Then, with the determination of a wife who will do anything to help her husband, Mary Ellen steeled herself and said; "Make sure you tell the psychologist about them, when you go this morning."

"I already did. He didn't make a big deal out of them."

"Oh, so you think that I'm making a 'big deal' out of them. Well, Paul, it *is* a 'big deal' when a man tells his wife that all of a sudden he is hearing voices in his head."

"Mary Ellen, that's not what I meant by that comment. I simply meant to convey to you that Nathan didn't react as if hearing voices in my dreams was of any great concern."

Anxious to end this conversation, Mary Ellen turned away from Paul and announced; "I've got to get ready for work."

Paul's jaw dropped, then he foolishly let out a sarcastic laugh; "You've got to get ready for work? Mare, it's quarter past five; you don't have to be at work for three and a half hours, for Christ's sake."

Mary Ellen kept retreating to the bedroom, as she responded; "Just leave me alone."

Paul chose to heed his wife's admonition, thinking that any further attempts to try to calm her down would be futile. He sat down at the kitchen table, drank his coffee and ate one of the muffins, while scanning the morning paper.

After his light breakfast, Paul showered, shaved and changed into clean clothes, then decided to use the time before his appointment with Nathan to go and look at a couple of jobs he had been asked to do. One was to wire up a new single-car garage someone was building in the northern part of town, near Larch's place, the other was more substantial and involved wiring the entire electric service for a small strip mall being built in the south end of the city.

The voice he had heard so clearly, both in his dream state and in his conscious state became a source of concern for Paul. It was on his mind as he dressed himself and he couldn't help but wonder if Mary Ellen was right to worry about his sanity. "*Where is this voice coming from, anyway? It has to be coming from some outside source. How the hell can I be warning myself against danger, when I couldn't possibly know it was there, in the first place? And why........why does it want me to go to the cemetery today? Does it want me to go first thing, or later in the afternoon? Or God forbid, at night? Well, I'm not going to go anywhere, until it tells me and I sure as hell am not going to say anymore about the voice to Mary Ellen. I should have kept my mouth shut about it altogether. Of course she thinks I'm nuts, what was I thinking?*"

Mary Ellen had busied herself in the kitchen after prematurely getting herself ready for work extremely early, much to her husband's unwisely-voiced amusement. Her irritation with Paul was evidenced by her silence when he entered the room. Pretending not to notice her mood, Paul came up behind her, encircled his arms around her shoulders and kissed her softly on the side of her cheek.

"I've got to go and look at two jobs before my appointment with Nathan, so I'm going to leave now, in order to have enough time."

Then, giving her shoulders a small squeeze, he said; "I love you, Mare."

Her response was to reach up with her right hand and pat his arm, as he slowly pulled it away, but her eyes had once again filled with tears and she knew she was unable to speak without breaking down. Paul mistook this to mean she was still upset with him and, in a way, she was. His pre-occupation with these 'voices' in his head, in combination with the increasing intensity of his nightmares had frightened her into believing her devoted husband was truly beginning to lose his sense of reality, if not his mind.

As Paul walked out the door, he said, without looking back; "Have a good day at work. I'll see you this afternoon."

Mary Ellen mumbled a low 'good-bye' and then bit her lip in anger at herself, for letting Paul leave while thinking she was angry with him. She glanced up at the clock, which showed that she still had two hours before work, as the time was six forty-five a.m. She grabbed a dust cloth, and went through the house, dusting off anything in sight. Then, she took a can of furniture wax and proceeded to wax all of the furniture. Finally, she washed and waxed the kitchen floor, then had to go and change her clothes again, but her plan to keep busy served two purposes; it managed to eat up most of the two hours and it also kept her mind off Paul's problems for a while.

At eight forty a.m., Mary Ellen started her car and drove to work.

CHAPTER FOURTEEN

6:50 a.m. Thursday, August 19, 2004

Paul decided to look at the job in the north end of town first, that way, he would be closer to Nathan's office when he finished checking the second job, in the south end of the city. The second job was much more involved than the first and Paul spent the better part of three hours measuring and figuring the cost of material he would need to bid successfully for the work.

When he completed the appraisal, he headed over to Nathan's office, which was less than ten minutes away. This time, he arrived fifteen minutes early and fully expected to be waiting quite a while, if the last visit was any indication.

Paul sat down and immediately glanced up at the tacky clock scene, which now seemed familiarly welcoming. He saw that the time was ten forty-eight a.m., but was unable to turn away from the scene. His eyes scanned the expanse of the bridge and he began to study the detail in the background. Noticing small buildings that he hadn't before, Paul chalked it up to nervousness in his first visit and now felt much more relaxed, even eager to update Nathan on the latest developments in his dream saga.

Hearing a low murmur inside Nathan's office, Paul's attention was diverted from the clock, then the murmur ceased.

Silently, the door opened and Nathan greeted Paul cheerfully; "Good morning, Paul; please come on in."

Paul rose and walked past Nathan, returning the greeting and headed for the comfortable chair he had chosen in his last session. Nathan walked to his desk, retrieved his clipboard and settled in the straight-back chair.

"Paul, you look much more rested today, I trust you had a good night's rest?"

"Yes, I did, but it was also a very active night, in terms of my dreams. Also, I've learned quite a bit more about certain events from the time period indicated in my nightmares."

"Such as?"

"Well, for starters, I found out that my friend, Larry, who has been in all of the dreams, was murdered on the same night that I fractured my skull. The police investigation apparently concluded that I had witnessed his murder and that the murderer then chased me. How I managed to end up in the road with my head bashed in, is anyone's guess."

"That certainly is a plateful. Did you experience any further dreams, as a result of this new information?"

"I sure did. The thing is, Nathan, you hit the nail on the head when you said the dreams would be more intense, but I'd also be more comfortable with them. I actually found myself anxious to go to sleep, in order to learn more, because they definitely are progressing. The only problem is that I still can't clearly see the face of the shadowy figure and that bothers the hell out of me."

The look of concentration on Nathan's face gave Paul the idea that he seemed to have some sort of solution on his mind and Paul asked; "Is there anyway I'll ever be able to identify that face, or is it locked away forever?"

"Nothing is locked away forever, Paul. It's just a matter of knowing when to unlock it. First, though, I want you to tell me of your dreams last night."

"I actually had two separate dreams, the first one started with me standing in front of the old cemetery and that voice I told you about commanded me to go inside. When I did, I saw a body, which, when I got closer, turned out to be Larry's. It was draped partially over a broken headstone, with most of the torso on the base of the stone. I leaned in close to the face, to see if it was really Larry and I saw the mouth moving, like he was trying to tell me something. But when I shook his head gently, maggots fell out of his mouth…….. they were disgustingly realistic. I got up and turned to run, but found myself looking directly into the face of some guy with leathery-looking skin, grinning at me and not saying a word……..just staring at me, with that insane grin. I just stood there, frozen in place, when suddenly a hand from the ground grabbed my ankle and pulled hard. I think it wanted to pull me into the ground, but I'm not so sure it was evil. Anyway, I woke up yelling."

Paul saw that Nathan was still writing and waited to ask his next question. When Nathan finished his notes, he asked the question for him. "Do you have any idea who this latest person in your dream might be?"

"No I don't. I'm sure I've never seen that face before, but there was definitely an aura of evil about him, no question."

"You say, Paul, that the hand which emerged from the ground gave you the impression it was not evil, but yet, you woke up yelling."

"Yeah, it scared the shit out of me. But, I felt strongly that it and the voice are good guys. That sounds strange, but it's what I get from them."

Nathan scribbled some more on the pad of paper attached to the clipboard and then focused his attention on Paul.

"Tell me about the second dream, Paul."

"Well, after I woke up, I was writing down these questions to ask you." Paul reached into his shirt pocket and pulled out a piece of paper and handed it to Nathan. "Then my wife came into the kitchen and said she heard me yell. I told her I'd sleep in my truck, so I wouldn't disturb her, but she wasn't too happy about that. I finally managed to convince her, well…….. I insisted. It didn't take me long to fall asleep and as my dream started I was on the dirt road, just entering the cemetery, when I heard a car approaching. That voice told me very distinctly to 'hide now'. I hid behind this tree, which was in the cemetery. There are no trees in there, or at least, there never were. Here is the strange part. I hid behind this tree, which was much too skinny to conceal me and when the car drove by, the same guy from the earlier dream, the one with the leathery face and the crazy grin……..he was driving the car……..AND HE NEVER SAW ME! Then, I felt the presence of someone else, or some *thing* else and turned around. The shadowy figure was standing, with its back to me, about fifty feet away. I don't think it knew I was there. All of a sudden, I felt this anger, almost rage, at this thing and I walked up and grabbed it by the shoulder and actually challenged it. I asked it what it did to Larry and it told me in this really wimpy voice that it didn't mean to kill him, but that Larry wouldn't do what he wanted. I took a swing at it, thinking I had nailed its jaw, but my punch felt weak and ineffective. Then, it just picked me up with one hand, like it had superhuman strength and threw me on the ground."

Unable to hold back a laugh, Paul told Nathan how he was able, in his dream, to leap to his feet from flat on his back, where he and the shadowy figure grappled, falling to the ground. Paul continued with his account of the dream.

"It was while we were on the ground that I saw the baseball we used in the game, the one that Larry was supposed to retrieve."

Nathan now wore a puzzled look.

"I don't understand, Paul. Were you boys playing ball in the cemetery?"

"Oh, I'm sorry, Nathan. I should have explained to you that the reason we were at the cemetery in the first place was because we were playing something called the 'graveyard game'. It was a game I came up with, to test your courage."

Then, leaning forward a little for emphasis, Paul said; "I just learned all of what I'm about to tell you last night, from an old friend, one of the four, actually. His name is Henry Stolarczek, but we call him 'Larch' and he came over to my house, at my invitation, to tell me about the game, along with what he knew about what took place on the night of my accident. Unfortunately, it also happened to be the same night that Larry was killed."

"Yes, you mentioned that earlier."

Paul dismissed Nathan's remark and continued; "Getting back to the game; the object of the game was to place a baseball with each of our special marks on it, in the cemetery during the day, then we would come back at night and one of us would have to walk down the dirt road by himself, retrieve the ball and bring it back to the other three, as proof. The first night we played the game, I was the one to get the ball. It was pretty scary. Larch went next, then Ritchie kept making excuses, but he finally took his turn. From what Larch told me, Larry had managed to work himself into a state about taking his turn. Larch and I tried to talk him out of going, because he looked like he was on the verge of a nervous breakdown, but he was hung up on not being called a sissy, so he went anyway. I sure wish we could have talked him out of it."

"Paul, your friend, Ritchie……..he doesn't seem to play an active role in either your narrative or your dreams. The only time you mention him, is in a passive way, as if he's just always there. Was this the case?"

"Yeah, it was, pretty much. Ritchie was always just along for the ride."

"Are you still in contact with him?"

"No. I hadn't seen him since our late teens. He died a few years ago, of a heart attack. He was only fifty-three."

"Prime heart-attack age, Paul."

"So I've been told."

"So you saw this baseball while you were fighting with the figure on the ground. What happened next, Paul?"

"Something very sinister. As I reached out to grab the ball, something grabbed me. It was a hand, which came from the ground and it latched onto my wrist with a tenacious grip. At first, I was terrified, but as I kept trying to pull away, I felt very strongly that the hand that was clutching me was not out to harm me. Instead, it seemed as though it wanted me to help it. That's kind of ridiculous, isn't it?"

Nathan spoke calmly and reassuringly to Paul; "Remember, Paul, to keep your mind open to all possibilities. Nothing we dream is totally without meaning. You very probably are receiving a subliminal message of some type. If I were you, I wouldn't be so quick to dismiss it as ridiculous."

"Okay, I'll remember that. Nathan........another thing happened, just before the dream ended, something which I'm a little embarrassed to tell you, but know I must. When my attention was diverted by the tug-of-war with the hand from the ground, the shadowy figure used the opportunity to mount my back. It started to get aroused as it choked me with its arm and I felt as though it was dry-humping me. When I woke up, I found the seat belt connection device was pressed into the crack in my butt and my neck was caught in the shoulder harness. Why does sex play a part in this dream?"

"That's a fairly easy one, Paul. In our first session, you related to me how this Roger Carey, whom, you'll recall, I suspect is your shadowy figure, tried forcing himself upon you, when you were a young boy. You successfully resisted his advances, but you never lost that helpless feeling you had when you felt trapped in his room, only to be set free, in the end, by his whim, more than mercy. The hand around your neck and you being pinned to the ground from behind are the expressions of the fear you still harbor. You were, in effect, back in his room, once again at his mercy. He will, I'm afraid, continue to be a problem for you, until you confront the issue head-on."

"But, Nathan........when I woke up, I was also aroused. I've never had any homosexual tendencies in my life. Do I have a problem, here?"

Nathan smiled and laughed softly; "Not at all, Paul. If you don't mind my asking, when was the last time you and your wife had sex?"

"A few days before the dreams started."

"Paul, we have another easy one. You haven't had sex in almost a month. The experience of arousal in your dream was a result of your body seeking sexual relief. Your mind will incorporate any possible scenario to achieve that relief. I suspect that, had you not awakened when you did, you would have awakened with a surprise, if you catch my drift."

Now it was Paul's turn to laugh. His relief was obvious.

"Yes, I do. Thanks for that reassurance."

Paul fidgeted in the chair, then posed a question to Nathan; "There's one other very important thing. This voice I've been hearing has been getting more insistent. It has ....I hope you won't think I've lost my marbles, but........the voice has been speaking to me, not only in my dreams but also when I'm awake. Worse than that, it told me this morning to go to the cemetery........today........for what, I have no idea. I made the mistake of telling my wife and she didn't handle it very well. She thinks I'm going crazy........she didn't come right out and say so, but I got the picture. Nathan, I'm worried about her, because she is having a harder time with these dreams than I am."

Nathan set his clipboard on the small table next to his chair, folded his arms and stared at Paul. His manner indicated to Paul that he might have something up his sleeve, but Paul had no idea just what that might be.

Finally, Nathan broke his silence; "Paul, normally, I employ a method where I gradually extract information from my patients in a series of visits. This allows them to dispense their thoughts in a timely manner, with a minimum of stress and a moderate amount of relaxation. Your case, however, presents an urgency, which must be dealt with and dealt with immediately, for fear of causing further and possibly permanent emotional distress. In addition, your marriage may be in jeopardy. What I'm about to propose to you is a technique with which I have enjoyed a rather high percentage of success, when I've employed it on patients whom I felt were most likely to benefit from it. It is called hypnosis-induced recollection. It is my feeling, Paul that you will benefit greatly from this technique. Here is what will happen, should you choose to accept this method. First, I will place you in a deep hypnotic state, where I will ask you to describe, in detail, the events you witnessed on the night your friend, Larry was murdered. This should shed some light on the dreams which are causing you such misery. Next, I will probe your mind for any connection between the original dreams involving the shadowy figure and the latest ones, where a new figure with a leathery face has appeared. I will also try to establish a reason for your vision of a hand reaching out from the ground, although I do have a theory on that, which I will not reveal to you without more facts. Finally, I will bring you out of the hypnosis. The story-book ending is that you will go home, your dreams will cease and you and your wife will live happily ever-after. Realistically, we are going from point 'B' to point 'W', but we need to get to point 'Z' to reach a satisfactory conclusion."

Nathan crossed his legs, leaned back in his chair and hooked both thumbs in the front pockets of his slacks, before finishing his proposal.

"I do, however, need your approval to initiate the process."

Paul sat quietly, digesting what Nathan had just laid out for him. Many questions bounced around in his head.

"You can hypnotize me?"

"Yes, I'm a licensed hypno-therapist. I've conducted several seminars on memory recovery through hypnosis at several major colleges throughout the northeast. In addition, several of my cases have been written up, anonymously of course, in the Journal of American Psychology."

Paul raised his eyebrows; "Wow, that's pretty impressive. Will I be able to recall everything that happened that night?"

"That depends, Paul, on several factors. First of all, if the memories are too intense, I may find it necessary to abort the procedure, for health reasons."

"Health reasons?"

"Yes. You're fifty eight years old, Paul. You appear to be in excellent physical health, but your age alone would require me to exercise caution, if you were to become too agitated."

"What else would prevent a recollection?"

Nathan uncrossed his legs and reached for his clipboard, setting it in his lap, where he cradled it in his right hand, while using his pen as a wand in his left hand to illustrate his points.

"The memories may simply be buried too deep to retrieve them. This has happened before and, unfortunately, no one in the profession has come up with a way of unlocking such secrets. There are memories which the mind, in its wisdom, decides to hide in a very deep recess of our brain, in an effort to protect us from the emotional trauma which would surely result if such memories were to surface. If this is the case in your situation, I'm afraid we will have hit a dead end."

"So, what you're saying is that you're not sure this will work?"

"On the contrary, Paul. From what you have described to me, your mind is willing and perhaps even eager to reveal what you have hidden away all of these years. I merely meant to point out some of the possibilities, albeit remote, that might occur. My feeling is that, in your case, we will be successful."

Paul leaned forward in his chair and smiled at Nathan.

"Then, let's go for it! When can we start?"

"Right now, if you wish. My next appointment isn't until three p.m., so we will have ample time."

Paul shifted in his chair, searching for the most comfortable spot, then asked Nathan; "So, what do I have to do?"

Nathan sat straight up and focused his eyes directly on Paul's, asking; "Just make yourself comfortable."

"That's not hard; I'm very comfortable in this chair."

As he spoke, Nathan arose from his chair and walked over to his desk, where he opened a side drawer and pulled out a small tape recorder. Holding it up for Paul to see, he said: "I want you to know, Paul, that I will be recording your entire conversation while you are under hypnosis. I find this to be more effective than my scribbled notes, which sometimes look more like hen-scratches. Do you object to being recorded?"

"No, I don't object, as long as you don't intend to play it on loudspeakers in front of City Hall." Paul flashed his old grin, which caused Nathan to smile broadly, the biggest display of emotion Paul had seen from him.

"I promise, that will not be the case, Paul. I *will*, however, ask you to turn off your cell phone and we can get started."

"I turned it off before the session, Nathan."

"Great!" Nathan sat down, turned on the tape recorder and held it a few inches from his face, while pressing the 'record' button.

"My name is Nathan Feldmar. Today's date is Thursday, August 19, 2004. I am about to place a patient, one Paul McCulloch into a hypnotic state, where I intend to bring the patient to a place in time where he underwent a most traumatic event, which resulted in defensive memory loss. The patient has recently been plagued with recurring nightmares, where he has experienced flashbacks related to the traumatic event. I am taping his comments made while under hypnosis, with his full consent, that consent now being verbally acknowledged by Mr. McCulloch."

Nathan held the recorder closer to Paul, who said; "My name is Paul McCulloch and I give my consent to having my comments recorded."

The recorder was placed on the small table, which Nathan had moved to a point midway between himself and Paul. It was then propped up with a book to better capture the voices. In his most reassuring tone, Nathan softly spoke to Paul.

"Excellent; Now, Paul, I want you to let your muscles relax, starting with the legs and arms, set them free of all strain. Now, concentrate on the muscles in your neck, shoulders and chest, letting them go limp. Rest your head against the back of the chair and close your eyes. You can feel the effect your relaxed muscles have on you and you begin to feel as though you are reclining in a relaxing chair. The cushions are made out of the softest fabric you can imagine and you have *never* been so comfortable. Now, I will ask you to block out any sounds you may hear, other than the sound of my voice. You will listen closely to my voice and recognize it as the authority in this state which you are in. I am going to ask you to take a journey with me. The journey will bring us to a place where you may become frightened, but you need not fear; I will not let anyone harm you. Are you ready to begin our journey, Paul?"

Paul, who has now settled back in the big chair and, for all appearances, looks completely relaxed, responds with a natural-sounding voice.

"Yes, I am."

Nathan, whose eyes remain riveted on Paul, continues.

"At this moment, Paul, we have just arrived at our destination. It is late summer of 1957 and Larch, Ritchie, Larry and you are at the junction of Crater Road, where it meets the dirt road to the old cemetery. You are getting ready to play the graveyard game for the last time. It is Larry's turn to retrieve the ball tonight and he is apprehensive about going to the graveyard, alone. Tell me, Paul, of the conversation that takes place."

In a solemn voice, Paul begins to recall the words that the boys spoke.

"Larry is really nervous. He is talking fast and his voice is starting to rise and become shrill-sounding. Now he is pacing back and forth, talking to himself, as if we weren't even there. Larch is looking at me……..he has a question in his eyes, but says nothing. I shrug my shoulders, because I don't know what to do, or say. Now, I see Larry has moved further away, so I walk over to him. Larch and Ritchie follow me, but I make a signal with my hand to stay there. I don't want to embarrass Larry. When I reach him, I put my arm around his shoulder and we walk further away. I tell him that if this is bothering him this much, he doesn't have to go, that no one will laugh at him, or make fun of him. I make the sign of the cross over my heart and say 'cross my heart and hope to die', but he just starts shaking his head and saying 'no, no, I *have* to go, I *have* to go!' Now Larch is there and he tells Larry the same thing. I look back to see where Ritchie is, but he's just throwing rocks at a tin can by the side of the road. Finally, I tell Larry not to go, because he is scaring me. He looks right at me and says; 'you don't understand, Paul, I *have* to do this and I'm *going* to do it.' We can't talk him out of it, so I do the next best thing. I tell him he better be fast, because if he's not back in ten minutes, we're going after him."

"What happened next, Paul?"

"Larry walked down the dirt road……..slowly……..very slowly. We all watched him go around the corner and out of sight. We waited and waited. None of us was wearing a watch, so I'm not sure how long it was, but it seemed to be about fifteen, or maybe twenty minutes. I don't know why we didn't go down after ten minutes, like I promised him, but we didn't. We finally went down to see what happened to him. Ritchie was complaining that he already had his turn and it wasn't fair for us to make him go again. Larch and I told him to shut up and keep walking. When we got to the cemetery, we didn't see Larry at first, so we walked through the gate and went inside. We were all huddled close together.

I saw Larry standing……..just standing at the back of the cemetery. I thought, maybe he caught his foot in a hole, or something like that and I walked toward him, with Larch and Ritchie right behind me. It was really dark down in the cemetery, because of all the trees around it, but there was moonlight shining down right where Larry was standing and we could see him clearly. He looked like he was frozen in place. He had been crying and he had also wet his pants……..really bad. It smelled awfully strong. When I looked down, I saw that he held the baseball in his right hand. I asked him; 'Larry, what's wrong?' He didn't say anything……..nothing at all!"

Nathan reached down and adjusted the tape recorder so it faced more in Paul's direction.

"Paul, can you give me any more detail on Larry's condition?"

"Yes, he seemed to be in a trance. His eyes were open, but he just stared straight ahead. I waved my hand in front of his face and he didn't blink. Ritchie started to cry. He said he was really scared and wanted to go home. Larch told him we had to help Larry first. I took hold of Larry's arm and pulled on it while my other hand pushed his back. He started to move and then……..."

"Then what happened, Paul?"

Noticing that Paul was having difficulty speaking the words his memory was now revealing to him, Nathan spoke softly, reassuringly.

"Paul, it's all right. No one will hurt you. You are not the twelve year old boy. You are simply remembering what happened to you when you were that age. What happened when Larry responded to your tugging and pushing?"

Paul's response to Nathan's calming words was evidenced by a slight droop in his shoulders, as his body gradually relaxed.

"The growl……..it was a low, terrifying growl, similar to what a wild animal would make, just before it attacked. Then we saw this…….. thing, running toward us."

"Describe the 'thing' that ran toward you, Paul."

"It was dressed in dark clothing, maybe black. I couldn't see the face, because there was a large hood covering most of it."

"And what was your response?"

"We ran like hell! We got halfway up the dirt road. Larch and Ritchie were ahead of me. I turned to see if the thing was still following us, but I didn't see it. I called out to them to stop. When I caught up with them, I told them we had to go back and get Larry. We couldn't just leave him there with that monster. Ritchie got hysterical and pleaded with us to let him go home. I told Larch to take Ritchie home, because I wanted to sneak back down there and throw rocks at whatever it was that had Larry."

"Were you able to do that?"

"When I got near the cemetery, I tried to be quiet and snuck along the side of the road, near the trees. Then, when I got closer to the cemetery, I heard someone talking. I could only distinguish one voice, a man's and he sounded as if he were trying to talk someone into doing something. The voice reminded me of someone, but I can't remember who. I snuck up closer until I found a good hiding spot in between some bushes. From there, I had a good view of the guy I at first thought was a monster. His back was to me and he was talking softly. Then he moved to the side a little and I saw Larry, but Larry still wasn't looking right. He wasn't in a trance anymore, but he was whimpering now. He kept saying 'no, please, no'. Then the man stepped toward Larry and I saw him unzip his fly. He sounded angry now and he reached out and grabbed Larry by the back of his head and pulled him toward his privates. I saw Larry stiffen up, but he seemed to still be terrified of this guy."

When Paul stopped talking, Nathan gave him a few seconds to see if he might be attempting to resurrect more memories. After a moment, he prompted his patient.

"Paul, what did the man do to Larry?"

"He……..he tried to make him put his penis in his mouth, but Larry clamped his jaw shut. I got really mad and pegged a stone at the guy. It hit him in the head, just above his ear. He hollered pretty loud and looked around. At the same time, I yelled to Larry to run. Larry pushed the guy away from him and swung his hand up into the guy's crotch. He still had the baseball in his hand and it must have got him square in the nuts, because he doubled over."

Again, Paul seemed to have difficulty bringing forth the words and Nathan gently prodded him along.

"What happened then, Paul?"

"The guy grabbed Larry's arm as he……..tried to run away. He swung him around very fast, like when a father swings his kid around in the air, except he wasn't playing. His other hand held Larry by the belt and when he spun him around in a complete circle, he……..let him go……..head first……..into a…….."

Paul sobbed once and then put his hand to his face, covering his eyes.

"It's all right to say it, Paul. You will feel better, when you tell me, what did the man throw Larry into?"

His face now contorted with anguish, Paul tried to speak, but found it difficult. In one loud outburst, he blurted out what Nathan expected to hear.

"A GRAVESTONE……..HE THREW LARRY HEAD FIRST INTO A GRAVESTONE. WHEN HIS HEAD HIT THE STONE, IT MADE AN AWFUL SOUND AND THE STONE BROKE. LARRY FELL ACROSS THE STONE……..HIS BODY WAS BENT STRANGELY AND LARRY WASN'T MOVING. THEN THE GUY TURNED AROUND AND POINTED HIS FINGER AT ME AND SAID; 'YOU'RE DEAD, MCCULLOCH! HE KNEW MY NAME AND I KNEW WHO HE WAS! SO I RAN……..I RAN AS FAST AS I COULD! I DIDN'T STOP RUNNING UNTIL I GOT TO THE LOWER FIELD JUST ABOVE BOUNDARY ROAD, ABOUT A MILE AND A HALF AWAY. I LEFT MY BIKE BACK AT THE DIRT ROAD, BUT I DIDN'T CARE! OH, GOD……..WHY DID HE HAVE TO KILL HIM? WHY…….. DID HE HAVE TO…….. KILL HIM?"

Overcome with emotion, Paul broke down completely and buried his face in both of his hands. Nathan let him get it all out and then decided to back off a little, perhaps with a short break.

"Paul, I'm going to bring you to a safe area for a few minutes, until you catch your breath. It is daytime, the sun is shining and warm and you and I are standing on Crater Street, near the dirt road to the cemetery. It is the present time. Would you like a drink of water?"

Paul finished wiping tears from his face and eyes with his handkerchief.

"Yes, I would like one, please."

Nathan went to the little refrigerator, hidden in the bookcase and removed a bottle of spring water. He handed it to Paul, who gulped half of the bottle, then let out a loud belch. Without excusing himself, he drank down the remaining water and set the bottle on the small table. Nathan studied him closely while he drank and when he had finished, Nathan wondered if Paul was ready to resume his memory recall process.

"Are you feeling better, Paul?"

"Yes, much better, thanks."

"If I accompany you, will you return to the cemetery with me?"

"I........I don't understand. Why do you want to go to the cemetery?"

"So you won't be alone, Paul."

"I'll be okay."

Nathan was more than a bit surprised at Paul's willingness to return alone to the place that had been the origin of his worst lifetime nightmare. He detected a clear strength of mind in his patient's determination to finish his story, a trait which impressed him. Nathan decided the time was right to get to the heart of the matter.

"Paul, we're going to leave this warm, sunny place. I want you to return to the cemetery. It is early in the evening, dark and you have just witnessed the death of your friend, Larry. You said that the man who killed Larry knew your name, but you also said that *you* knew *his*. I want you to tell me his name."

With his lower lip quivering slightly, Paul stammered; "I........can't."

"Why can't you, Paul?"

Paul sat still, staring straight ahead, but did not answer. Nathan attempted to ease his anxiety.

"Remember, Paul, you are no longer the twelve year-old boy; instead, you are simply visiting the place where you witnessed your friend being murdered and you are remembering all of the details about that murder, including the person who committed the crime. You have nothing to be afraid of. You spoke earlier of the anger you felt at that man, for trying to force Larry to perform oral sex on him. Now you can use that anger to reveal his name, so that Larry's murder can be avenged. Use that anger, Paul."

Paul continued to sit motionless, then his body seemed to convulse, as if two forces inside of him were battling for control. His face reddened and tiny beads of sweat trickled down his forehead, some catching in his eyebrows. His lips pursed and then moved, with no sound emitted, until finally, the words came hard and loud.

"ROGER CAREY……..IT WAS ROGER CAREY! HE KILLED LARRY! THE SON OF A BITCH THREW MY FRIEND INTO THAT HEADSTONE SO HARD THAT I HEARD HIS SKULL CRACK. THEN HE DIDN'T EVEN BOTHER TO SEE IF LARRY WAS OKAY……..HE JUST TURNED TO ME AND SAID HE WAS GOING TO KILL ME TOO, BECAUSE I SAW HIM DO IT."

Calmness settled over Paul as he took a deep breath. One large tear overflowed from his left eye and swiftly traveled down his cheek, to his jawbone, where it followed the jaw to his chin, hung for a second and dropped to his shirt. Softly, almost inaudibly, Paul repeated; "He didn't even bother to see if Larry was okay……..all he wanted was to kill the kid who could identify him."

For Nathan, the hypnosis had been an overwhelming success. Paul had been able to utter the words that had been stored away in some remote area of his memory bank all of these years. He had faced his demon, so to speak, and won. Even so, Nathan wanted to be sure there were no residuals left to cause any future problems and for that reason, he probed a little more.

"Paul, was anyone else, in addition to Roger and you, present at the cemetery when Roger killed Larry?"

"No. Larch and Ritchie were both gone."

"I want you to think very hard, Paul. Did you see anyone, perhaps a man with a leathery-looking face, either on your way to the cemetery, or when you were running home?"

"No, I saw no one."

Nathan picked up his clipboard and flipped through his notes from the first session, then, finding what he was looking for, asked Paul; "Tell me, Paul, what happened when you ran down the animal path that night?"

"I wanted to get to Boundary Road, because I thought it would be safer than going home through the woods. Then I realized that I'd have to pass right by Crazy Roger's house and I got really scared again. But, when I thought about it, I knew there was no way possible that he could have gotten to his house ahead of me, so I kept on running. When I got to the steepest part of the path, just before the big stone retaining wall next to the road, I knew I was going too fast and might not be able to stop, but I planned to leap off the wall onto the road. Just before the wall, something caught my ankle. It felt like a very strong, thin, string. I remember doing a summersault in the air and then I saw the asphalt right before my face. All I saw next, was a bright flash of light, then after a while, I heard old Mr. McQuade's voice. I also heard his wife's voice. She was very upset. I tried to talk, but I don't think anyone could hear me. Then, I heard the voices of some of the people who lived in that neighborhood. Some of the ladies were crying and people were saying how they didn't think I would live, but Mr. McQuade got really mad at them and told them to be quiet. I heard the ambulance siren and felt a man pushing a cloth hard against my face and forehead. It felt like he was going to break my nose, but it didn't hurt at all. Just before they put me into the ambulance, I heard some of the people mumbling under their breaths. They were saying "Look who's coming up the street. What's he been up to?" Then I heard Mr. McQuade saying "What happened to your head, young man? You have a nasty cut there." I heard

Roger Carey's voice answer him. He said; "It's nothing, I just ran into a tree branch, that's all." Then I heard Roger say; "What happened to him?" When I heard his voice, I got very scared, just terrified. The next thing I remember is hearing a woman's voice at the hospital, asking me to wiggle my toes if I could hear her. I tried to, but I guess they didn't move, because I heard her say; "Still no response, doctor."

At this point, Nathan could see no further reason to pursue the process any further. Speaking to Paul in the same, confidently soothing voice, he softly said; "All right, Paul, I want you to close your eyes. We are going to leave this place and time and return to the present. I want you to listen very closely to what I am about to tell you. When I issue you the command to awaken, you will, but not without remembering everything that you have recalled in this conversation. You will remember clearly, all of the events of August 22, 1957. In addition, you will remember that you lost your memory for quite some time, as a result of the accident in which you suffered a skull fracture, but that memory has now been completely restored. Having told you this, I now will tell you to step back into the present time and place, here in my office and be fully conscious and aware."

Quickly and easily, Paul's eyes opened. He looked directly at Nathan and said; "How did we do?"

Nathan, smiling broadly, said; "You hit a home run, a grand slam, actually."

Paul shifted in his chair, not taking his eyes off Nathan.

"Something feels different, in a strange sort of way. It's a peaceful sort of feeling, a more relaxed feeling than I've had in quite a while.

"Paul, you were one of, if not the most informative patients I have ever encountered. Your mind was more than willing to give up the secrets it had locked away for all these years. I carefully monitored your mental and physical state while you were under hypnosis and you exhibited very little signs of stress, other than what should normally be expected, of course, when you were relating some of the more gruesome details of the events of August 22, 1957 and for this reason, I enabled you to retain those memories........"

"Wait a minute, Nathan……..how did you know that was the date? I don't recall telling you…….. unless…….. did I tell you while I was under?"

"I did some research yesterday afternoon, after you left." Nathan got up, walked over to his desk and opened one of the drawers. He pulled out a yellowed copy of the local newspaper and handed it to Paul.

"For a small fee, I was able to obtain this from the publisher's archives."

Paul took the paper from Nathan and scanned the front page. The date of the paper was Friday, August 23, 1957. The lower section contained two articles, one of them bore the headline; "Sheridan Boy Seriously Injured" and detailed the account of how Paul McCulloch was found lying in the street by his elderly next-door neighbors. There was no mention anywhere in the article of Larry, confirming what Larch had told him; that Larry wasn't found until the next evening. The article went on to say that the on-the-scene police investigation revealed that the boy had been running down a path toward the road, when he had tripped on some nylon fishing line, which had been strung across two small trees, at a height of about six inches off the ground.

"So that's what happened. I'm willing to bet I know just who strung that line, Nathan."

"Judging from what you've told me, Paul, if your guess is Roger Carey, then you're probably correct."

"Nathan, did I hear you right, when I heard you say that you enabled me to retain the memories of that night?"

Nathan smiled and held out his hand in a welcoming gesture.

"Well, let's try a test, Paul. Why don't you tell me what you said to Larry when he was adamant on going down to the cemetery, despite your and Larch's efforts to talk him out of it?"

Paul thought hard, lowering his head in concentration, then lifted his head up, eyes bright with excitement, as he said; "I told him we'd give him ten minutes and if he wasn't back by then, we were coming after him. Oh, my God, Nathan……..I remember that……..I can actually remember that. Thank you……..Thank you so much!"

Nathan walked back to his chair and sat down. His voice became solemn as he addressed his patient.

"Paul, one of the reasons why I felt it important to enable you to retain your memory of that night is the fact that you told me, in recall, that you had indeed, been a witness to murder. That declaration has literally solved two mysteries: that of your recurring nightmares and as such, is a statement of tremendous impact. It also should help to close a case which I'm sure has puzzled the local police department for many years. It does, however, present me with a delicate problem. My first obligation is to you, the patient and your right to privacy and confidentiality. This, I will protect. You have stated to me, under hypnosis, that you were witness to a murder. Legally, I must inform the authorities of that fact. This does not, in any way, violate the patient privacy law, as my obligation is to reveal any statements made, which do not implicate you, as long as I do not reveal any details of your conversation which do not pertain to the crime. My intention is to call the state police, inform them of what you have told me and the conditions under which you told me and let them do with the information what they must. I would advise you to contact them also. The tape that I made of our session will not be given to the police, unless they obtain a court order, as I consider that privileged information........"

"That's okay, Nathan. You have my permission to let them have the tape, if you wish. I don't feel as though I have anything to hide."

"Well, Paul, that's not the point. You are very casual in your approach and there is something to be said for that. Not every patient, however, is as open-minded as you. They want their privacy protected at any cost. If I were to make the tape recording of your session easily available to the authorities, I might be setting a dangerous precedent. If they want it, they must fight for it."

Paul, who was still on a high from the knowledge that he had his full memory of that fateful evening back, simply shrugged his shoulders and said; "Whatever." Then, as a second thought, he said to Nathan; "There is one favor I'd like to ask of you, Nathan."

"Yes, Paul. What would that be?"

"I have a good relationship with Bill Fenton, who happens to be the Chief of Police in Sheridan. I intend to report this information to him and I am asking you to do likewise."

"That's fine, Paul. I'll be happy to oblige. It is, after all, in his jurisdiction."

"Thank you, Nathan. I'm curious to see just how much information on this case is still available after all these years."

"Paul, I wouldn't get my hopes up, if I were you. Sometimes old files are thrown out by over-zealous cleaning people, or folks just wanting to make more room."

Holding up both hands to show he had crossed his index and middle fingers, Paul said; "Here's hoping that everything is still there."

Fidgeting in his chair uncomfortably, Paul struggled for the right words and asked; "Nathan, even though I feel a hell of a lot more relieved and relaxed than I have in a month, there's still……..I don't know how to say it……..still something bothering me. It's very confusing, because at times, it seems evil and at the same time, seems good. I just have a funny feeling that there is something more……..still to come; and I think this 'voice' has a lot to do with it. What do you make of that?"

Nathan reached over to the little table and picked up his clipboard once again. He thumbed through the notes he had taken, set the board in his lap, put his two hands together, as if he were about to pray and spoke to Paul.

"Paul, I want to be sure that you understand the significance of what has transpired during this session. This series of nightmares which you have endured can best be compared to an abscessed tooth, which we have now removed. Even though we have removed the source of your problem, there will still be some lingering pain for a while. It is an integral part of the healing process. To be perfectly candid with you, I'm not sure I understand why this 'voice' is speaking to you, but I must caution you not to put too much stock in what it says…….."

"So, you're suggesting that I don't go to the cemetery today?"

"I'm suggesting very strongly that you do not go to the cemetery today. You are still vulnerable to subliminal suggestions, Paul, as a result of your dream experiences. My advice to you, after you talk to the police chief, is to go home, inform your wife of what we were able to accomplish today, take her out to dinner and a movie, preferably a comedy and try to put all of this behind you. You have accomplished a great deal today. You have defeated your evil dream tormenter by exposing him for what he was and is; a perverted killer. Now is the time to turn the information over to the authorities and let them handle it from here. You need to rest, for one thing. It might not be such a bad idea to take a week or two off and just relax. You don't have to go away; a quiet spot in the yard and a lounge chair will do just fine."

"Boy, my wife will be glad to hear that. She's been after me to do just that."

Nathan stood up, signaling that the session was over. He held out his hand and shook Paul's, saying; "I want to see you one more time, to be sure that you are not suffering from any lingering effects of your dreams, which I seriously doubt, will happen. We could set something up in a week to ten days, if that would be all right?"

Paul nodded his approval and Nathan walked to his desk and consulted his appointment book. Looking up, he asked; "Thursday the twenty-sixth, at one p.m. Will that suit you?"

"That works for me."

Nathan walked Paul to the private exit, where the two men said good-bye. Paul walked out to his truck, got in and drove away. He glanced at the dash clock, noting the time as one thirty-five p.m. As he drove up Juniper Parkway, he turned his cell phone on again. It rang immediately.

CHAPTER FIFTEEN

The voice on the phone was barely distinguishable, amidst a background of sobs and disjointed phrases. Nonetheless, Paul instantly recognized it as Mary Ellen's.

"Paul……..Oh, Paul……..It's Marilyn…….."

At the mention of Marilyn's name, Mary Ellen completely broke down and cried miserably. Paul's mind raced, as he began to think the worst. Had she been hit by a car? Had someone shot her in a robbery at the store?

"Mary Ellen, what about Marilyn?"

Paul waited; his wife still unable to control her sobbing. After a few moments, far from regaining her composure, she blurted out; "SHE'S GONE!"

The crying intensified, as the words she had just spoken, hit home. Paul was now left to wonder what 'gone' meant. Was it 'gone', as in dead, or had Marilyn packed up and left town?

"What do you mean, 'gone'?"

The voice which answered his question now rang with anger at his inability to understand the meaning of what Mary Ellen had just said.

"SHE'S MISSING! Oh, Paul……..Please come and get me……..I NEED YOU!"

"Are you at the store?"

Again, the voice flashes with anger, mixed with distress and worry.

"YES!"

"I'll be right there."

Paul immediately disregarded his plans to drive to the Sheridan Police Department and instead, focused his attention on this new problem. He was well aware of the bond of friendship that had grown between his wife and Marilyn and he understood why. Despite her reputation, there was an inner quality which Marilyn possessed, a sort of trustworthiness which seemed to transcend what most people expected from her. He smiled to himself, as he thought that even though she flirted openly with him, there was no way she would ever betray her friend, by sleeping with her husband. His thoughts now ran through some hastily-devised scenarios as to what could have happened to her.

"Let's see, she gave Mary Ellen a ride home yesterday afternoon…….. She would have gone back and finished her shift……..No, her shift would have been just about done when she dropped Mary Ellen off, so she most likely would have gone straight home. Would she have gone out on the town on a Wednesday night? Most people wouldn't, but we're not talking about most people, here, we're talking about Marilyn and she marches to a different drummer. So, if she went to a bar and got picked up, she might still be with the guy at his apartment, nursing a hangover, or…….."

Paul shuddered, as he thought of another possible scenario, one in which harm had come to Marilyn. He, himself, had grown fond of her, as she was outgoing and friendly and had the ability to grow on you after a while.

Before he knew, he found himself turning into the parking lot of the small shopping plaza where the Paragon Gift Shoppe was located. He found a space next to Mary Ellen's car, shut off his ignition and went into the store. Emily, the high school girl who worked full-time in the summer, was on the register and Paul went straight to her.

"HI, Emily. Can you tell me where I can find my wife?"

As she carefully placed two birthday cards in a bag for a customer, Emily turned to Paul and said; "She's in the back room, Mr. McCulloch. Ralph is with her. You can go right in."

As Paul pushed his way through the two large swinging doors, under the sign which read 'Employees Only', the sight which greeted his eyes was heart-wrenching. Mary Ellen was sitting in a swivel-style office chair, her head buried in her hands, shoulders lurching, seemingly inconsolable. Ralph, one of the brother-owners, stood helplessly in front of her, holding a box of facial tissues. The look of relief on his face when he turned indicated to Paul that he was at his wit's end. He had tried, unsuccessfully, to provide some measure of comfort to Mary Ellen, to no avail.

Paul quietly approached his wife and slid his arm around her shoulder, at the same time crouching in front of her. He then cupped her hand in his and reached up to gently stroke her hair. As she lifted her head, Paul was shocked by the image he saw. The woman in front of him looked so completely different from the wife he had said goodbye to earlier this morning. Her entire face was blotchy red and swollen from crying, with wrinkle marks from the contorted position she had held, while trying to restrain the sobs. Her eye shadow had run, creating small dark tell-tale lines along her cheekbones. Her eyes had lost the sparkle for which she was so well-liked by her co-workers and friends and loved by her husband and family. They seemed devoid of any hope and it was when he looked into those eyes, that Paul realized the gravity of the situation. And when Mary Ellen looked into Paul's eyes, she saw the compassionate man she had fallen in love with all those years ago, the man who had always been there for her and was, once again. As she fell forward into his arms, the only words she was able to utter before lapsing into another spell of unrelenting sobs, lurches and tears was; "Oh, Paul! I think something terrible may have happened to her!"

Ralph moved to steady the swivel chair, which had started to roll backward, fearing it might roll out from under Mary Ellen. Paul went to one knee, in order to steady himself and hugged his wife tightly, saying nothing, but looking up to Ralph, in an effort to find someone who could provide information as to what happened to Marilyn. He silently mouthed the words "What happened?" and Ralph, who was the complete opposite of his brother, Jack, softly answered.

"Paul, the police came in here late this morning. They said they needed to ask us all a few questions. They wanted to know who had been the last person to see Marilyn yesterday. Your wife said that Marilyn had dropped her off at her house around two thirty p.m. and Jack had given her a ride back to the store to pick up her car. Emily then said that neither of them had come back to the store and she called me at five thirty to inform me that she was alone in the store and she needed me to close at six p.m. I asked her where Jack was and she told me about what happened to Mary Ellen and how Jack was supposed to follow Marilyn in his car and drive her back to the store, but that they never showed up. The poor kid was alone all that time. I asked the police why they wanted to know about Marilyn and they said her car was found early this morning in the old Madison Shoe factory parking lot."

Ralph paused here and made a polite attempt to speak softly enough so that Mary Ellen would not hear.

"They said there was blood on the back of the front seat and the keys were in the ignition."

Paul now wanted to ask the obvious question.

"Did they talk to your *brother?*" Paul tried hard to control his rising anger, but he couldn't bring himself to say the word 'Jack', when referring to the man whom he had only recently learned, had caused his wife so much dismay. Paul had always held Ralph, however, in the highest regard and it was that sentiment that helped to keep his temper in check.

"Yes, Paul, I'm afraid they did………The police have placed him under arrest and he is being held without bail. When I finished closing the store last night, I drove over to Jack's apartment. He lives by himself on the west side. I wanted to ask him why he left that young woman all alone in the store. I was extremely upset with him and fully expected that he must have had a medical problem, as that was the only excuse I could accept for doing what he did. When I got to his apartment, he wouldn't answer his bell, so I rang it several times and yelled through the door, saying I knew he was in there, because I saw his car in the parking garage. By this time, I assumed that he was unable to answer the door and used my emergency key to open the door. When I walked inside, I couldn't believe my eyes. Jack was standing there, in his underwear, his face and undershirt covered in blood. He had a wet towel, also soaked in blood, in his hand and he seemed disoriented, almost unaware that I had come in. His nose was swollen to almost twice its size and both eyes were blackened. When I asked him what happened, he told me he had been mugged. I asked him if he had called the police and he changed his story, saying instead, that he had gotten into a fight with someone younger than he. He refused to let me drive him to the hospital, or to accept any medical treatment whatsoever. I yelled at him, telling him that no matter what had happened, he should not have left young Emily alone for that long. I also told him I was tired of hearing his lies and that we would deal with this in the morning. I love my brother, Paul, but if he has caused Marilyn any harm, then……..."

Paul could see that Ralph was also on the verge of breaking down and wisely decided to resist any more questioning. Instead, he stood up, gently pulling Mary Ellen up with him.

"Let's get you home."

Nodding her head in thankfulness for the prospect of leaving this place which had been the source of so much sorrow for her, Mary Ellen shuffled along beside Paul, leaning into him for support. Ralph hurriedly caught up with them.

"Paul, I can bring your truck around back, so Mary Ellen won't have to walk past anyone who might be in the store. Mary Ellen, who was slowly regaining her composure, due to the comforting presence of her husband, turned to Ralph and said; "Thank you, Ralph, but I'll be all right now."

In a gesture which he hoped would convey his feelings, Ralph looked directly at Mary Ellen and said; "I'm so sorry!"

Reaching out, she patted his hand and taking a deep breath, replied; "I know. Let's just pray that she's all right."

Paul, who had been sidetracked picturing in his mind what possibly could have happened to Marilyn, thought; *"She's gonna need a lot of them, Mare."* As far as he was concerned, this didn't look good, at all.

Ralph's thoughts were on his brother, Jack and he wondered how a man who had come from the same loving parents as he, could be capable of causing harm, or killing, another human being. It just didn't seem feasible, but he had been wrong about Jack once before, several years ago, when one of the more buxom young women who worked at the store, complained to Ralph that Jack was watching her while she was in the ladies room. Ralph had vehemently denied that Jack could do such a thing, until she later showed him where Jack had cut a small peep hole in the wall, just under the mirror, opposite the toilet.

The wall where the hole was made was at the rear of Jack and Ralph's office. When Ralph went into the office to see why he hadn't noticed the hole before, he found that it had been covered by a newly-hung painting that Jack had been anxious to install. Ralph remembered confronting Jack, who feigned innocence, saying it must have been the cleaning people who came into the store at night. Knowing this was preposterous, because why would someone drill a hole to spy on women in a bathroom when they would never have the opportunity to do so; Ralph thought about raising that question to his brother and, perhaps fearing the answer, let the matter drop.

Now, as he stood there, he suddenly felt partly to blame for what happened to Marilyn. Had he spoken to his brother and told him to get help, maybe things might have turned out differently. His mood became increasingly somber as he muttered to himself; "Heaven help me, if something terrible has happened to Marilyn. Heaven help *Jack* if something's happened to her."

CHAPTER SIXTEEN

Police Chief William G. Fenton closed the bottom drawer of the file cabinet marked "Unsolved". Leaning his right arm across the top of the cabinet, he pondered his next move. Since receiving the rather bizarre phone call from a psychologist named Nathan Feldmar earlier this afternoon, he had been unable to locate the file from the Guernette murder case of 1957.

Bill Fenton remembered the case well, despite the fact the murder occurred when he was barely two years old. When he joined the Sheridan Police force in 1978, fresh out of a four-year stint in the military police, the case was still talked about on a regular basis. The then police chief, John Yates, had never given up on the theory that a somewhat wild local teenager named Roger Carey had been responsible for the boy's death. There were, as Fenton recalled, many tantalizing little tidbits of information, which all seemed to indicate culpability on Carey's part, but the investigators had been unable to come up with any solid proof. This afternoon's call would change all of that, giving police a first-hand eyewitness testimony from a well-respected lifelong town resident. Fenton shuddered slightly however, thinking of the field day a defense lawyer would have with this witness, a man who suddenly regained his memory after almost fifty years. That would be a hard sell.

"They'll have him for breakfast" he thought.

Nevertheless, it was Chief Fenton's job to act on any information he received and he had placed a call to Paul McCulloch's home, leaving a message to return his call a.s.a.p., as he wanted to interview him.

The Graveyard Game

Now, as he leaned on the file cabinet, Fenton thought of one last possibility; the file must have been transferred to the archives in the Town Hall at some point, in a space saving measure.

Reaching for his phone, the chief dialed Rosemary, the Town Clerk. When she answered, Fenton said; "Hello Rosie, Bill Fenton here."

"Well, hello Bill. Gosh, I don't get calls from you on a regular basis, something must be wrong. Did someone see me running a stop sign on my way to work this morning……..because if they did, I'll deny everything."

Without cracking a smile, the chief replied in his most solemn voice; "It wasn't just the stop sign, Rosie……..it was the two parked cars you sideswiped when you were ogling those young construction workers on Pleasant Street."

Laughing heartily, Rosemary responded; "Like that would happen! Now, how can I help you?"

Chief Fenton assured himself of one indisputable fact; if the case file had been moved to the Town Hall anytime within the past thirty seven years, which happened to be the length of time that Rosemary O'Bryan had served as Town Clerk, then Rosie would know not only if it had, but would likely be able to tell him the year it was transferred, as well as the present location. She was known for her ability to recall dates, names and places of events that occurred in town, as well as ages of most town residents and their addresses. Rosie O'Bryan was, dollar for dollar, perhaps the most valuable town employee in terms of hours that she had saved department heads in comparison to the relatively meager salary she received. The chief was aware that many folks in various town offices relied heavily on Rosie to bail them out, which she did efficiently, usually with only a quick 'thanks, Rosie' as a reward. He didn't like the thought of adding to the burden of this overtaxed worker, whose good nature he felt was slightly abused by those others in need. However, he now found himself in the same situation that prompted others to rely on her help; he had not a clue as to where the case file would be in the Town Hall, if in fact, it was even in the building. There was also the possibility that it had been thrown out, either by mistake, or by an overzealous file clerk, hoping to create badly needed space. Whatever the case might be, the one person who could set him straight was on the other end of the line.

"Rosie, I've got a bit of a problem here. I need to locate a case file from a murder which occurred here in town back in 1957........"

"That would be the little Guernette boy........sad case. Right after John Yates retired in 1982, that hotshot they hired to replace him, Nelson Landers, cleaned all files older than ten years out of his office and had them lugged over here. They filled a pick-up truck. I told him that he could just haul them all back, because there was no way we could store all of them here. He compromised and sent over everything older than twenty five years, which cut it down to three good-sized boxes. I had an un-used file cabinet in the basement, so I let him use that, on the condition that he would send someone over to properly file them. Well, he sent someone all right, but the knucklehead just tossed all the files into folders in a mish-mash. They looked neat enough, but trying to find a particular file is a different story. The file is here, but if you're looking to punish one of your men, send him over to look for it; I guarantee he won't cross you again. You say you've got a bit of a problem; well, the way I see it, your only problem is finding the file before getting overcome by the musty smell down there........whew! It's horrid!"

With his head spinning a little from the rapid-fire voice at the other end of the line, Chief Fenton could only shake his head in admiration.

"Rosie, you're amazing!"

"Well, you'd better hold your praise until you find your file."

"I'll send Andy over to have a look. Thanks a bunch, Rosie."

"Yeah, yeah. I want to know when you're going to buy me that steak dinner you keep promising me."

"I told you, as soon as the selectmen vote to give me a raise."

"That means I'd better get used to peanut butter sandwiches, because those guys are tighter than paint on a new car."

Rosie succeeded in getting a laugh out of Chief Fenton, who quickly agreed; "You're right about that, lady."

"Tell Andy I'll have cream and no sugar, I'm sweet enough."

Again laughing, Bill Fenton answered; "You sure are, Rosie; you sure are!"

Before she hung up, Rosie pointed out something to the chief.

"Bill, make sure Andy sees me before going down to the basement. I have the only key to that file cabinet here in my office."

"Will do, Rosie."

Chief Fenton sauntered over to his desk, where he keyed the mike on the two-way radio.

"S-one to Unit 4, come in 4."

The radio crackled and Patrolman Andy Fine answered; "Go ahead, Chief."

"Unit 4, head into the station, if you would."

"Roger that, Chief. My E.T.A. will be six minutes."

Andy Fine was one of the newer members of the Sheridan Police Force. Bill Fenton had been impressed with him from day one. He readily accepted his assignments, was thorough in his paperwork and perhaps most importantly, showed the patience and street smarts to become a good cop. Bill knew he could trust Andy to plod through the file cabinet and come up with the Guernette file without the whining and grousing he would be sure to get from most of the other patrolmen. Besides, Andy and Sergeant Tom Skinner were the only ones working this afternoon and he couldn't take Skinner off the road.

While he waited for Andy to return to the station, he re-dialed the McCulloch residence, but still got only the answering machine.

Leaning back in his chair, Chief Fenton began to assess the information he had so far. A respected psychologist had informed him that a patient of his, while under hypnosis, had recalled witnessing his childhood friend being murdered. The patient, a lifelong resident of Sheridan, was known to Fenton as a hard-working local electrical contractor, solid citizen, who gave no indication whatsoever that he wasn't playing with a full deck at all times.

"I've talked with Paul McCulloch dozens of times. He's as solid as they come. I'm looking forward to hearing him tell me the details, it should be interesting. This could end up being the most exciting thing to happen around

here in a while, so I better prepare for a media blitz if the story leaks out. I want to keep a lid on it for a while, anyway, if that's even remotely possible. These things have a way of leaking out."

Fenton's thoughts were interrupted by Andy's knock on the chief's open door.

"You wanted to see me Chief?"

"Come in, Andy."

Andy walked over to a spot in front of the chief's desk, where he dutifully stood, a little nervously, wondering if he had messed up somehow. Chief Fenton, sensing this, put his young charge at ease.

"Andy, I need you to locate a rather important file, actually a *very* important file. It sits somewhere in a filing cabinet in the basement of the Town Hall. The case is a murder, which was committed in 1957. The victim's name was Lawrence Guernette, a young boy who was eleven or twelve years of age, I believe. Now, Rosie tells me that the files are all thrown into the cabinet in a haphazard way, so it may take some time to find it. I've just received what appears to be a reliable lead in the form of an eyewitness who has come forward, so I *need to have* that case file. See Rosie and she'll give you the key to the cabinet and either tell you where it is or escort you down there, if she has the time."

Relieved that he wasn't in trouble and eager to head off on his new assignment, Andy turned and headed for the door after assuring his boss that he'd get right on it. As he neared the doorway, Chief Fenton called out; "One other thing, Andy; if anyone asks, you're just updating some of the older files so we can put them on hard disks and toss out the paperwork. We're doing them one at a time, okay? Absolutely *do not* disclose our true reason for being there. It may be difficult, but try to be as discreet as possible."

"I understand, Chief. I won't let you down."

"You wouldn't be going there if I thought you would."

"Thanks, Chief."

As his patrolman disappeared into the hallway, Bill Fenton's phone rang.

CHAPTER SEVENTEEN

The ride home was a silent one as Mary Ellen sat quietly in the passenger seat of her husband's pickup truck. Paul, not wanting to say the wrong thing, for fear Mary Ellen would become upset again, pretended to be concentrating on the traffic, which had gotten heavy along Main Street.

About halfway home, the inner voice spoke to Paul in a sudden, adamant tone.

"YOU MUST GO THERE TODAY!"

Startled by the directness and clarity of the voice which Paul thought for sure Mary Ellen must have heard, he instinctively turned to her and said; "What?"

Her face still puffy from crying, Mary Ellen glanced in Paul's direction with a bewildered look, then quietly said; "I didn't say anything."

Again, the voice spoke to Paul, with the same intensity as before.

"DO NOT LET ANYTHING DETER YOU! YOU MUST GO THERE TODAY!"

The clearness of the voice, combined with the insistent message caused Paul to respond to its unrelenting demand.

"All right, I'LL GO!" he half-shouted at the determined inner being, not knowing its origin, only the persistence it displayed.

Mary Ellen jumped, shaken from her thoughts of Marilyn by her husband's unexplained outburst.

"PAUL, WHAT IS WRONG WITH YOU? MY GOD, YOU SCARED ME HALF TO DEATH. WHO ARE YOU TALKING TO?"

"I'm sorry, Mare. I was just thinking out loud."

"Paul, *please* don't tell me you were talking to that voice in your head."

Betrayed by his lack of response, Paul fidgeted in his seat, reaching for the controls for the radio, in a fruitless attempt to convince Mary Ellen that he was, in fact quite sane, despite the outward appearance that he was displaying. She was far from convinced.

"It didn't go well for you this morning, did it? I mean……..at the psychologist's office."

"Actually, it went very well. But, I don't want to trouble you with that business right now. I just want to get you home and let you lie down and rest."

"Paul, I *want to know*, is that voice in your head still telling you to go to that cemetery?"

"Don't worry about it, Mary Ellen. I'm not concerned about that voice right now."

"Well, I am, Paul. I don't know what's going on in your head, but I *do not* want you to go to that cemetery alone. That's just not a good idea."

Paul did not respond to Mary Ellen's stated concerns. He knew any response would just lead to bickering, which would only aggravate his worried wife further. Mary Ellen, too tired to continue her line of questioning, settled back in the truck seat silently for the remainder of the ride home.

Once home, Paul went into the bathroom, where he started the water running in the bathtub, uncomfortably hot for him, but just the way Mary Ellen liked it. She had gone into the bedroom and sat on the bed, intending to lie down.

"I'm running a nice, hot bath for you. You'll feel a lot better after you soak in there for a while."

"Thank you, honey. That *will* feel good."

He opened Mary Ellen's closet door and retrieved her favorite summer robe, laid it out on the bed, along with her plush slippers and helped her slide her shoes off. Taking her hand, he helped her off the bed, grabbed the robe and slippers and led her into the bathroom, where he kissed her tenderly on the forehead before closing the door, leaving her alone. Paul set about making a light snack for his wife, along with a steaming hot cup of tea, timed to be ready just as she exited the bathroom. Then, he went into the bedroom and turned back the covers on Mary Ellen's side of the bed.

When Mary Ellen came out of the bathroom, she looked a lot different than before her bath. The swollen look was gone from her face, although her red eyelids bore proof that she continued to be upset over her missing friend. When she saw the neat little setup Paul had prepared for her on the kitchen table, she smiled and walking toward the table, said; "Is this for me?"

"Knowing you, I'm willing to bet you haven't eaten all day, so you should eat a little something and then lie down. You'll feel better."

"You're so thoughtful. I'm sorry I've been........well, I haven't been very nice to you today, Paul. And now, with this thing with Marilyn, I'm........just a mess."

"It was Roger Carey."

"What?"

"It was Roger Carey who murdered Larry. Mare........ Nathan put me under hypnosis and I was able to recall everything about that night. Not only that, he enabled me somehow to retain the entire memory. I can picture it in my mind now as if it happened yesterday."

"Paul, I don't know what to say. That's wonderful, I guess. But, are you bothered at all with those memories? I mean, they must not be very pleasant."

"No, they're not, but you know Mare, I was just so glad to be able to recall everything about that night and remove this blank spot from my life, that the horror of it all hasn't seemed to bother me. Besides, I've seen it all replayed in my dreams for the past three and a half weeks........it just doesn't seem as bad in my conscious memory as it was in my dreams. They were brutal."

"Does he think the nightmares are over?"

"He does, but I'm not so sure I do."

"Why, Paul?"

"Mare……..in the last day or two, there has been a new presence in my dreams……..a sinister……..very *evil*, person. This character really worries me. The best way I can describe him is that he reminds me of those pictures we used to see in comic books of the grim reaper. He has this constant grin on his face and he appears to be very muscular and strong. He sort of has a California beach-boy type of look to him with hazel eyes that seem to burn right into you like lasers. He has long blond hair and he is probably the most unlikely terror figure you can imagine, with all those handsome good looks, but……..he is absolutely frightening. I get this strong feeling that he is still someone I'm going to have to deal with in my dreams. He seems even more evil than Carey."

"Is he the voice in your head?"

"No, Mare. The voice I hear doesn't give me the impression that it is in any way evil. You've got to believe me when I tell you I am not losing my marbles. This voice isn't telling me to go kill someone or anything wacky like that…….."

"No, Paul……..it's just telling you to go and stand in a cemetery at night, so that some God-awful thing can happen to you. I'm sorry, but I can't accept this part. Having nightmares is one thing; hearing voices is just too much for me to understand."

"Mary Ellen, even the psychologist doesn't understand why I'm hearing it. What I'm trying to tell you is that, if the voice was instructing me to do something terrible, then I would think I might be losing touch with reality. But all it has done so far has been to warn me of danger. It warned me in my dream not to run past Roger Carey's house. It told me to go into the cemetery in another dream and when I did, I found Larry's body. Now, it's telling me to go to the cemetery again. I have a strange feeling Mare, that if I don't do what it asks, I may live to regret it."

"*If* you live to regret it."

"All right, I'll tell you what. I'll call Larch and ask him to go along with me, okay?"

"That doesn't really satisfy me, but it is better than you going there alone, I guess. Paul, I know I'm not going to be able to talk you out of this foolish idea, so just be sure to take your cell phone and *keep it on!*"

"Mare, I'm not going to leave you alone tonight."

"That's nice to know, at least."

Paul stood up from the table and motioned for Mary Ellen to get up, as well.

"Let's get you into bed, now. You need to get some rest. I'm going to call the police chief and try to explain how I've come about being a witness to a forty seven-year old murder. I'll also see if he has anything new on Marilyn."

"Thank you for doing that, Paul."

"Maybe he'll have some good news for us." Paul wanted badly to ease Mary Ellen's concern for her missing friend.

"Maybe."

Mary Ellen downed some aspirin before going into the bedroom, where Paul kissed her on the cheek and left her alone to rest.

He picked up the portable phone on his way through the kitchen and went out to the sunroom, where he dialed his son Mike's number. As expected, neither Mike nor his wife, Heather, were home, so Paul left a message, instructing Mike to call home. He then called daughter Kathy's cell phone, which she answered on the second ring.

"Kathy, this is Dad."

"Hello, Daddy, I can barely hear you. We don't have a good connection."

Paul spoke louder and told Kathy he would hang up and try again on his cell phone. He dialed Kathy's number again and this time got a clear connection.

"Hi, Daddy; is everything okay?"

"Well, we've got a little trouble here, but your mother and I are physically okay. Do you remember her friend Marilyn, from the gift store?"

"Yes."

"She didn't show up for work this morning and the police found her car later on, abandoned in a parking lot........"

Upon hearing this, Kathy let out an audible gasp. Paul continued.

"There were blood stains in the car and it's not looking too good."

"Oh, my God! Mommy must be heartbroken."

"She's taking it pretty hard. That's why I'm calling you. I'd like you to........"

"Daddy, I just finished my shift and I'm in my car. I'll be there in less than an hour."

"Thanks, sweetheart; but don't rush. I just got your mother to lie down, so she should sleep for an hour or more."

"Okay, Daddy; I love you."

"I love you too, Kathy."

As Paul disconnected, he immediately dialed the number for the Sheridan Police Department. When the dispatcher answered, Paul asked to speak to Chief Fenton.

"I'll connect you, Mr. McCulloch."

Paul at first wondered how the dispatcher knew his name, but then he remembered that the town had recently put in place the new system, which displayed the name and address of each caller on the computer screen. In a few seconds, he heard Bill Fenton's voice.

"Hello, Paul. Gosh, you're a hard man to get a hold of. I tried your business line and your home phone and was just thinking of driving by your house."

"I'm really sorry about that, Bill. I just got home from picking Mary Ellen up at work. She is very upset, because her best friend went missing sometime yesterday afternoon or evening."

"Oh, yes; the Duran woman; we got an advisory from the state police."

"Is there anything new on it?"

"Not anything more than what you've probably heard on the news reports. It just said that her car was found in the old Madison Shoe Factory parking lot, with the keys in the ignition. There was blood on the driver's side headrest, which the state police crime lab is now checking. They're also checking several prints, which were found on the driver's door. They have a man in custody, apparently her boss. He was covered in blood, as was his clothing and he's not talking. It doesn't sound good."

"That's what I was afraid of. I told Mary Ellen I'd ask you for an update, but I'll skip the details and just tell her there is nothing new. She's upset enough already."

"Taking it pretty hard, is she?"

"She's a mess, Bill. They were very close."

"I'm sorry to hear that. Now, I understand you have something very important to tell me, but I'd rather interview you in private. Can you come up to the station?"

"Would it be possible to do it here, at my house? I'm not sure that Mary Ellen is asleep yet and I don't want to leave her alone."

"Yes, we can do that."

"Bill, would you come in through the sun room in the rear of the house. We can sit there and talk without disturbing Mary Ellen. I'll watch for you."

"Not a problem. I'll be there in a few minutes."

Paul set his cell phone down on the window ledge, set about tidying up the sunroom and waited.

CHAPTER EIGHTEEN

Chief Fenton had just put the phone down from his conversation with Paul McCulloch, when the dispatcher buzzed him that he had a caller with information on the missing woman. The caller's name was Henry Stolarczek. As he picked up the phone and pressed the blinking button, his heart jumped a little at the thought that this new information might be of a positive nature, as this caller was known to the chief as another well-respected businessman in town.

"Hello, Henry; this is Chief Fenton."

"Chief, I just heard the news report about that missing woman. I had heard part of it earlier, but just now heard the part where they mentioned that her car was found in the Madison Shoe lot. I saw something there yesterday........"

"Henry, I'd rather you didn't say any more over the phone. Can you come into the station?"

"Yes, I can. I can swing over there right now, if you'd like."

"I'll tell the dispatcher to let you into my office."

The chief hung up and called Paul McCulloch to tell him that he would be delayed and would be over in an hour or so. In a few minutes, Larch walked into his office, the dispatcher at his side.

"Come in, Henry and sit down. Would you like some coffee?"

"No, thank you." Larch sat down and in his typical fashion, wasted no time in getting to the point.

"Chief, I saw something yesterday afternoon as my crew and I were waiting for a state environmental agent to inspect an oil leak on a construction site next to the old Madison Shoe complex. While we were waiting, I wandered over to the property line next to the complex. I was standing there, looking at the buildings and thinking about how they could be utilized, when I heard a woman scream. It sounded as if it came from the area in front of the main building and I started to walk over there to check it out, when my foreman called out to me that the agent had arrived, so I turned away to go back to the spill site."

"What was the approximate time when you heard the scream?"

"It was just about three thirty p.m."

"How many times did this woman scream?"

"Just once."

"Did anyone else hear the scream?"

"I doubt it, Chief. I was a lot closer than any of my crew to where it originated."

The chief picked up his pen and jotted down a note on a scratch pad.

"I'll have to send someone over to interview them. When are they all together?"

"You can catch them all at seven a.m. tomorrow. I'll hold them in until your officer arrives."

"Thank you, Henry, for your co-operation. I'll make sure we don't keep them any longer than necessary. Did you hear or see anything else?"

"Yes, I did. As I was walking back toward the spill site, I saw a car speeding out of the driveway to the complex. Whoever was driving must have been in a hurry, because the car was kicking up broken pieces of asphalt."

"Can you describe the vehicle?"

"It was a dark sedan, a late model, nice-looking car."

"Were you able to get the license plate number?"

"Unfortunately, no; the car was too far away."

"Did you notice any obvious damage to the vehicle?"

"None that I could see."

"Were you able to see how many occupants were in the vehicle?"

"Yes, but it was strange. When the car turned and headed west on Main Street, I saw only one person, a man, driving the car, but he appeared to be struggling with someone. But, I didn't see anyone else, so he might have just been trying to keep something from falling off the seat."

"Or he was trying to keep some *one* from climbing back *onto* the seat." Chief Fenton made some more notations and asked the next question.

"Can you describe the driver?"

Larch was apologetic as he said; "I'm sorry Chief, there were enough shadows from the trees that it was only possible to determine that it was a man, but other than that, I can't give you anything else."

"Don't apologize, Henry. I appreciate your honesty. We sometimes get witnesses who think they have to make up something in order to satisfy us. Then, when they get to the courthouse and realize they could face perjury charges if they're found to be lying, or see a defendant sitting before them and know that their testimony could send him away for a long time, all of a sudden they say what you just said, that you're not sure. It is so much easier to have you tell me that now, than to hear you back off in your sworn statement, before the judge. Now, you say the vehicle headed west, towards Sheridan?"

"That's correct. I watched it until it drove out of sight."

"Is there anything else you want to add?"

"No. That's all I can tell you."

Rising from his chair to signal the end of the meeting, Chief Fenton ushered Larch to the door and out into the lobby, where he thanked him for coming forward with the information.

"I'm sure the state police will be in touch with you. They'll want to hear it from you, all over again."

Larch reached into his shirt pocket and pulled out his business card, which he handed to the chief.

"Tell them the best way to get me is by my cell phone number on the bottom, or they can leave a message on my office phone. I check them several times a day."

The chief smiled a knowing smile as he said; "I'm sure they won't have any trouble finding you."

As Larch drove away, the chief got into his cruiser and, as he drove to McCulloch's house, he patched into the West Dale barracks commander and gave him the rundown on this latest information. He read off the numbers on Larch's business card and asked to be informed of any developments in the case. Fenton continued on, arriving at his destination, where he went around the back, as instructed, to find Paul waiting at the door to the sunroom.

After an exchange of pleasantries, the men sat down at a large wooden trestle table in the well-lit sunroom. Paul poured each a cup of freshly brewed coffee and the chief was the first to broach the subject at hand.

"Paul, this fellow, Nathan Feldmar, says that you were able to name, under hypnosis, the person who is responsible for the murder of the Guernette boy, back in 1957, is that correct?"

"Yes, it is."

"And who is this person?"

"You mean, he didn't tell you?"

"No, he said he would leave the details to you. I've got to say, Paul, I'm a bit confused by all of this. I've always been under the impression that someone who has suffered memory loss is only able to recall certain events while actually in the state of hypnosis. Has he left you in such a state?"

Paul laughed as he said; "No, Bill, I'm not in a hypnotic state. Actually, I used to think the same way you do, but Nathan was able to enable me to retain everything I recalled while in hypnosis. You don't know how good it is to have this lost portion of my life returned to me. I owe a lot to that guy."

"You were going to tell me the suspect's name?"

"Bill, 'suspect' is the right word, because this man has been a suspect right along, from what I hear. The man I saw murder my friend is Roger Carey. I'm as sure of that as I am of my own name."

"Okay, Paul, why don't you describe to me just exactly what you saw happen as your friend was murdered. Don't leave out any details. Just give me a minute here."

Bill Fenton lifted his shirt collar closer to his mouth and spoke into the tiny transmitter.

"S-1 to S-2."

The receiver on his belt crackled with the reply from Sergeant Skinner.

"S-2"

"Give me a land line."

"Right, Chief."

Chief Fenton fumbled around in his briefcase, searching for something.

"I wasn't going to bother taping your initial statement, but then I remembered how these things have a way of biting you right in the ass........"

Paul nodded, as if in agreement, even though he hadn't the slightest idea how his statement could bite the chief's ass, either physically or hypothetically.

Now the cell phone in the chief's hand rang. Fenton flipped it open and spoke.

"Tom, I need you to find a Roger Carey for me. I'm going to need a current address, along with a place of employment and home and work numbers."

Turning to Paul, Fenton asked; "How old would he be?"

Paul replied; "He'd be about sixty three or sixty four years old."

"He's in his early sixties, Tom. He grew up in Sheridan in the fifties."

Again turning to Paul, the chief asked; "You got any idea where he lives now?"

"No. He joined the service shortly after Larry's murder, but he never came back to Sheridan, as far as I know."

"Check military records if you can't locate him. He left Sheridan in 1957 and apparently never returned. Tom, he's being I.D.'d for murder, so we need to find this guy. I've got a lot of questions for him."

Sergeant Tom Skinner hesitated only a few seconds before answering.

"Chief, I'm showing a Roger Carey at 1477 Arlen Street, in Providence, current age of sixty three. He's a thirty year Navy veteran. He's got three arrests, two for assault and battery and the third for aggravated assault. He's been clean since 1992. Providence P.D. lists him as having a violent disposition."

"Sounds like our man. See if you can verify his former address as Boundary Road in Sheridan. If you succeed, try contacting him and let him know that we'd like to speak to him about the Guernette murder in 1957. If he is our guy, that should provoke some sort of interesting response. If you have to go into the station, feel free. Thanks, Tom. Is it staying quiet out there?"

"It is so far, Chief."

"Get back to me as soon as you can."

"Will do, Chief."

The chief took out a pocket-size tape recorder, into which he spoke..

"This is Sheridan Police Chief William G. Fenton. The date is August 19, 2004 and I'm about to take a statement from one Paul McCulloch, who was a witness to the murder of one Lawrence Guernette, on August 22, 1957. It is approximately four twenty p.m. and Mr. McCulloch will now make his statement."

Carefully standing the small recorder on the table between them, the chief positioned the device so it would catch both ends of the conversation.

"Go ahead, Paul."

Paul hesitated at first, then he slid his chair closer to the table and leaning forward, spoke.

"My name is Paul McCulloch and I live at……."

Chief Fenton interrupted.

"I just need you to state your name, Paul."

"Oh! Sorry, Bill……..uh, Chief."

Paul was surprised at feeling a little flustered and tried to arrange his thoughts in the order in which he felt they should be stated.

"My name is Paul McCulloch. On the night of……..I mean, in the *early evening* of August 22, 1957, myself and three friends rode our bicycles up to the old cemetery on the dirt road which runs off Crater Street, in the town of Sheridan. Our intent was to continue playing a game of daring, in which three of us would wait on our bicycles on Crater Street, while the fourth boy would walk down the dirt road to the cemetery, retrieve a baseball, which we had placed on a gravestone earlier in the day and walk back to the waiting three guys, showing them the ball, as proof that he had completed the……..mission, I guess you would call it."

At this point, Chief Fenton asked; "What did you mean when you said your 'intent was to continue' playing this game?"

Paul sat up straight, pulled his chair in closer, still and spoke in reply.

"We had been playing this game, which, by the way, we called 'The Graveyard Game', for a couple of weeks. We all had taken a turn going after the ball, except for Larry, who kept putting us off with different excuses as to why he wasn't able to do it. We finally called his bluff and he agreed to take his turn that night."

The chief cut in once more.

"Was anyone else aware that you boys were going there on this particular night?"

"There might have been, Chief. We had all sworn a vow of secrecy, but, one of the boys, Ritchie Bledsoe, after he took his turn, had bragged about it at school the next day. Some of the older boys seemed really interested."

"Your parents knew you were there, didn't they?"

"No. We all knew that none of our parents would have allowed us to go that far away from home after dark, so we told them we were going to be playing at the very end of the street we lived on, Hillside Road. We knew that none of them would look for us there, because the road was unpaved, full of ruts and unlit in that section. Besides, we all had pretty much of a green light until nine thirty or ten o'clock."

Paul was beginning to feel elated at the ease in which his mind was remembering the events of that fateful evening; events which, until this morning, he thought had been lost forever.

"Please continue, Mr. McCulloch."

Mildly amused at hearing the chief address him this way, Paul smiled and emitted a silent laugh, more of a small gasp. The chief, aware of why Paul was so amused, returned the smile and pointed to the recorder. Paul went on.

"Anyway, on this particular evening, Larry was really nervous about taking his turn. He was high strung to begin with, but that night he was really off the wall. He kept talking to himself on the bike ride out there, then when we arrived at the dirt road he seemed to be trying to psych himself up to do it. He was sort of freaking us out a little, so we told him he didn't have to do it if he didn't want to. He just looked at us and said that if he didn't do it, then everyone at school would think he was a coward. I took him aside and told him that it would stay with us. He smiled a sarcastic smile and looked in Ritchie's direction and I remember clearly what he said to me. He said; "Do you really think *he* could keep his big mouth shut?" Then I told him he was really scaring me and he said; "You don't understand, Paul. I have to do this and I'm going to do it.""

Paul took a moment to sip some coffee and continued with his story.

"He just turned away and started walking down the dirt road. I yelled out to him that we would give him ten minutes and then we would come looking for him. We ended up shooting the bull for what must have been fifteen or maybe even twenty minutes, when I told the guys we'd better go look for him, because he had been gone way too long. Well, when we got to the cemetery, we found Larry just standing there, like he was in some sort of trance. He had wet his pants and I remember how it smelled so strong. He *did* have the baseball in his hand, though. I asked him what was wrong, but he wouldn't answer me. All of a sudden, this guy dressed up in a dark hooded cape came charging at us, growling. He scared the hell out of us and we started screaming. At first, we all ran off, scared to death, because we didn't know whether it was human or not. I turned around, but the guy wasn't following us, so I told the other two guys to stop, because we couldn't just leave Larry there. One of the guys, Ritchie, got hysterical, so I told Larch to take him home and I would try to sneak back and hit the guy with a rock, if I could."

Pausing, Paul pushed his chair back, crossed his legs and said; "When you're twelve years old, you don't think about what will happen if you miss."

Chief Fenton was tempted to say "Or, if you hit", but bit his tongue.

Picking up the narrative again, Paul spoke; "I did manage to creep back to the cemetery, staying low, along the edge of the road, using the trees and bushes for cover. When I got closer, I heard a voice talking low, almost softly and then I found a good vantage point, where I could observe what was going on. Larry wasn't in the trance anymore, but he was sobbing and whimpering. He kept saying 'no, please, no'. I saw the guy unzipping his fly and he was getting really pissed at Larry. He grabbed him roughly by the back of the head and pulled his face toward his exposed privates, but Larry wouldn't give in. Now I got pissed and threw a stone at the guy and I caught him a good one, just above his left ear. He yelled and turned in my direction; then I yelled to Larry to run, but instead, Larry pushed the guy and swung his hand, with the baseball in it, up into the guy's crotch, which made him bend over in pain."

Paul took a deep breath, looked at Chief Fenton and continued.

"I'm sorry, but this part is a little tough."

Fenton calmly reassured Paul.

"Take as much time as you need."

Taking another deep breath, Paul sat upright and went on.

Larry........tried to run, but the guy was too quick. He grabbed Larry's arm and swung him around hard. He grabbed Larry's belt with his other hand to spin him even faster, then he let him go. Larry went headfirst into a........gravestone. He hit the stone with so much force that it broke in two. God, what an awful sound........I'll never forget that sound his head made against that stone. I knew right away that Larry was dead, because his head and neck were twisted in a way that was humanly impossible."

With Paul's voice faltering and his hands shaking noticeably, Bill Fenton reached over and stopped the tape recorder.

"What do you say we take a little break here, Paul?"

Although phrased as a question, there was little doubt that Paul did not have a vote on the matter. Clearly shaken, Paul's eyes filled with tears, as he tried to apologize once again to the chief.

"I'm *really* sorry, Bill. I thought I'd be able to get through this without any difficulty."

The chief was quick to respond.

"Maybe if you were some kind of android you could. You're human, Paul. To be honest, I wouldn't think much of you if you didn't break down at some point. Now, just relax a minute and let me know when you think you can go on. You don't mind if I pour myself another cup of coffee, do you?"

Smiling, Paul replied; "Help your self."

Fenton refilled his cup, returned to the table, sat down and took a sip of the black coffee. Paul adjusted his chair yet again and told the chief he was ready to resume his statement. Chief Fenton reached over and started the recording device.

"Mr. McCulloch, what happened after you realized your friend, Larry Guernette was dead?"

"The guy turned toward me once more and pointed at me. He screamed out; 'YOU'RE DEAD, MCCULLOCH!' It was then that I recognized who he was. It was Roger Carey. He lived in our neighborhood, down on Boundary Road. I just took off, running for my life."

"Did he pursue you?"

"At first, he did……..but, he must have stopped, because after the first hundred feet or so, I never heard his footsteps behind me and when I finally stopped running to catch my breath, he was no where in sight when I turned around."

Chief Fenton rested his chin in his left hand, which was propped on the table.

"Mr. McCulloch, has Roger Carey contacted you in any way since that particular night?"

"No."

"Do you have anything you wish to add?"

Paul's first impulse was to launch into a diatribe about how he had been plagued with horrible nightmares for the better part of a month now, nightmares which had necessitated his having to go to a psychologist for relief and which had put an obvious strain on his marriage. He wanted to scream out that it was all the fault of Roger Carey, the Roger Carey who he now knew had murdered his friend and who had terrified him in an upstairs bedroom in the Carey home, so many years ago. He wanted to speak into the tape recorder loud and clear about the hatred he had carried for Roger Carey throughout most of his adult life, a hatred which, because of time and age, had slowly dissipated in intensity, but still remained in his memory, sometimes flaring up in angry thoughts, but always there.

He knew, however, that any such tirade would only taint the statement which he had just given, as it would appear to anyone listening that Paul had an axe to grind with Carey. Paul did not want to do or say anything that would hinder the arrest of this killer.

"No, Chief, I do not."

As Paul started to push his chair away from the table, Bill Fenton held up his right hand, index finger pointing up in a gesture to wait a minute. Paul stopped in mid-push and sat back in the chair, where it was.

The chief spoke in the direction of the recorder.

"Mr. McCulloch, I need you to state why it took so long for you to come forward with this information."

Paul leaned forward, at the same time pulling his chair back in closer to the table and spoke.

"The reason it took so long is a rather complicated one. It all started on the night of the murder. As I was fleeing from Carey, whom I thought was still chasing me, I tripped over some fishing line, which someone had strung between two trees in the path on which I was running. I plunged head first onto Boundary Road, fracturing my skull in the process. I spent three weeks in a coma and lost all memory of the events of that night. That memory loss continued throughout my life, until recently, when I began having recurring dreams of seeing my friend, Larry in the cemetery, along with a hooded figure. The dreams had a negative effect on my daily life, as one would expect. I finally ended up going to see a psychologist, Nathan Feldmar, who was able to discover the reason for my dreams. He also enabled me, through a procedure called hypnosis-induced recollection, to recover my memory, permanently and completely. The memories I have of the events of that evening are as vivid to me today as they were on that night. This total memory recall was only just completed earlier this afternoon, upon which I immediately informed you, Chief Fenton."

Fenton reached over, picked up the little recording device and held it close to his mouth. Speaking softly, he said; "This concludes the interview with Mr. Paul McCulloch."

Fenton put the recorder in his briefcase and opened his mouth to say something to Paul, but, before he was able to speak, his cell phone rang. Paul watched, as the chief answered. Fenton's demeanor was that of a good police officer, not prone to showing his true feelings and able to keep his emotions in check. Completely unable to detect any positive sign on Bill Fenton's face, in what he assumed must have been news about Marilyn, Paul observed until the chief completed his series of 'uh-huhs' and hung up. Still holding the phone in his hand, Chief Fenton looked directly at Paul, smiled and said; "Andy was able to find the file on the Guernette murder. I told him to bring it over here. I may have some more questions for you, Paul, once I get a chance to read it. There's no sense in wasting a trip, as long as I'm here, now. Do you suppose I could have some more of that coffee?"

Paul stood up from the table, grabbing the half-empty carafe as he rose and said; "Sure thing. I'll make a fresh batch. I could use another one myself."

As Paul went about making the coffee, Chief Fenton spoke from his sitting position.

"Paul, I want you to know that if this thing goes to court, you're going to literally be run through the ringer by Carey's defense attorney. He'll have a field day with this memory recollection thing."

"Yeah, I was thinking about that, Bill. It will sound pretty bizarre to a jury, too."

Fenton turned halfway around in his chair, so that he was now facing Paul.

"Don't get me wrong, I'm not trying to talk you out of anything, but I want to be sure you know that Carey's lawyer will do whatever it takes to discredit your testimony. He will probably try to make it look as though you have some mental problems and, if he's good, will be able to subtly suggest that to the jury. He will dig into your private life and use whatever he can dig up against you. In other words, he will make every attempt to bring the focus of the jury on your mental state, simply because the basis of your testimony is as a result of your visit to a psychologist."

As Paul listened to Bill Fenton, he thought about the voice which had been speaking to him and knew that he could never tell anyone about it. He had seen what an adverse effect his telling Mary Ellen had created and he could only imagine what a defense attorney would do with that knowledge. His thoughts were broken by the ringing of Chief Fenton's telephone. Paul watched, as the chief answered, still showing the poker face, as the first words he spoke were several 'yeahs' murmured into the phone. Finally, Chief Fenton said something which got Paul's attention.

"Did he sound upset at all, when you told him?"

There was a pause as Fenton listened to Sgt. Skinner's answer.

"Good. I was hoping that would be his reaction. Alert Providence P.D. to keep a close watch on him, in case he turns into a runner. I'm going to have you run down there and meet up with one of their guys first thing tomorrow, so you can make the arrest and bring him back here. We *could* have *them* make the arrest, but I want to see what this guy does overnight. I'll fill you in on all the details when you finish your shift. Good work, Tom."

Fenton hung up the phone and turned to Paul.

"Well, it seems as though Mister Carey suddenly developed a stammer. Was his voice that high-pitched when he was younger?"

The chief smiled broadly, as Paul began to laugh.

"No, Bill; and he never stammered either. This guy was proud of being known as 'Mister Cool'."

Pausing for a moment, Paul asked the chief; "Bill, I heard you ask whoever was on the phone if Carey sounded upset when he told him. If you don't mind my asking, what exactly did he tell him?"

"It was Sgt. Skinner on the phone and he told Carey that we would be coming to visit him so we could ask him some questions about the murder. He also told him there has been a significant new development in the case, which links him. As soon as Carey heard that, his voice got really high and he sounded very nervous. We'll see what transpires overnight. His behavior in the next sixteen hours will tell me a lot."

As Paul walked over to the trestle table, his eye caught a glimpse of someone moving quickly past the window outside. He was about to walk to the sliding door to see who it was, but, just as suddenly, Patrolman Andy Fine appeared at the door. In his hands he held a large box, filled with papers and several bags marked in bold black letters as 'evidence'. Paul slid the door open and Andy began to identify himself, but was interrupted by Chief Fenton.

"Come in Andy. He knows who you are."

Andy excused himself and stepped past Paul to the big table, where he deposited the heavy box.

"This is everything she had, Chief."

Chief Fenton immediately dove into the box like a young boy opening birthday presents. Pulling out the evidence bags one at a time, he carefully opened each one, peeked inside and just as carefully re-closed each of the bags. He paused at one bag, staring at the contents and drew in his breath. Fenton set the bag down and thumbed through the files, finally locating the one he had been looking for. Totally oblivious to the two men who stood watching him, the chief intently read through the report detailing the autopsy results. For the first time, Paul thought he could detect a rising anger in the heretofore stoic police chief. His suspicion was confirmed as Bill Fenton slapped the file folder down on the table. Fenton looked at Andy, then turned to Paul and announced:

"Larry Guernette was sodomized……..possibly after he died."

Turning back to his patrolman, he said; "Andy, run this over to the State Police Crime Lab and tell them I want a complete D.N.A. analysis done on this pair of underwear."

Andy hesitated as he accepted the bag from Fenton.

"But, Chief; these clothes are almost fifty years old. There isn't much chance of…….."

Chief Fenton angrily interjected in a loud voice.

"I DON'T RECALL ASKING FOR YOUR OPINION! I DO, HOWEVER, RECALL GIVING YOU A DIRECT ORDER."

Andy snapped to and responded; "Yes sir!" He quickly turned and exited the sunroom without saying another word to either Paul or the chief.

Fenton looked at Paul and gave him a wry smile.

"Now you know why the son of a bitch didn't run after you."

Paul, shaken by this suddenly-revealed detail, only nodded his head solemnly, in affirmation.

Bill Fenton picked up the box and slung it under one arm, then said; "Paul, do you have a disposable cup? I'm afraid I'm going to have to make my coffee 'to-go'."

With the thought of his friend, Larry still in his mind, Paul was unaware that Fenton was addressing him.

"PAUL……..did you hear me?"

"What? Oh, yeah. Just take it in the mug, Bill. Don't worry about returning it. We have plenty of them."

As he filled the mug with coffee, Fenton thanked Paul for coming forward with his information, told him that he had a million things to do before he could go home tonight and left. As he slid the door closed behind him, he leaned in and announced; "I'll be in touch, Paul."

The chief hadn't reached his cruiser when the voice in Paul's head spoke once more.

"*Tonight is the night. You must go there tonight!*"

CHAPTER NINETEEN

Paul watched, as Fenton backed out of his driveway. As the chief started to go forward, another car pulled up, with its left directional on, indicating a turn into the McCulloch driveway. Chief Fenton signaled with a wave of his hand for the other driver to cut in front of him. Paul could see that it was his daughter, Kathy. He glanced over at the large, oval-shaped clock that hung on the wall. Mary Ellen had spotted it in one of those discount hardware stores and liked the background of pink roses, painted neatly in the center of the timepiece. She thought it would compliment the décor in the sun room. The clock read five fifty-five.

No sooner had Paul turned to clean off the table, than Kathy burst through the sliding door.

"Daddy, why were the police here? Is anything wrong?"

Paul smiled and wrapped his arms around his daughter.

"Yes, Kathy, I'm fine. And how are you?"

Kathy, sensing the bit of rudeness in her entrance, responded.

"I'm sorry, Daddy. I guess I just panicked. How is Mommy?"

Paul released his embrace and gave her cheek a gentle pinch between his index finger and thumb.

"She's still sound asleep in the bedroom. Kath, your mother has had a rough month. There have been some things happening which have upset both of us, but these last few days have been exceptionally difficult for her, in particular, the last twenty four hours or so."

"Daddy, what's been going on to upset her?"

"Well, part of it is why the police were here. It's a rather long and complicated story. I've just brewed a fresh pot of coffee, so why don't you pull up a chair and I'll fill you in."

Kathy McCulloch sat and listened, as her father explained how he had been besieged with nightmares for almost a month now and how her mother had begged him to see a psychologist, which he finally agreed to do, albeit reluctantly. He told her how Nathan Feldmar had been so successful in getting to the root problem of his horrible dreams and how he had, through a process called hypnosis-induced recollection, been able to not only recall the events of the evening of his friend's murder back in 1957, but was also able to retain those memories.

Kathy McCulloch sat transfixed, as her father talked. Never in her life had she heard him speak in such hushed tones. Never before, had he ever told her that something had frightened him, until now and it was clear that the latest figure in his dreams had truly scared him. Her mind traveled back to her childhood and the recollection of her father as a big, strong man, afraid of nothing, who would lift her high on his shoulders when they walked in the deep grass in the field behind their home, because she was so afraid of snakes. She remembered the night when his truck broke down on that dark country road, on their way home from a visit with friends. Her mother had been nervous and, even at the tender age of eleven, she knew why. It was a road frequented by rowdy teenagers, looking to raise hell and their predicament presented the perfect opportunity to do so.

Her father had remained calm, quietly going about the task at hand, which was getting the truck to run well enough to get them home safely, which he did. Only one car had driven by, with three boys, who asked if they could help. Kathy hadn't liked the way one of the boys looked at her and her dad had told the driver that everything was under control and they wouldn't need their help. When the driver didn't move the car, she remembered how her father strode over to the driver's window and got really close to his face and told him in a strong voice that he appreciated their offer, but it would be better for everyone if they moved on........ now! The teenaged driver must have seen something in her father's eyes which un-nerved him, because he promptly drove away, leaving her mother to breathe a deep sigh of relief.

Now, this same man was sitting across from her at the old trestle table, which had been moved from their old house and upon which they had all shared so many family meals and telling her that he had seen a man's face in his dreams which had terrified him. He had also told her that he had been hearing a voice, coming from deep inside of him, which had warned him, in his dreams, mind you, of danger. This same voice was now telling him repeatedly that he must go to the same cemetery he had been dreaming about, complete with all the terrifying faces of his dreams and it was telling him to go there tonight.

Convinced that she was witnessing the breakdown of her beloved father, Kathy was unable to hold back her tears. She daubed at her eyes with a tissue and reached out to hold her father's hand.

"Oh, Daddy........you need to get help. Don't you see why Mommy is so upset?"

Paul, who was caught completely off guard by the realization that his daughter thought he was going crazy, tried to convince her otherwise.

"No, Kathy, you don't understand. I'm not losing my mind. These dreams are real and so is the voice. I've tried to convince your mother of this and didn't do a very good job. Please believe me. I don't know why this voice is telling me to go there, but I know it isn't for an evil reason. I just have a strange feeling that I'm the only person who can do whatever it is I'm supposed to do there."

With a new wave of tears streaming down her face, Kathy loudly proclaimed; "Daddy........LISTEN TO YOURSELF........for God's sake, Daddy, you're talking about going to a cemetery alone at night, not knowing why, or what you're supposed to do there........because a VOICE IN YOUR HEAD TOLD YOU TO? Doesn't that strike you as abnormal behavior?"

Unable to convince his daughter that he was in full control of his senses and now beginning to wonder if he really was, Paul decided to give up the battle.

"I guess it *does* look as if your old man is going nuts. But, the one thing that really makes me crazy is the awareness that both you and your mother think I am…….. I don't know what else to say, Sweetheart, except that I love you and your mother very much and I would never intentionally do anything to hurt either one of you. The same thing goes for Mike, also. Will you at least do one thing for me?"

"What's that, Daddy?"

"There's this………feeling I have………also deep inside of me. I can't explain it, but I'm sure it is true……..that all of this is going to end tonight. What I'm asking you, Kath, is not to give up on me just yet. Hang in there tonight and if I'm still hearing voices tomorrow, I promise I'll check myself in at the state hospital. Will you agree to that?"

Kathy managed a brief smile and said; "Daddy, that's a little overkill. I just want you to go back to that man you've been seeing and tell him about the voices and let him take it from there."

Paul thought about telling Kathy that Nathan already knew about the voice and didn't seem overly concerned about it, but decided to let sleeping dogs lie.

"That's all?"

"Yes, Daddy; that's all I would like you to do."

"Then we've got a deal, Sweetheart."

Excusing himself, Paul arose and went into the bathroom. As he stood in front of the toilet, the now-familiar voice in his head spoke again.

"*You must leave now. You must drive to the cemetery now, but you must not leave your car where it can be seen from the cemetery road. GO NOW!*"

The restless feeling he had felt throughout most of the afternoon began to subside, replaced by a sudden urgency to take action. Paul knew he could not disobey the command he had just been given. The voice had succeeded in instituting a type of comradeship with Paul, which led him to believe he was taking the correct course of action in following its instructions. Afraid of becoming like one of the blind-faith zombies in one of those late night movies, Paul questioned the enigma, softly mouthing his words so Kathy would not hear.

"Why do I have to go now? Can't I go later on?"

Answering in a tone which suggested not anger, but more a sense of immediacy, the voice responded; *"You must go now, before it is too late!"*

Paul zipped up his fly, washed his hands and faced the mirror, staring at the face before him, wondering if his wife and daughter were correct.

"Am I going crazy? I'm hearing a god dam voice in my head, telling me to go to the scariest place I've ever known, alone, in the dark……..and I'm GOING TO GO! I've got to be fucking whacky!"

As Paul exited the bathroom, he glanced over at the clock and saw that it was now coming up on seven thirty p.m. He walked to the table and said to Kathy; "I've got to go out for a while, Kath. I'll be back shortly. If your mother wakes up, be sure to tell her that I'm going to get Larch and ask him to come along with me, okay?"

Kathy, who had been sitting at the table with her chin resting in the upturned palm of her left hand, now leaned back in the chair and looked directly at her father

"I don't suppose there's any way I'm going to convince you *not* to go to that cemetery."

Paul glanced down to where his daughter was sitting, proud of what she had become; an intelligent, strong-minded woman, not afraid to confront any issue. She deserved more than a cursory good-bye as he rushed out the door. Instead, he pulled out a chair and slid it over to a spot closer to Kathy and sat down beside her. Reaching over, Paul slipped one hand under his daughter's and cupped his other hand over hers.

"Kathy……..I wish that I could tell you why I'm going to do this. The truth is, I don't even have a clue. But, I *can* tell you one thing for sure; I didn't spend a lifetime loving your mom and raising two great kids, one of which has produced two precious grandchildren, to go and get myself hurt. I *will* be careful. I know how to take care of myself. I also know that I can't prove to you that I'm not going nuts. All I can do is ask you to believe in me. I won't let you down."

With moist eyes, Kathy squeezed her father's hand and said, forcing a smile; "You never have, Daddy."

Paul quickly got up from his seat and leaned over to give Kathy a kiss on her forehead.

"If your mother wakes up, don't forget to tell her that I'm going to ask Larch to come along with me and……..tell her that I love her."

Kathy stood up and rubbed Paul's arm as he turned for the door.

"I will, Daddy."

"I'm not expecting to be gone for long. She may still be sleeping when I return. She was really exhausted."

As he pulled the slider shut, Paul peeked in and said to Kathy; "Love you. Bye."

Kathy held up her right arm and slowly waved her hand back and forth as her father walked away. She fought back tears, as she wondered if her *real* father would ever return to normal and fought off panic, wondering if he would return at all.

Hearing a noise in back of her, Kathy abruptly turned and let out a frightened squeal, as she came face to face with her mother, or at least the woman who appeared to be her mother. Kathy's jaw hung in stunned disbelief, as she regarded the pathetic figure standing before her, clad in a tattered old bathrobe, which was held tightly closed by both hands, in an attempt to stave off the sudden chill that comes upon someone who has just gotten out of a warm bed. Once the sun went down, the sunroom had quickly cooled off on this late summer evening and Mary Ellen felt the chill.

In the moment before recognition was complete, Kathy's eyes scanned the face of her mother and saw that it was swollen from either sleeping or crying, or both. Her eyelids were rimmed in red and there were wrinkly lines running in unorthodox patterns across her face, from both eyes to her lower jaw, confirming the conclusion that at least some of them were caused by the weight of her head on the pillow.

For what seemed like an eternity before the process of recognition was completed, but, in truth was only a couple of seconds, the singular thought in Kathy's mind was that she could not recall ever having seen her mother look so disheveled. The one thing Mary Ellen always made sure of was that her hair was neatly brushed. Now, it clearly was not. Kathy's hand involuntarily rose to her mouth, in a failed attempt at stifling the squeal.

"MOMMY; you scared the heck out of me!"

Before Mary Ellen could reply, Kathy embraced her in a tight hug, holding on long enough for Mary Ellen to know that something wasn't right.

"What is it, Sweetheart?"

Gathering up all of her strength of mind, Kathy was determined not to cry as she related her conversation with her father to her mother.

"It's Daddy. What is going on with him, Mommy? He just told me this crazy story about having nightmares and hearing voices and now he's gone off to the old cemetery off Crater......"

"HE WENT TO THE CEMETERY? WHEN DID HE LEAVE?"

"He just left a minute ago. I tried to talk him out of it, but he said he was going to ask Mr. Stolarczek to go with him and that I shouldn't worry, but I am worried, Mommy. Do you think we should call the police?"

"That's exactly what I'm going to do. Kathy, I don't know what's gotten into your father. The bad dreams were bad enough, but this thing with the voices in his head is just making me crazy. This past month has been a living hell."

Mary Ellen walked over and picked up the phone, dialing the standard number for the police department, rather than the 9-1-1 line. When the dispatcher answered, she asked to speak to Chief Fenton and was told that he was very busy in his office and had asked not to be disturbed.

"I think you need to disturb him for this. My husband may be in extreme danger. He is a witness to a murder and he has gone to the location of that murder, because someone told him to do so."

There was an awkward moment of silence, then the voice replied; "I'll get him right away, ma'am."

CHAPTER TWENTY

Paul felt a stronger sense of urgency now, as he drove along Chestnut Street. He thought about what he would do once he arrived at the cemetery. Should he wait in the car? The voice said to leave the car where it couldn't be seen from the cemetery road. If it said to leave the car, he reasoned, it must have wanted him to walk away from the car, probably in the direction of the cemetery.

"What am I worrying about?" he said aloud. "It hasn't been bashful about giving me orders so far."

He didn't like the idea of leaving Kathy when she was obviously upset, but he knew Mary Ellen would be even more so when she awoke and learned where he had gone. Paul felt somewhat like a little kid, who had snuck out of the house to go and hang out with some friends of whom his parents not only disapproved, but specifically forbade him to associate with. He knew he was going to have a lot of explaining to do when he returned home, but it didn't seem to matter much at the moment. Something drove him on, towards the old cemetery off Crater Street; something that he hoped wasn't setting him up.

Suddenly, Paul remembered his promise to Mary Ellen, that he would call Larch to see if he would accompany Paul to the cemetery. He reached down for his cell phone, but the holder was empty. Thinking at first, that he had lost it somewhere, Paul tried to remember when he used it last and then it came to him; he had set it down on the window ledge in the sunroom, after talking to Bill Fenton. If he reversed direction, he could turn left at the corner of Main Street and use the pay phone in the parking lot of Forbes Breakfast Nook, but that would add another ten minutes to the ride to the cemetery. Still, Paul slowed down and pulled to the side of the road, intending to turn around. The voice had been unusually silent, so Paul saw no harm in taking the extra time to make the call to Larch. In the instant that Paul started to turn the truck around, the voice announced itself in a loud and clear tone.

"YOU MUST NOT WASTE TIME! KEEP MOVING AHEAD, TOWARD THE CEMETERY! DRIVE AS FAST AS YOU ARE ABLE, OR IT WILL BE TOO LATE!"

Paul stepped down hard on the accelerator pedal, acknowledging the critical time window, which he could feel evaporating. He still had no idea why he needed to hurry, but he knew he must; nor did he know why he needed to be there, but he also knew he was, in some strange way, an integral part of whatever was about to take place in, or near the cemetery. It was a sensation that was both invigorating and frightening at the same time and his heart raced with anticipation.

As the last colorful rays of sunlight disappeared over the horizon, Paul turned the truck right onto the far end of Crater Street, about a mile and a half from the dirt road that would lead to the cemetery. The truck lights automatically turned on, as he drove down the dark, tree-shaded road.

Once again, the insistent voice implored him to hurry.

"You MUST go faster!"

Paul's patience was wearing thin.

"ALL RIGHT, I'M GOING OVER THE SPEED LIMIT NOW, FOR CHRIST'S SAKE."

"It is not fast enough! Go faster, still!"

Pushing his foot all the way down on the pedal, Paul heard the truck engine roar and felt the back end fishtail slightly, as the truck rapidly gained speed. He glanced at the dash clock, which read seven forty-four p.m., but he amused himself with the realization that it didn't matter what time it was, because the voice was only filled with immediacy, not time, as we know it.

When he turned around the last bend before the dirt road, the voice quickly spoke.

"*Pull over well before the dirt road and shut off the motor.*"

Paul turned onto the dirt shoulder at a high rate of speed, stopping the truck in a cloud of dust, dirt and rocks. He shut down the engine and climbed out. The voice spoke to him as if it were a companion at his side.

"*Walk very quickly! Run, if you must, but hurry down the road toward the cemetery.*"

Paul obediently complied with the orders being barked at him by the mysterious internal vocalization, which sounded more like a gunny sergeant leading his platoon into battle. He walked at a brisk pace, but picked it up to a trot as he turned down the dirt road. Sweat began to roll down his face and he felt his shirt begin to dampen, as his torso unleashed tiny droplets into the fabric. His heart pounded wildly, reminding him briefly of the way it pounded that cool August evening, forty seven years ago, when his dream monster was, or was not chasing him. It was important, he knew, to slow down the pace, or someone would be finding *his* body here tomorrow. He could make out the wrought-iron gate of the old cemetery, about three hundred feet ahead, on his left. Just as Paul started to slow down, the voice issued its latest command.

"*Get off the road and hide; NOW!*"

As the voice spoke, Paul heard the sound of a motor vehicle approaching from the east end of the dirt road, from the same direction he had come, at a fairly high rate of speed. He instinctively jumped off the road, into the thick brush, just as the vehicle, a late-model pickup truck, rounded the curve, about four hundred feet behind him. Before Paul could get himself situated in the brush, the truck whizzed by, kicking up stones and leaving a huge, trailing dust cloud. Although he tried, he was only able to catch a glimpse of the driver, enough to see that it was a rugged looking man, who drove with both hands on the steering wheel, for better control on the rut-filled road.

Paul leaned forward from his hiding spot, hoping to follow the path of the truck, but was chastised by the inner voice.

"*Stay hidden. He must not see you, or he will kill you!*"

Feeling a lump forming in his throat at the sound of those words, Paul swallowed hard and felt the dryness burn in his esophagus. If only he had brought the water bottle he had left in his truck.

As he listened, Paul heard the truck slow, and then it stopped, in what sounded like the area in front of the cemetery. Then, he became aware of the sound of the vehicle backing up. He peered through the bushes, but was only able to see one unidentifiable section of the truck, glistening in the twilight. Listening closely, he was able to distinguish muffled sounds of objects being moved around. Around him, mosquitoes gathered, occasionally darting in and striking his skin with piercing little daggers. The longer he stayed in the brush, the more aggressive the little insects became; landing and stinging at will, sometimes two and three at a time. Paul slapped as quietly as he could, but once in a while, the stings were exceptionally sharp and his response was to slap harder. The voice remained silent.

Frustrated at not being able to see what was going on, Paul eased himself out of the brush onto the road. He took one careful step toward the parked truck, alternating his glances between the pickup and the rocks on the ground, cautiously avoiding any contact with the stones. Mindful of the warning the voice had issued earlier about being killed if the driver saw him, Paul picked his way carefully along the edge of the road, using the dense growth nearby as cover. Because of the angle he was at, Paul was unable to see anything but the grill and about half of the hood on the truck. Knowing that if he were to cross the street, his field of vision would improve markedly, Paul was about to cross over, when a loud clanging sound startled him into a crouching position, where he froze momentarily.

Paul peered into the darkness and saw the shadow of the man's head barely visible through the overhanging tree branches between himself and the truck. In the brief moment in which he glimpsed it, the head moved toward the front of the truck and then he heard the door opening.

Knowing he must get off the road, but fearful of tipping off his presence by stumbling on a rock, Paul waited for the sound of the door closing, so he could time his move to the starting of the engine. He waited, but the door didn't close.

"Come on, close the damn door! What is he waiting for? Maybe he saw me. Just remember your combat training. In a camouflage situation, be absolutely still. It almost always works for deer and rabbits."

Paul remained frozen in place, his eyes fixed upon the area where he suspected the man was located. Seconds passed, but still, there was no sound of a door closing. Trying to remain still, Paul felt his throat tighten up and tried to swallow, but the small bit of saliva he mustered up dragged down his parched throat, seeming to sear the delicate tissue along the way.

"I'll bet he's watching me. He's probably spotted me and is trying to decide if I'm an animal, a human, or just a shadow. I've got to stay still. How could he possibly see me? After all, I can't see him. Yeah, but the view he has might allow him to see you without you seeing him. Come on, buddy, CLOSE THE DAMN DOOR AND START THE FREAKIN TRUCK!"

Without moving his head, Paul's eyeballs scanned from left to right and to his relief, he was completely enveloped in the shadow from a large swamp maple. He knew it was improbable that the man had spotted him, but he remained still. Now he could feel the muscles in his calves tightening up, the right one, in particular, meaning a leg cramp was forthcoming. No sooner had he come to this realization when the cramp hit. It instantly tore into his calf, locking the muscle into a solid granite-like limb, turning that part of the leg rock-hard.

The pain was intense, causing Paul to lose his balance and pitch forward, where he quietly placed both hands on the ground in front of him to stabilize himself. Despite the pain he was in, Paul never took his eyes off the parked truck and sucked his breath in deeply, clenching his teeth and wincing. For one, brief second, Paul thought about standing up and jumping off the road into the undergrowth, where he would be able to rub his aching calf muscle, but he knew he could not risk such a foolish move. Tears of pain formed in the corners of his eyes, as his anguish reached a fever pitch. The pain throbbed on in waves and just when Paul thought it couldn't possibly get any worse, it did; as yet another spasm gripped his lower leg in an unrelenting torrent of agony.

Then, like a blessing from heaven, Paul heard the door of the truck close and the sound of the engine turning over. Instantly, he was on his feet, but the muscular cramping had left him unable to move. Forcing his body to turn, he felt his right leg give out from under him and he tumbled forward, face first into the brush. Now, a new pain hit him, as the left side of his face was punctured by a small branch, just missing his eye.

Hearing the sound of the truck beginning to move, Paul scrambled to get his legs completely off the dirt roadway and under cover. His body racked with pain, he clawed his way in about five feet off the road, stopped and listened. The ground beneath him was wet and soggy, as it lay on the perimeter of the swamp. Paul turned his body enough so that he was lying parallel to the road. From this position, he would not be able to see the driver as he drove past, so he forced himself once again into a crouch, this time stretching out his right leg in a straight line, angled away from his body, similar to an outrigger on a construction backhoe. Through the discomfort, he clung to a small sapling, using it for support and waited for the truck to pass by.

Paul could feel blood begin to run from the wound beneath his eye, but dared not lift his hand to brush it away. Any movement would easily be seen by eyes that had grown accustomed to the darkness, eyes that might suspect someone was watching.

As Paul waited, he grew aware that the sound of the truck had changed. Instead of proceeding at a high rate of speed, as it had on its way to the graveyard, the vehicle sound indicated that it was crawling along at a slow pace, without its lights turned on. This was not a good sign and Paul wished he had stayed lower to the ground. He could picture the driver scanning both sides of the road, looking for whoever had been watching him.

"He couldn't have seen me! But why did it take him so long to close the door. Could the son of a bitch smell my sweat? There's no way he can possibly know I'm here."

Taking a long, deep breath, Paul tried to steady himself.

"I can't panic. I know the guy doesn't know I'm here. Relax, man! Just freeze, that's all. Be like a rabbit in a thicket."

Remaining motionless, Paul fixed his gaze on the approaching truck and was startled to see a small bright flash appear in the cab of the vehicle. The pickup started to gain a little more speed.

"The guy was driving slowly because he was digging for a cigarette, that's all!"

Despite the slight increase in speed, the truck was not moving all that fast and Paul wondered if maybe it wasn't just a cigarette the driver had been searching for. The cramp in his leg had slowly started to ease, but Paul didn't notice. His only concern at the present was the driver of the pickup and whether or not he knew Paul was lurking in this undergrowth.

Once again, the truck began to gather speed and was quickly nearing Paul's little hiding area. As the vehicle started to draw abreast of Paul, the driver took a long drag on his cigarette, temporarily lighting up the inside of the cab, along with his face. Paul moved only his eyeballs, as he followed the path of the pickup. He felt his heart race as he moved his eyes up and into the interior, but it jumped at the sight which he saw before him.

"THIS CAN'T BE TRUE!" Paul screamed inside his mind. The driver, casually sucking on the lit cigarette, was a blond-haired younger man, looking as if he was smiling to himself, but the smile wasn't really a smile. It was more of a grin, the *same* grin as the one Paul's last dream monster wore. Paul's eyes bore into the features of the driver and he was convinced it was the same hideous face of his latest nocturnal tormenter.

As the truck passed by, Paul saw that the man had clasped the cigarette between his upper and lower teeth, as he reached with his left hand toward the dash. The headlights suddenly came on, as the truck simultaneously picked up speed again, this time in earnest. He maintained his motionless position until he heard the pickup reach the junction of Crater Street, turn and head south, by the sound of the engine.

Paul stood up, pulling on the tiny little tree as he did and almost ripping it from the soft earth. The sapling held, however and Paul made it to his feet, where he gingerly tested his sore leg. Although it still ached a little, Paul was able to step forward, where he got himself back on the road. After taking a few steps the muscle began to relax and allowed Paul to walk with his full weight on the leg. He had only taken two or three steps, when his familiar little advisor again spoke.

"Hurry, before it's too late!"

Startled somewhat by the re-emergence of the inner voice, which had remained quiet since warning Paul to take cover, he responded, aloud.

"Too late for what........will you please tell me what the hell is going on, here?"

Paul listened for an answer, but no voice spoke, either imagined, or real. Nonetheless, he picked up his pace considerably, swinging his arms back and forth, as he quickly moved closer to the graveyard.

As Paul neared the entrance to the old burial ground, a wave of apprehension enveloped him. The old, wrought-iron gate remarkably stood partly open, in the same position it was in the last time he was here, more than thirty years ago. He had come here with Mary Ellen, for reasons he still was not aware of and had broken down miserably, not having the slightest idea why. Mary Ellen had walked her sobbing husband back to their car and Paul had vowed that he would never come here again. Trying hard not to think about that last visit, so many years ago, Paul turned his attention away from the gate and into the enclosure, where, as far as he could tell, nothing appeared to be out of the ordinary.

"What the hell am I supposed to do now?" he thought, as he stood at the entrance. The old cemetery was dark, except for two or three luminous shafts of moonlight, which had managed to snake their way

down through the dense canopy of tree branches which overhung the graveyard. As he looked around, Paul expected to receive another urgent command to hurry, but none was forthcoming. His gaze was interrupted by the first moonbeam, shining brightly on an open patch of moss-covered soil. As if by an unspoken celestial order, Paul turned his head slowly to the next shaft of light, which poured across the top and side of a centuries-old headstone. The ground to the right of the stone was also bathed in moonlight. This piece of earth, however, appeared somehow, to be different. The ground was not smooth, as was the earth under the first beam. Paul moved steadily closer, his vision confirming what he had suspected. The top soil had been disturbed. Not only that, but there was an object, a spherical shape, about two or three feet to the left of the uneven ground.

A new revelation hit Paul. This was the destination! THIS WAS IT! The object looked more and more familiar the closer he got to it. Within fifteen feet of the object, Paul was now able to clearly see the stitched seams and what appeared to be writing, or at least some type of markings.

"That's our old ball! But, why is it here? Why didn't the police take it as evidence? Is that why I had to rush to get to this place? Maybe that guy is coming back. Don't be ridiculous; that guy is probably ten miles from here, by now."

Paul proceeded to where the ball lay on the ground, knelt down slowly, placing his right knee on the ground in order to keep the pressure off of his sore calf. He divided the support between the knee and his right hand, which he also placed on the ground. As Paul leaned forward, he felt the calf muscles begin to tighten and quickly moved his left knee to the ground in order to further relieve the tension on the right side. Secure in this kneeling position, his left hand reached out and grasped the sphere. He drew it nearer, noting that the ball was caked with dirt.

Emotions ran swiftly through the fifty eight year-old man; exhilaration at discovering the artifact; sadness, as he recalled the last small fingers to grasp the ball, the fingers of his boyhood friend; a life lost at a tender age, in a far too brutal fashion; and finally, a burning anger, bordering at this very moment on hatred, for the sick son-of-a-bitch that had caused so much heartache in a grieving family; so much so that they were forced to move far away from a town they had loved, without leaving so much as a forwarding address to even their closest friends.

Paul's thoughts led him to remember his last conversation with Larry.

"At least he knew I cared." he reminisced, as the memory of his last words to his friend rang clear in his brain; "RUN, LARRY, RUN!" were the words Paul spoke to his cherished friend just before Roger Carey slammed him head first into one of the old gravestones.

Paul turned his head to the left and sure enough, the old, broken stone, upon which his friend's corpse had lain all night and all of the next day, was standing upright once again, displaying a noticeable separation running diagonally from the lower right section to the upper left corner of the ancient marker. Paul pictured in his mind's eye, someone, perhaps a caretaker, carefully drilling out the broken piece and installing two iron rods, then carefully aligning the top and bottom, before setting it in place. His eyes followed the crack upwards to a name, which was barely visible, having been worn by the passage of time. He was barely able, in the faint glow of moonlight, to make out a woman's name; 'Martha Lynden, b. 1801, d. 1849' and wondered for a moment how she had come to die and what her life had been like.

Lost in thought, Paul did not see the ground trembling, only inches from his right hand, which still acted as a partial support. So deep was his reverie that he did not immediately feel or respond to the clutching grasp, which encircled his wrist.

Then, startled by the sudden dawning of reality, Paul instinctively glanced down at his wrist, thinking fearfully that some type of small animal must have somehow grabbed him in this manner. Nothing, however, could have prepared him for the terror of what he saw, a dirt-encrusted hand, coming out of the ground, as in some old re-run of a horror movie and clamping itself tightly to Paul's wrist.

Paul's initial reaction was of sheer terror, as a spasmodic chill coursed through his entire being. Screaming out, in the cry of someone who is about to die, he tried jerking his hand free, but the grip tightened. Once again, he yanked, this time with more force and easily pulled free of whatever zombie-like creature from this hell, disguised as a graveyard, had clutched him. Paul's effort not only succeeded in setting him loose, but also sent him reeling backwards, off balance and landing on his rear, where he was able to stop himself from falling any further back by putting both hands on the ground.

As he sat in this position, Paul continued to cry out in a series of obscenities and invectives, aimed at the appendage which had gripped him so tightly, seemingly in an attempt to pull him down into its subterranean abode.

This couldn't be happening to him! The entire episode was too real. How was it possible to dream a horrifying series of nightmares over a period of a month, only to have them come true?

"*This isn't real! I must have fallen asleep somehow and I'm dreaming this. Dear God, let me be dreaming this!*"

Remembering that other sinister fiends had been present at the cemetery in all of his previous dreams, Paul looked nervously around him, but all he saw were the shadows of the overhanging branches, gently moving from side to side, as if swaying to a slow dance tune being played on some invisible woodland radio. He quickly turned back to the hand, expecting to find it gone, but it remained; only now it had started to claw at the ground around it. Paul watched, in a combination of fright and fascination, as the slender arm started to emerge a little more from its prison.

Confused and shaken, immediate flight presented itself as his best option, but, as Paul began to get up off the ground, his attention was drawn to something twinkling faintly in the tiny ray of lunar illumination. Afraid to move any closer, but curious as to what had caught his eye, he leaned forward and saw what appeared to be a bracelet, hanging loosely on the half-buried wrist. Suddenly, the arm went limp, falling softly to the ground, where it started to raise up and fell once more, this time without moving again.

As Paul kneeled on one knee, his heart began to slow from the rapid beat of a few seconds before. The revulsion and sheer terror which had previously engulfed him began to subside, replaced by a sympathetic desire to assist whatever was trying to dig *out* of the earth, not pull him in, as he formerly believed.

Expecting to hear some sort of guidance from the voice, which hadn't been shy in advising him what to do and when to do it up to this point, Paul hesitated for just a moment. The voice again was silent.

Moving forward on hands and knees, Paul crept ever so tentatively toward the limp arm. As he drew nearer, he kept staring at the glittering object, which he confirmed to be a bracelet. The arm and hand were definitely those of a young woman, someone who could not possibly be a threat to him.

Paul began to fully grasp what was going on here. The guy in the truck must have tried to bury her alive. He reacted quickly now, reaching out and gently lifting the arm, while grasping her hand with his right hand. She immediately gave Paul's hand a soft squeeze. She was losing strength.

"I've got to uncover her face, before she suffocates!"

Maintaining his tender grip on her hand for comfort, he carefully brushed away the soil from the area where he calculated her head to be, but felt only a stringy wetness.

Paul instinctively pulled his hand back and held it up to his face for a closer examination. His fingers were covered in blood. The woman's hand gave his another weak squeeze, as Paul tried to reassure her, not knowing if she would even hear him.

"Hang in there, honey, I'm going to get you out of there. CAN YOU HEAR ME?"

Again, he felt a caress.

Paul resumed his effort to uncover the woman's head and released her hand in order to use both of his to dig. In a few seconds, he was able to make out the outline of her face, covered in blood and dirt. He gently brushed away the dirt from around her mouth and nose, saying a silent prayer that she would still be breathing. There was no movement from her head. Paul slid his index finger down under her jaw, trying to locate a pulse, but was unable to detect one. Fearing the worst, he tilted her head back and bent down, preparing to give her mouth a couple of quick breaths. Hesitating for only a second or so at the sight of her blood-covered face and mouth, Paul placed his mouth on the woman's, moving his lips in an attempt to create a seal. Before he was able to blow in the first breath, the body of the unfortunate woman convulsed and she coughed sharply, spewing dirt and saliva into Paul's mouth.

Paul withdrew and spat on the ground. Below him, the woman writhed, renewing her effort to pull herself free from the makeshift grave. Without hesitation, Paul began to dig furiously, running his hands alongside her prone body and scooping out handfuls of dirt, tossing them aside. He used his left arm as a plow to drag the eight to ten inch layer of soil which had covered the torso and legs. When he felt he had removed enough dirt to successfully raise her up, he slid his left arm around her neck and gently lifted the woman to a point where he then lowered the arm behind her back. From this position, Paul was able to extricate the woman from the trench. Upon doing this, Paul could see, in the dim moonlight, that the woman was naked.

Pulling as hard as he could, Paul felt the muscles in his back begin to tighten, but gave one last tug and the body of the lady who had reached out from the ground for assistance was at last freed. The momentum from the final lifting effort caused Paul to fall onto his back, with his rescued victim falling on top of him. Her body rested heavily on top of Paul's and he pushed against her, trying to roll her off of him. Paul knew by the lack of effort on the part of the woman that she was weakened seriously by her ordeal.

Bracing his right leg, he rolled to the left and felt the helpless body slide off of him, almost falling back into her hole in the ground. Paul held on, however and managed to pull her away from the trench far enough so she wouldn't slip in.

The woman appeared to be slightly more alert now and began to moan, reaching her right arm up to her head and gently touching it. As Paul looked closer, he saw a large gash just above her forehead, running along the hairline, about four inches long and quite deep. Blood was caked in and around the opening, as well as in her hair. Removing his handkerchief, Paul daubed at the wound, noticing that blood was still oozing from the laceration.

"It's no wonder why she's so damn weak." Paul thought.

He covered it evenly with his handkerchief and applied pressure, all the while talking to his injured party.

"You're going to be okay, honey. I'm going to get you out of here, but I need to go and get my truck. It's parked…….."

Suddenly, a wild-eyed look came over the woman and she clutched at Paul, shaking her head and moaning out loud; "NO, NO……..DON'T LEAVE ME……..PLEASE!"

Paul froze upon hearing the woman speak. Her voice, even in its weakened state, was unmistakable.

Leaning closer to her face, he whispered; "Marilyn?"

Through the mud and blood surrounding them, her swollen eyes filled instantly with tears and Paul, filled with joy at the realization that his and Mary Ellen's dear friend was still alive cried out; "Oh, Marilyn, THANK GOD you're alive.

Scooping her up in his arms, while in a kneeling position, Paul hugged his weakened friend, then, feeling her arms feebly wrapping themselves around his back, he placed his hands on both sides of her cheeks and kissed her forehead, nose, eyes and finally her mouth, all the while exclaiming; "Oh, Marilyn, sweetheart; I'm so happy you're okay. You're going to be okay, honey; I promise. We thought for sure we had lost you. Oh, God bless you, you're okay."

Paul felt Marilyn's body convulse in spasms of gratefulness and joy, at not only having her life spared, but that her rescuer was her best friend's husband. The wailing sobs that emanated from her throat sounded like music to Paul's ears as he thought of how truly ecstatic Mary Ellen was going to be when she learned that Marilyn, her beautiful friend, whom everyone had given up for dead, had survived this terrible ordeal.

The couple held their tight embrace for a long time. Paul did not want to let go until Marilyn had finished her sobbing. He calmly and gently stroked her hair, whispering; "That's okay, sweetheart; go ahead and cry. Let it all out. God knows what you've been through. I won't leave you alone, I promise."

Marilyn clung as tightly as she could to her friend, afraid to loosen her hold. Just as Paul thought she might be all cried out, another wave of convulsive sobs began. Each time, Paul held her more tightly, rocked her gently from side to side and soothingly whispered to her, establishing a bond of love that would run deeper than any two friends, or lovers, for that matter, could ever expect to achieve in a lifetime.

The one thought that kept ringing in Paul's mind was; *"What kind of a sick bastard could do this to her? To ANYONE!"*

Paul thought about telling Marilyn that he was sure he had seen the man who hurt her drive away, but quickly and wisely dismissed the idea, as it would more than likely upset her even more. Feeling her embrace loosen, he started to lower Marilyn to the ground, but she only clutched more fiercely at his arms and it wasn't until Paul looked at her eyes that he saw the look of utter and complete terror, as she stared beyond him, saying; "No, no……..NO, NO!"

Sensing impending doom, Paul felt the chill start at the base of his spine and continue up the vertebral column, where it splayed out across his shoulders, finishing with an involuntary shudder. Before he was able to turn around, he heard the ominous voice boom out.

"WELL, NOW; ISN'T THIS SWEET! THE BIG HERO RESCUES HIS LITTLE GIRLFRIEND."

Paul spun quickly around, Marilyn still clinging to him and looked up to see a true-to-life horror monster, standing over the helpless pair, holding in his hands a long-handled shovel. It was the young, sinewy, blond-haired figure who had, only minute before, driven his pick-up past a huddled Paul; the same man who had tormented him in his last two or three dreams, wearing the exact same devilish grin Paul had seen so vividly in those dreams. Stunned by the sight of such a frightful fiend that had now presented itself to him in true-to-life form, Paul was unable to move momentarily.

"WHAT'S THE MATTER, HERO? HAS THE CAT GOT YOUR TONGUE? OR SHOULD I SAY 'THE PUSSY'?"

When he finished speaking, the grinning man laughed a maniacal laugh and Paul knew he had to come up with some kind of attempt to defend himself and Marilyn. But, how do you defend against a younger, stronger opponent with a shovel, when you're sitting on the ground and he's poised above, ready to strike?

Paul could hear Marilyn whimpering beside him. It was the sound of someone who knew she was about to die; knew also that it would be a sudden, violent death. She clung ever so tightly to Paul's arm, pulling herself close to his body with all of the strength she was able to muster.

Bracing his body with his right arm in back of him, while holding Marilyn with his left, Paul's hand reached out slowly, searching for a rock to grab hold of. The man with the shovel sneered down at them, focusing his anger towards Marilyn.

"I BET YOU THOUGHT YOU LUCKED OUT, BITCH. I GUESS YOU THOUGHT WRONG. NOW YOU'RE GONNA BE THE ONLY WHORE TO DIE TWICE IN THE SAME DAY. CHEER UP, SLUT! THIS TIME YOUR BOYFRIEND GETS TO DIE WITH YOU."

Grinning man raised the shovel.

"THIS TIME, YOU AIN'T GONNA DIG OUT OF YOUR GRAVE, BITCH. I'M GONNA MAKE SURE OF THAT."

Paul's right hand searched furiously and then he felt it bump a familiar object.

"The ball…….that beautiful old ball."

Paul carefully secured a grip on the old baseball and, when grinning man had raised the shovel almost all the way up, he let out a loud scream, which startled Marilyn enough to make her jump and brought his arm around in a side-arm movement, releasing the ball with enough velocity to take a man's breath away with a well-placed groin shot. The ball soared up towards the assailant, covering the short distance in a nanosecond. It struck with a thud, but to Paul's horror, a foot above its intended target, landing squarely in the aggressor's abdomen.

Another burst of raucous laughter came forth from grinning man, as he lowered the shovel.

"YOU EVEN THROW LIKE A PUSSY, HERO."

Then, looking back at Marilyn, whose face was now buried in Paul's shoulder, he said; "YOU REALLY PICKED A LOSER, BITCH. THIS LITTLE FAIRY CAN'T GET THE JOB DONE."

He then ripped his shirt open to reveal a granite-like abdomen.

"YOU HAD THE CHANCE TO HAVE A REAL MAN AND YOU CHOSE THIS! YOU MUST REALLY THINK……."

Paul cut him off in mid sentence.

"If you're such a 'real man', then why don't you put that shovel down and fight me like one?"

The grin disappeared quickly from the man's face as he responded.

"BECAUSE, FAIRY BOY, THERE'D ONLY BE TWO SOUNDS; THE FIRST WHEN MY FIST SMASHED YOUR JAW AND THE SECOND WHEN YOU HIT THE GROUND."

Sensing a weakness in the man's quick to anger response, Paul pushed it a little further.

"I think the real 'fairy boy' is standing in front of me."

Nostrils flaring visibly, grinning man responded.

"IF YOU'RE TRYING TO PISS ME OFF, YOU'RE DOING A GOOD JOB, ASSHOLE."

Paul kept up the taunting, giving his adversary a taste of his own medicine.

"I've seen guys like you, before. You act real tough, but only when you've got a weapon in your hands. I'll bet you've never even been in a real fight, have you, tough guy?"

Paul's last remark hit home, as grinning man flew into a rage.

"SHUT UP! SHUT THE FUCK UP!"

Pushing the envelope just a little further, Paul snapped back.

"Oooh! What are you going to do, tough guy, punch me? No, because you've never had the guts to stand up to a man before, have you? I bet you've won a lot of the fights you've had with girls though. But that........"

Grinning man screamed in fury, dropping the shovel and putting both hands to his ears.

"THAT'S IT, FUCKHEAD! NOW, I'M GONNA BEAT THE LIVING SHIT OUT OF YOU. THEN, WHEN I'M DONE, I'M GONNA BEAT THE BRAINS OUT OF YOUR LITTLE WHORE........WHILE YOU WATCH!"

Paul removed his arm from around Marilyn, who whimpered all the more loudly, grabbing and clutching at him, in fear of being left alone, at the mercy of the man who had already tried to kill her. He began to stand up, but grinning man quickly picked up the shovel and stepped forward, swinging wildly, but with deadly force. Paul raised his left arm to deflect the blow, but the steel blade of the shovel came down hard on his forearm, sending a searing pain deep into the bone and knocking him backwards. No sooner had he completed the swing than grinning man started a return swing. Again, Paul lifted his arm, but this time a bit too late and he heard and felt the heavy clang, followed by a loud ringing in his right ear, as the shovel scored a direct hit on the right side of his head, immediately opening up a deep gash above his ear.

Paul fell to the ground and saw the bushes off to his left, spinning in a crazy circle, as he felt blood pouring down the side of his face. He could hear Marilyn screaming, but she sounded so far away. Someone was holding him and saying something, but the voice was muffled and unintelligible. As he looked up, he saw grinning man raising the shovel high above his head, but knew he was powerless to stop him. His gamble had failed. He had hoped to taunt the man enough so he would drop his weapon and engage him in a fistfight, where Paul thought he might at least have a slight chance of winning and now he knew he was about to die.

In one last feeble attempt to defend himself, Paul forced himself into a propped-up position, where he leaned on his elbows. He reached out with his right hand, knowing he didn't have the strength left to ward off any further strikes. Marilyn clung to his left side and he tried to wrap his left arm around her head to protect her as long as he was able. But the intensity of the pain in his forearm convinced Paul that it had been broken by the blade of the shovel. Now, there appeared to be two grinning men standing over the helpless couple, as Paul's head reeled with dizziness.

Suddenly, Paul heard what he thought was another voice and he knew that grinning man heard it too, because he stopped in mid-swing. The new voice seemed to be a distance away, but he heard it say; "FREEZE, POLICE! DROP THE SHOVEL! NOW!"

With his head spinning, Paul was still able to discern that a cop was holding a gun on grinning man, but was not quite sure just where the officer was. He struggled to lift his head and turned it enough to see Bill Fenton and Tom Skinner standing about twenty feet behind and to the right of, grinning man. He looked up at the man who had just been about to kill him, smiled and quietly said; "Go for it, tough guy!"

Eyes wild with hatred and wanting only to smash the shovel down hard on this taunting man lying on the ground, grinning man again lifted the shovel high and began the downward swing, screaming a loud, primitive scream at the same time that two shots rang out. The first shot hit grinning man in the upper right shoulder area, instantly spinning him around, where the second entered the lower part of his chest, below his heart, sending him reeling backwards, where he stumbled past Paul and Marilyn, falling. His rear end hit the ground at about the same time as the back of his head hit a gravestone. Grinning man slumped at the base of the stone, his mouth opening and closing, as if he were speaking silent phrases, in desperate gasps for air. A few seconds later, blood spurted from the orifice which only moments before had spewed forth the vilest torrent of invectives and then, his head slumped to the side, eyes wide open and unblinking.

Paul stared, transfixed by the unfolding drama played out before his eyes and despite the blinding pain in his head, he saw that the stone that grinning man had fallen against was the very same stone upon which his friend, Larry Guernette had met such a brutal death. The rods which had been installed to repair the stone held and this time the stone did not break in two.

Satisfied that Marilyn was in no further danger, Paul tried turning his head back toward Bill Fenton, who approached, along with Sgt. Skinner, guns held out, stiff-armed, in front of them. As he struggled to raise his arm and give a thumb's up to Fenton, Paul felt a sudden tranquility overtake his mind and body. All the pain ceased and the only awareness of discomfort was a sodden, numbness on the right side of his head. Making eye contact with the chief, as he passed by to verify that the man with the shovel was dead, Paul McCulloch smiled, as his world turned colorless before him, fell against his friend, Marilyn Duran and closed his eyes.

CHAPTER TWENTY ONE

8:35 a.m., Saturday, August 21, 2004

"Is there anything else I can get for you, Ms. Duran?" asked the nursing assistant, as she fluffed the pillow, carefully placing it behind Marilyn's back.

"No, thank you. I'm fine, for now."

"Someone has been waiting outside to see you. She was here yesterday also, for several hours, but you weren't quite ready for visitors. She has been very patient. May I send her in?"

"Please do."

Marilyn cocked her head to the side to see who would be coming through the doorway. Her mouth, stitched in two places, opened into a wide smile as her best friend, Mary Ellen McCulloch walked into the room, carrying a large bouquet of red roses. Mary Ellen's eyes were red-rimmed from crying, but her joy and relief from seeing her friend alive and well overwhelmed her so completely that she ran to Marilyn's bedside, dropping the bouquet on the bed and hugging her tightly.

"Marilyn!" Mary Ellen whispered, as she ran to her.

Both women cried tears of joy for many minutes, luxuriating in the closeness of their friendship and the love it had fostered, as they embraced each other.

"Oh, my dear, dear friend." Spoke Mary Ellen tenderly, as she wiped the tears from Marilyn's cheeks with her thumb and, unable to staunch the flow, brought out a tissue. "I prayed so hard that God would spare you and he did."

The two women again cried with each other, rubbing each other's arms, until Marilyn locked her hands on to Mary Ellen's.

"Mary Ellen……..about Paul…….."

Marilyn raised one hand to her mouth as she saw her friend's face contorting, trying to hold back even more tears.

Now, Marilyn burst into a new round of tears as she hugged her friend.

"Mary Ellen……..HE SAVED MY LIFE!"

"I know, honey, I know." Mary Ellen replied, as the two women came together again, in a tearful embrace.

"HEY! Isn't this supposed to be a happy reunion?" The voice asked from the doorway.

The two women turned to see Paul, sitting in a wheelchair, his head wrapped in a large wad of gauze. His left arm was encased in a plaster cast and the wheelchair was being pushed by a smiling Bill Fenton.

Marilyn was overjoyed at the sight of Paul and screamed with delight; "PAUL! YOU'RE ALIVE!"

Paul looked up at her and replied; "The last time I checked, I was, anyway."

Her emotions out of control, Marilyn drifted between sobs of joy and near hysterical laughter in the happiness of the moment. Finally, the emotion overcame her and she lapsed into a series of spasmodic sobs, enough so, that Chief Fenton left his post at Paul's wheelchair, rushed over and with Mary Ellen, tried to console and calm the distraught woman.

Paul motioned to Mary Ellen to push him closer to Marilyn's bedside. When she did this, he stood up, a little shakily and reached out with his right hand to softly caress her cheek. Marilyn responded to his touch by cradling his hand in both of hers, kissing his fingers.

When she had calmed enough to speak, she quietly said; "You saved my life, Paul. I will never be able to thank you enough for that."

Tenderly squeezing her hand, Paul tried to lighten the moment.

"Hey, I promised I wouldn't leave you alone, but that's all I can take credit for." Then, motioning his head in the direction of Chief Fenton, Paul said; "There's the guy that saved both of our lives. If it wasn't for him and Tom Skinner, you and I wouldn't be around for this conversation."

Chief Fenton rested one hand on the bed rail and gestured in the direction of Mary Ellen.

"We were just responding to a call from your wife, Paul; which brings me to the question of how you came to be at the exact place where this lady almost became a murder victim. We're going to talk about that, later. Right now, I've got to try and make sense of this entire mess, so I can put together a statement to present to the news media. You may not know this, but there are several television news vans in the parking lot, along with a couple of dozen reporters and advance people in the lower lobby, all waiting to get a crack at interviewing either or both of you. Captain Monroe from the City P.D. was kind enough to position one of his officers outside of the trauma area. He will allow that officer to accompany you, Ms. Duran, when you are moved to a standard room, but was unable to supply more than one officer, so I've assigned Andy Farland to stand guard outside your room, Paul, when that becomes necessary. In addition, the hospital staff has assured me that they will try and protect your privacy. I will caution both of you, in the event that someone from the media does make contact with you, to choose your words carefully when answering their questions."

Paul looked directly at the chief and then at Mary Ellen, finally returning his focus on Fenton.

"Bill, I didn't have any prior knowledge of what went on at that cemetery.........if that's what you're suggesting."

Chief Fenton answered, rather quickly.

"I just need to have some questions answered, that's all. But, we'll do that later."

Angered by the insinuation that he was even remotely connected with grinning man, Paul shot back; "No, Bill, I want to talk about it now. I don't want this woman lying here, thinking that I was in any way involved with what happened to her, other than trying to help her. Now, what questions did you have for me?"

Stepping away from Marilyn's bedside, Fenton crossed his arms in front of him and said; "All right, Paul; we'll do it your way. When your wife called me last evening, she said that you had gone to the old burying ground by yourself and she thought you might be in danger. I want to know why she thought that and I also want to know what made you go there. It's not the sort of thing a person would normally do."

Paul stared across the bed at the chief, eyes unblinking and answered.

"I honestly don't know, Bill. I wish I could give you a good reason, but I just had a very strange compulsion to go to that cemetery at that particular time. This may sound odd, but the feeling was one of extreme urgency. I don't believe that it was just a coincidence that I was there at that exact time. Call it what you will, but I know that I was meant to be there."

Chief Fenton moved his head forward, as if waiting for more of an explanation and then said, in mock disbelief; "That's it?"

With tightened lips, Paul replied; "Yes, that's it!"

Mary Ellen shifted her weight from one leg to the other, as she held on to Marilyn's arm. Her eyes gazed down at the floor and then darted between her husband and Bill Fenton, in order to gauge his reaction to what Paul had just told him. She thought about it and came to the conclusion that Paul really hadn't lied to the chief, he just omitted the part about the voice in his head, which she felt was a wise thing to do, under the circumstances.

Noticing Mary Ellen's nervousness, Chief Fenton once again asked Paul; "You're sure there's nothing else you want to tell me?"

Paul's voice remained firm as he answered.

"Nothing that you would want to hear, Bill. Look, why don't I give my psychologist a call and I'll ask him to explain this whole business about the dreams and all the whacky stuff that went with them. I'm sure he can clear things up for you."

Chief Fenton lowered his head, deep in thought. When he raised it, he gave Paul a half-smile and said; "That won't be necessary, Paul. I've known you long enough to tell by the way I've ruffled your feathers that you're telling me the truth. I'm just going to indicate in my report that you told me you were out for an evening's walk, because you had some things on your mind you wanted to sort out, if that sounds okay to you."

Paul smiled broadly and replied; "Actually, Bill; that's pretty much the truth."

Then, as an afterthought, Paul asked the chief pointedly; "What about the guy that……..you know……..tried to kill us?"

"He was D.O.A. at the hospital. Captain Monroe's preliminary investigation turned up quite a bit."

Turning to Marilyn, he continued; "It seems that he had come into the gift shop several times and was attracted to you, ma'am. According to an older gentleman who would wait in his car to pick up his wife, who also works in the gift shop, he noticed this man sitting in his truck on more than one occasion. The older man said that this guy would watch Ms. Duran walk out and then he would leave. It appeared to the older gentleman that the suspect followed Ms. Duran at a far enough distance so as to avoid detection. He really became suspicious when, on the night you were abducted, the suspect showed up in a dark sedan. He informed the city police after he heard about you coming up missing the next day. He was able to provide them with a partial license plate number, which, along with the description of the vehicle, allowed investigators to narrow down the search, eventually turning up our suspect. It seems he worked at the construction project near the gift shop and had heard about you from some of his co-workers. They said that after he had gone into the shop and seen you, he began to talk about you to them more than what they considered normal. Apparently, he became obsessed with you and that led to your abduction…….."

Suddenly, Marilyn broke in; "He didn't rape me……..at least not in the *true sense* of the word."

Chief Fenton flushed a little and responded; "You don't have to talk about this now, ma'am."

Marilyn pulled at the raised side railing, trying to lift herself higher in the bed. Mary Ellen slid the pillow further down her back for better support, then grabbed a spare pillow from a small table near the bed, doubled it over and placed it behind Marilyn's head. Marilyn smiled at her friend, thanked her and continued.

"I don't mind talking about it, Chief Fenton. He tried to rape me. He tried several times, in fact. He couldn't get himself hard enough to penetrate me. Each........"

Mary Ellen backed away from Marilyn's bedside, uncomfortable at hearing the intimate details of her friend's ordeal. Gesturing in the direction of Paul, who had resumed his seat in the wheelchair, she said, in a half-whisper; "We'll just go for a little walk. Paul should get back to his bed, anyway."

With a look of surprise on her face, Marilyn pleaded with her friend.

"Mary Ellen, please stay! I want you and Paul to hear this. I need to get this out and you two are the closest I've got for family. In fact, you *are* family to me, so you need to hear it........please?"

Feeling herself misting up once again, Mary Ellen grasped her friend's hand and said; "Oh, sweetheart!"

Holding on firmly to Mary Ellen's outstretched hand, Marilyn continued her story.

"He took me to an old, run-down cabin; I'm not even sure what town it was in. We drove out Old Charter road and I remember seeing the sign that said we were entering Preston. It was hard to see much, because he kept pushing my face down on the seat. I was kneeling on the floor, facing the passenger seat and he said if I sat up he would kill me, but I knew that was a lie, because he wouldn't do that until he had his fun with me. I knew he would kill me eventually, because he made no attempt to blindfold me."

At this point, Chief Fenton interrupted Marilyn's narrative to raise a question.

"Excuse me, Ms. Duran, but your car was found at the old Madison Shoe Factory parking lot, with a small amount of blood on the headrest of the driver's seat. Can you tell me how your car got there?"

"Yes, I drove it there. I had been there a half an hour earlier and had to fend off an unwanted sexual advance from that slime ball boss of mine. In the process, I lost a precious necklace........well, at least it's precious to me. It has a strong sentimental value for me. Anyway, I had gone back to look for it and I never saw this guy coming. The next thing I know, I'm being dragged backwards and this guy is telling me to shut up or he'll kill me. I screamed, but he punched me really hard, right in the mouth. It hurt so badly, I just cried. That blood on the back of the seat, though; that wasn't mine. I head-butted my boss to get him off of me. He had me in a bear hug and was groping me all over. When I got out of his car, I saw that his nose was bleeding badly. I threw my shoe and hit him square in the crotch. Then, I walked back to the gift shop parking lot and got in my car. When I drove by Madison's, I didn't see his car in the lot, so I drove in to look for my necklace. That's when this other guy grabbed me."

Fenton scribbled a few notes in his small, worn notebook and urged Marilyn to continue, thanking her for answering his question so completely. She went on.

"We must have driven for twenty minutes to a half an hour, before he turned off on this really bumpy road. We drove on that road for a long time, maybe another five minutes and he slowed down and turned again and I saw branches scraping the windows on his car. When we stopped, he got out and opened my door. He dragged me out and pulled me towards that old cabin, which was more like a shed, than anything else. I remember my legs burning in pain as he pulled me through some picker bushes. When we got inside, I saw that he had a dirty mattress on the floor and an old comforter folded up on top of the mattress. He threw me down on the mattress, put his fist right in front of my face and told me not to move or he would punch me again. Then, he went back out to his car. I thought about getting up and running, but I knew he'd just catch me and……..my mouth hurt so much that I didn't want to get punched there again…….."

Marilyn sobbed once, wiped her eyes with the back of her hand, then Mary Ellen handed her a tissue, running her right hand over Marilyn's forehead, straight back over the top of her head in a gentle stroking motion. As she regained her composure, Marilyn resumed the gruesome account.

"I laid there on that mattress, wondering if I should try to resist him, or let him have his way. I thought about this pamphlet I read once, that said if a rapist gets you into a car, that's the worst scenario, because now he can transport you anywhere. It told how you should fight as hard as you could to avoid that and all I kept thinking was; 'Yeah, but it didn't say what to do if somebody surprises you and punches you so hard that you see stars.' Then I heard his car door slam and he came back in, with a six-pack of beer in his hand. He opened up a beer and drank it down so fast that some of it rolled down his neck and then he just crushed the can in his hand, like it was made of Styrofoam. He looked at me to be sure that I saw that and then he knelt down beside me and tore my blouse open. He never even *tried* to undo the buttons. Next, he pulled out this knife from his back pocket and I was afraid he was going to stab me, but he slid it under the middle of my bra and sliced it open. I was *so* scared!"

As he listened, Paul thought of his own encounter with Marilyn's abductor and how big and strong he had appeared. Paul himself had been more than a little intimidated as the grinning man had stood over him, taunting and yelling. He could only imagine how terrified Marilyn must have been, knowing that this man not only intended to rape her, but most certainly would kill her, probably in a violent way, which he almost succeeded in doing. He listened closer, as Marilyn continued.

"Next, he knelt down beside me and started fondling my breasts. He was starting to breathe heavily now and his hand went down to my privates. He pulled my skirt off, along with my panties and penetrated me digitally. He was so rough and he made no attempt to even spit on his finger. It hurt an awful lot. All I could think was that this guy had never been with a woman before; he was totally clueless as to what to do. Then, he stood up, unbuckled his dungarees and pulled them and his underpants down to his knees. When I saw that he was only partially erect, I knew we were going to have a problem and we did. He knelt down in front of me and pushed my legs apart. This idiot actually tried to enter me with that floppy thing, but then a bad thing happened. He started cursing and yelling at me, picked my butt up off the mattress and pulled me hard against him, but I could feel how soft........"

Chief Fenton cut in and said; "Ms. Duran, I don't think it's necessary to go into this much detail. We get the picture. The man obviously had a performance problem. I want to hear what he did to you in a little less explicit clarification, if you don't mind."

Both Paul and Mary Ellen breathed an inaudible sigh of relief upon hearing Fenton speak these words, as everyone had become more than a bit uneasy with Marilyn's description of her tribulation.

Marilyn responded in an apologetic tone of voice.

"I'm sorry, Chief Fenton. I thought you needed to hear all of the details."

Chief Fenton reached out and patted the back of her hand.

"You don't have to apologize, just omit the intimate details and try to briefly describe each event, as it unfolded."

Marilyn put her head down, as if trying to think of how she would go about phrasing the next part of her story.

"Anyhow, the guy really got upset when he wasn't able to........screw me. He somehow blamed it all on me and started hitting me. He slapped me hard twice, once on each side of my face. Then he started kneading my breasts really hard........"

Fenton rolled his eyes and glanced over at Paul and Mary Ellen, cocking his head to one side, in a gesture of defeat, as Marilyn rolled on.

"........and got more angry when that failed to get him excited. Finally, he got up and drank another beer. When he finished his beer, he kicked me in my upper thigh, got down on his knees and tried to do it again, but he still couldn't do anything. I could tell he was getting embarrassed, because he wouldn't look at me. Then, when he sensed me looking at him, he yelled; 'what are you looking at, bitch?' and he started to beat me; badly enough that I lost consciousness. When I woke up, it was dark and he was asleep next to me, with his arm around my chest. The smell of stale beer on his breath was making me sick to my stomach, plus, I had a splitting headache and both arms were sore and I realized it was from trying to fend off his punches. Plus, my back was stiff from being in the same position, so I tried to roll over, but when I moved, he didn't wake up all the way, just enough to move his hand to my breast, which got him aroused. Now he woke up and tried to do it again, this time he actually did it almost right. He kissed me on the lips, which I didn't understand, because my lips were swollen and bloody; the blood was scabbed on them, in little lumps and it must not have been very appealing, but maybe he was drunk enough not to notice. I knew he must have drunk a lot of beers after I passed out, because he was slurring his words. He was actually sweet-talking me and being gentler than he was before. Then, he just fell asleep, or passed out, from drinking. I lay there all night, without falling asleep. I tried to think of every conceivable way I could to get away from him, without waking him up, but nothing seemed like a good plan. I couldn't even move, without disturbing him. His breath was putrid. The shack was full of mosquitoes, which kept stinging me all night. By the time morning came, I actually felt hopeful that he would spare my life, because he told me he was going for food for us. He taped my mouth, tied my hands and feet together and left me alone. I tried to get loose from the ropes, but he had them tied so tightly, I couldn't undo them. I was so frustrated, because this was a golden opportunity to get away and I couldn't even get off that damn mattress.

    He must have been gone for only a half hour or so and when he came back, he untaped my mouth and untied my hands, but left my feet tied together. He threw a bag at me, which had one little cheeseburger in it. I had to choke it down, because I was so thirsty. I asked him for something to drink and he yelled at me to shut up, but after a while, he gave me a sip of his beer. He started looking at me funny and when he finished eating, he took all of his clothes off and started on me again. He did everything a man could do to a woman, except he never got himself off, which pissed him off to no end. I had to pee really badly, but I was afraid that if I asked him, he would beat me again. I thought that if I could just pee a little, without him knowing, he would think that he had gotten me wet and would be able to complete what he started. I slid myself up higher on the mattress and let out a little, but too much came out, before I was able to stop. I slid down to cover the wet spot, just as his hand was reaching down there again and I pretended to be getting aroused. It seemed to work, until he tried to enter........"

Chief Fenton had clearly had enough and let Marilyn know of his displeasure.

"Ms. Duran, please! Just stick to the basics."

Marilyn, unable to comprehend why the chief would not want to know the complete story of her ordeal, looked questioningly at Fenton.

"I was just getting to an important point, Chief."

Fenton, in an agitated tone, replied; "Then please try to get there quickly. I do not *need* or *want* to hear about every time he touched you intimately. The man is dead, so there is no reason to........" then, regaining some of his composure, the chief calmly added; "I'm sorry, Ms. Duran. But, please try to be brief. My hand is cramping from writing so much."

Fenton smiled at the bedridden woman and she returned his smile with one of her own.

"When I was a little girl, my mother would always quote a line from Shakespeare's 'Hamlet', when I rambled on about something. She would say; 'Brevity is the soul of wit', but I never understood just what that meant.

Unable to resist the opening, Fenton laughingly replied; "That has become obvious to all of us here."

The four people gathered in the small room at the end of the trauma wing all laughed, brought together by tragedy, while finding friendship among themselves, rooted in patience and compassion for the one among them who had been through such a horrific experience, yet, not only was able to discuss her torment, but found comfort in the gentle teasing of the others.

"All right, then." Marilyn said. "I'm going to try my hardest to keep it short and……..well; there really isn't anything sweet about the next part. The bottom line is that he couldn't get it up, no matter what he did, or tried and he took his anger and frustration out on me……..all day long. He ranted, punched me, screamed some more, kicked and punched me again until I began to feel numb all over my body. When I thought he might be starting to calm down, he would look at me lying there on that mattress and start all over again. I've never been much of a religious person, but I actually prayed that he would knock me out, so I wouldn't have to endure any more of the beatings. I wondered how he would kill me. Would he strangle me, or beat me to death? I prayed really hard that he wouldn't stab me with that terribly sharp-looking knife. I was petrified of being stabbed to death. All the time, he was drinking and getting nastier. Late in the afternoon, he tied me up and left me alone again, while he went out in his car. When he came back, about a half hour later, he had a bag of fast food, but he didn't offer me any, so I asked him for some, because I was so hungry. What he said next, made my heart sink. He said I wouldn't need any more food where I was going, because I was just a……..useless whore that no one cared about……..and that no one……..would miss…….."

Marilyn buried her face in her hands, overcome, both by the emotion of the moment and the strain of recalling the specifics of her captivity. Mary Ellen hugged her, while Paul and Chief Fenton cleared their throats and glanced at each other uncomfortably. It was Fenton, who spoke next, in a surprisingly soft tone.

"Ms. Duran, you don't have to continue. We can do this on another day."

Lifting her head, Marilyn responded; "No! I want to finish this now! Just give me a minute."

Mary Ellen handed her several tissues, which Marilyn used to wipe her eyes and nose, took a deep breath and went on.

"He rolled me over and did some awful things to me with his fingers. He was like a little kid in a candy shop who didn't know where to start, so he did a little of everything. I just lay there, hoping it would be all over soon. I was sore all over, my throat was parched and dry and I was very hungry. But, most of all, I was terrified of what was to come. He tried to make me perform oral sex on him, but I wouldn't. He got mad and beat me some more. That's when I decided I had had enough. I was going to die anyway, so I might as well make him as miserable as I could before I did. Sure enough, after he drank another beer, he tried to get me to go down on him again. This time, I did and bit down hard. He punched me in the side of the face a bunch of times. I could hear him screaming in pain and cursing me out. Then, I felt a dull thud above my ear and it was lights out. When I woke up this time, I was on the floor of a house; actually it looked like a back porch of some type. I couldn't really see, because there was blood and matted hair in front of my eyes. My ears were ringing, but it was more like a buzzing, a constant buzzing. It was dark and I knew I must have been unconscious for some time. Then, I heard him saying something from the next room. I lifted up my head, but it hurt too much to hold it up for long. I could see a light in that room, but it was too bright and I looked away. The next time he spoke, I could hear him saying; 'You think you're pretty tough, whore? Well, let's see how tough you really are. You almost bit my dick off, you useless piece of shit. Now you're gonna pay, bitch.' Then, he came over to where I was lying and reached down and touched my neck, like he was feeling for a pulse and then he grabbed my ankles. He pulled me by my ankles out into a driveway. I felt my head bumping over a threshold, but it was just a dull pain. When he got me in the driveway, he continued to pull me along and the back of my head felt like it was burning in pain. Then I realized that my back was also being scraped along the asphalt and every so often, I got a shooting type of searing pain that radiated up to my shoulders. I tried to cry, but I didn't even have the strength to do that, let alone scream. I was aware of being totally naked and didn't even care, at that point. I was so weak, that my resistance was gone. Finally, he stopped pulling me and I heard him open a door. Then I felt his arms sliding under me and I had the sensation of being lifted up and dropped, into what felt like the back of a pick-up truck. He pushed me toward the front part of the truck bed, up near the cab and covered me with a heavy tarpaulin. I felt something heavy land next to me, on top of the tarp, then another. I heard him get into the truck and start it up. He drove slowly, at first and when he got on a paved road, he drove a little faster. It dawned on me that there was a possibility that he thought I was dead. I guess I hadn't quite given up, because I felt a twinge of hope that, maybe he might drop me off in the woods somewhere and leave me for dead. I had heard of a case where that actually happened and the girl was able to crawl a long way to a farmhouse. She survived……..which gave me hope."

Marilyn paused and reached for her water glass. Mary Ellen quickly secured it and handed it to her. She took a sip and then drank the glass down. Setting the glass on the small table beside her bed, she resumed her narrative.

"When I heard the truck slow down and stop, I got really scared. I knew this was it. This was where it was all going to end. It's funny, but all I thought was 'Don't let it be in a pond, or some dirty landfill. Let me die in an open field, where the sun will shine on me in the morning and I can travel up to heaven on a sunbeam.' Then he…….."

Mary Ellen sobbed once, daubing at her eyes with a tissue and apologized.

"I'm sorry. Oh, honey, you must have been so terrified."

Now, it was Marilyn's turn to offer comfort and she reached over and gently rubbed Mary Ellen's arm. She looked back at Chief Fenton and said; "Then he pulled the tarp off of me and pulled me towards the back of the truck. He felt my neck again and I prayed that he wouldn't find a pulse, thinking that it might be too slow to detect. I tried to act dead, but that isn't as easy as it would seem. I heard him clunking some kind of tool around in the truck and then he walked away. The next thing I heard was a digging sound, which lasted for only a few minutes, along with a scraping sound. This would have been the perfect time to escape, if I were going to. That was totally out of the question, as I wasn't even able to lift my head, let alone my body, off the bed of that truck. I heard him walking back toward the truck and when he got there, he tossed the shovel into the bed, in back of me. Part of it hit me on the side of my head, but I remained frozen, as if I never felt the hit. It worked, because, as he lifted me out of the truck, he said; 'You gave it up too soon, bitch. I wanted you to pay for what you did to me, you cheap whore, but I guess it's too late for that, now.' And then, he carried me a short ways and dropped me down hard, on the ground. It hurt so much that I wanted to cry out, but that would have given it away. My arm was touching the side of what felt like a shallow impression in the ground; my grave, I surmised. As scared as I was, I held out hope that, if this *were* to be my grave, then perhaps he might not cover me with too much dirt and I would possibly be able to dig myself out. He cursed and ran back to the truck, whimpering to himself as he ran. When he came back, I remember him saying; 'How about one for the road, bitch?" Then I felt a sharp pain in my forehead and my head started buzzing again. He must have hit me with the shovel. I guess he wanted to be sure I was dead and I wondered if maybe I really was and didn't realize it yet. Still, I had enough of a sense of awareness to feel the dirt being shoveled over me. I don't know if he was too tired or possibly too sore, as he kept moaning in pain as he shoveled. Whatever the case, my wish came true, as I could tell by the weight of the dirt that he had covered me with no more than six or eight, maybe ten inches at the most. I prayed that I could hold my breath long enough for him to leave and prayed also that his departure would be quick. It wasn't. I wasn't able to hear the truck start and I began to panic. Then, in desperation, I slowly tried to move my left hand, which had flopped under my chin before he started shoveling the dirt on me. I was surprised when it moved. If he were still standing there, he might see the dirt moving, but I had to take that chance, as I was running out of breath. After a few seconds, I was able to raise my hand along my neck and up over my mouth and nose, where it cupped a small breathing space for me. Dirt was going up my nose each time I breathed and I wanted to cough, but dared not. Now the dirt seemed to be weighing heavily on me and I knew I couldn't move enough to get myself out of this grave. Even when I heard the truck finally start up and drive away, I felt a terrible aloneness. I almost wished I had made enough noise to make him clobber me over the head with the shovel again and put me out of my misery. I said what I believed were my last prayers. I asked God to send me to heaven with my mom and I also asked him to bless you, Mary Ellen; and you too, Paul, my two dear friends."

Mary Ellen tilted her head and sighed, eyes brimming with tears. Paul looked away, eyes blinking rapidly. Still, Marilyn continued.

"The last prayer I said was to ask God to forgive me. I told Him that I knew I was far from pure, but I had always tried to be a good person and I had never in my life tried to hurt anyone else. As soon as I finished, this feeling of peacefulness came over me. I noticed the air was getting harder to breathe, but it didn't cause me to panic. Instead, I just started to relax and give in to the inevitable. All of a sudden, I heard footsteps and I somehow knew that it wasn't that guy coming back. I *knew* that his was a good person and that he was here to help me."

Marilyn paused and looked in Paul's direction. Paul, sitting in his wheelchair with one arm propped on the armrest and his hand supporting his head on his index finger and thumb, merely smiled and winked at the friend whose life he had helped to save.

"It took every bit of strength I had left, but I pushed with all my might and managed to force my right arm up enough to punch my hand through the surface. I felt the cool night air on it and I wanted to *live* again! I wanted to *breathe* that air! I felt around and found Paul's wrist, but I had no idea it was *him*. When he jerked his hand away, I knew I had scared him and I prayed he wouldn't run away. I heard him cursing in fright, but then he became silent. Then he lifted my hand and I gently squeezed his, to let him know I posed no danger to him. I felt myself slipping away into a peaceful place, once again, but Paul wouldn't let that happen. I heard a voice saying; 'Hang in there, honey........I'll get you out of there.' And my heart jumped with joy. I recognized Paul's voice instantly. I had no idea how he found me, but I knew God had answered my prayers. He had sent Paul to me. You guys know what happened next and it wasn't pretty."

Marilyn focused her gaze on Paul and Chief Fenton, who had taken up a position behind Paul's wheelchair.

"As long as I live, I will never be able to repay you men for what you did for me. I love you both so much."

Fenton cleared his throat, smiled and said; "Ms. Duran……..you have got to be the most courageous woman I have ever met. Your bravery throughout your entire ordeal is admirable, along with your will to live. As you were relating your story, I was amazed at your power of recall. Captain Monroe, from the City P.D. briefed me this morning on what his investigation had turned up so far and I found it remarkable that, despite your severe injuries, you were able to correctly recall significant facts in your abduction period, such as waking up on the suspect's back porch and being dragged to his truck. Monroe's men found blood on the floor of that porch and bloody drag marks out through his driveway, just as you recalled. I'm sure tests will show that it's your blood. Our suspect must have been quite sure that he could dump your body, return to his house, clean up the mess and return to work the next day, with no one being the wiser. He might have succeeded, if it weren't for this guy, here."

Fenton reached out a big paw and rubbed Paul's shoulder.

"Your testimony in the Show Cause hearing for Sgt. Skinner and me will be invaluable in clearing us of any wrongdoing in the suspect's death. No one will be able to dispute your excellent skills in recall. You say that you don't think you'll ever be able to repay Paul and me for what we did? Well, ma'am, let me tell you something. I consider it an honor to have been involved in your rescue. The best way to repay me, if you feel the need to, is, when you get to feeling better, go out and enjoy your life. Have a ball, because you deserve it. You are one *hell* of a woman!"

Fenton walked over to Marilyn's bedside, reached out his big hand and shook hers. Then, in an uncharacteristic gesture, he leaned over and warmly hugged her. Marilyn returned the hug and said; "The first thing I'm going to do when I'm well enough, is ask you out for dinner."

The small contingent burst into laughter, as they realized some things never change. Fenton responded by saying; "You've got yourself a date."

As the group laughed, the charge nurse came into the room, slightly perturbed and admonished them to break it up, as they had overstayed the ten minutes allotted time for visiting. Taking a look at Paul, who had become visibly pale, she said; "You shouldn't even be out of bed, Mr. McCulloch."

She then shooed Chief Fenton out into the corridor, turned to Paul and wheeled him out and into the third room on the left, from Marilyn's, where she carefully helped him back into bed, before taking his readings. Mary Ellen stayed at Marilyn's bedside for a few minutes, before heading back to be with Paul.

As the chief proceeded down the hallway, his cell phone rang. He continued walking as he answered it and then stopped in his tracks. His voice was incredulous as he asked; "Would you mind repeating that, Tom? That's what I thought you said. That is truly amazing. This job *never* ceases to amaze me. I know someone who should be relieved to hear that. Thanks for the update. Oh, by the way; we've got a rock-solid witness in that young lady who was abducted. We shouldn't have any problems with the hearing."

Spinning around, Fenton hurried back down the hallway to Paul's room, where the nurse was just finishing up with him. When he entered the room, she started to speak, no doubt to rebuke the chief for disobeying her order to leave, but he held up the index finger on his right hand and pleaded; "I just need two or three minutes with him. Believe me, what I have to tell him, should pick up his spirits."

Seeing the determination in the chief's eyes, the beleaguered nurse breathed a deep sigh and sharply answered; "Make sure it's no longer than three minutes. This man has a serious head injury and must get some rest."

Then, looking at the broad grin on the face of the visitor, she scolded; "I'm not kidding, officer. You're not in charge in this facility, do you understand?"

Chief Fenton was a little taken aback at the apparent over-reaction of the nurse, but at the same time, he knew she was right; Paul needed to get some rest. He nodded his head and said; "Yes, ma'am. I won't stay a minute longer, I promise."

Once she was satisfied that she had made her point, the irritated woman turned and walked away. When she was gone, Fenton quietly closed the door and approached Paul's bedside. In a soft voice, he began to speak.

"I just got a phone call from Tom Skinner. Because of the shooting we were involved in, we were unable to interview our suspect in the Guernette case. Providence P.D. agreed to extend the surveillance another twenty four hours. Well, they just informed Skinner that the officer who was assigned to watch Carey's apartment heard a gunshot coming from the apartment building, around three fifteen a.m. He called for backup and when they got no answer to knocks at Carey's door, they had the building super let them in. He was lying on the floor, next to an overturned kitchen chair, in a pool of blood. They found a thirty-eight across the room, probably thrown from a spasmodic reflex action. He blew his brains out, Paul. There were some old newspaper clippings about the murder of Lawrence Guernette lying on the kitchen table. Scrawled across one of the articles were the words; 'I'M SORRY. I NEVER MEANT TO KILL HIM.' He was still breathing when they got to him, but he died on the way to the e-room."

Paul sat up in his bed; his back supported by a pillow and stared at the wall ahead, absorbing the impact of what he had just been told. His mind raced, as he thought of that night, some forty seven years before, when Larry Guernette's world ended. Now, his killer had met his own violent death, one night after another friend had been spared from one.

Chief Fenton spoke again.

"I thought you might rest easier, knowing this."

Turning quickly toward the chief, as if wakened from a trance, Paul said; "What does it all mean, Bill? The nightmares........Marilyn's kidnapping........me having an inexplicable yearning to go to the exact place where Larry was murdered at the exact time that I needed to be there? You and Skinner getting there just in time to save Marilyn and me from getting our skulls bashed in? What the *hell* does it all *mean?*"

Bill Fenton reached out his hand and laid it on Paul's shoulder, patting it twice. "I'll be damned if I know, Paul. I'll be trying to answer that question when I attempt to make out some kind of a believable report. Maybe your psychologist friend can help you with your answer. In the meantime, I better beat feet out of here, or that nurse will be lighting into me again. You go ahead and get some rest. I'll be back tomorrow and we'll talk some more."

As Fenton turned to leave, Paul asked; "Bill……..you knew he'd do this, didn't you?"

The poker face gave no indication of Chief Fenton's mindset in this matter, as he bluntly replied; "I thought he'd run."

Police Chief William Fenton walked out of the room, coming face to face with Mary Ellen. He smiled and said; "He should rest easy, now." Then he walked away. Mary Ellen entered Paul's room, wanting to ask what would make him rest easier, but Paul had already closed his eyes and fallen fast asleep.

She pulled a chair close to his bed, sat down and reached for his hand. Gently, she caressed him, at the same time lowering her head, until it rested on the mattress, next to her husband's chest. Letting out a long relaxing sigh, Mary Ellen, in turn, closed her eyes and whispered a soft prayer of thanks.

CHAPTER TWENTY TWO

8:15 a.m., Saturday, September 4, 2004

    Mary Ellen sat at the kitchen table, drinking a cup of freshly-brewed coffee and reading the newspaper. Paul had made the coffee just before going into the shower. She listened carefully, fearing he might become dizzy and fall. The doctor had warned him not to try to shower, as turning around in such a small space could lead to a dizzy spell. But Paul had been insistent, claiming that washing while sitting in front of a sink just wasn't doing it for him. She relaxed a little, as she heard the water turn off and the sound of Paul drying off with a towel. Then, she heard the clatter of his razor, as it swished back and forth in the water. Soon, Paul emerged, towel around his waist and said; "Oh, good! You're all dressed. I told Marilyn we'd be there at eight thirty."
    Mary Ellen looked up from the paper and replied; "Then you better get moving, nature boy, or we'll be late."
    "I'll be ready in a jiffy."
    Paul ambled into their bedroom, where he got dressed in a few minutes and returned to the kitchen. Mary gave him a disapproving look.
    "Paul, I'm really not sure this is such a good idea. Marilyn just got home from the hospital yesterday. Maybe this will be too much for her."
    Grabbing the keys to Mary Ellen's car off the table, Paul handed them to his wife and answered; "Mare, *she's* the one who asked *us* to take her there, remember?"

Without answering, Mary Ellen took the keys from Paul and they headed out to the car.

As soon as they had backed out of their driveway, Mary Ellen pulled the car back in and shut off the ignition.

"What's wrong?" asked Paul.

"Paul, there's something I have to say to you." Mary lowered her head, as she carefully chose her words. "I'm so ashamed of myself for……..not trusting you. I really thought you were losing your mind and I……."

"Whoa, stop right there!" Paul leaned over and placed the back of his right hand on his wife's cheek, lowering it to her chin and gently rubbing, as he continued.

"Sweetheart, *I* thought I was losing my mind too, so don't beat yourself up over a silly thing like that."

"You don't understand, Paul! I was angry with you, because you seemed so……..fixated on listening to that voice, that I thought you were going to……..either kill yourself, or get yourself killed. Along with that, I was a wreck with worrying about Marilyn and what happened at work and…….."

"Mare, do you think anyone else would have, or *could* have handled it any better than you did?"

Without waiting for an answer, Paul continued; "My God, you were scared half to death by your boss at work, you injured your arm, your best friend was missing, with the evidence not looking good and your husband was telling you that he had to go to a cemetery in the middle of the night because a voice in his head was telling him to! I think you did pretty damn well keeping it together as well as you did."

"I just wish I had trusted you more. I've always trusted you and you've never given me reason not to, but that *voice*; that was just *too* much for me to handle!"

"Mare, don't you understand? The voice……..that wasn't some figment of my imagination, or some alien being trying to take over my body. The voice was ME! It had to be some part of my subconscious mind. Think about it! The first time I heard it, was when it warned me in my dream not to go near Crazy Roger's house. I didn't remember why, but my subconscious mind sure did! Remember how I told you that Nathan felt as though I possessed some sort of extra-sensory perception. He was right about that! I knew that something would happen at the cemetery! Only, I didn't know what. But, I knew it was something bad and that I needed to be there, to help, in some way, to either prevent it from happening, or……..I just *knew* that I was needed there! That was the……..sixth sense, or whatever you want to call it. I'm telling you, Mare, I felt that very strongly. For God sakes, I *saw* that guy in my *dreams*, the guy that kidnapped Marilyn and tried to kill her. I *saw him at that same cemetery* in my *dreams*! How do you think I felt when I was going through this? I'll *tell* you how I felt Mare. I felt god dam scared, that's how! Then, when it all started to play out that night at the cemetery; *that's* when I knew it was all about a single purpose. I was *chosen* to be there. I don't know by whom, or why, but I know one thing; it couldn't have been a coincidence that you were sleeping when I left and weren't able to talk me out of going."

Mary Ellen raised her head in recognition and looked at Paul.

"If I had, my best friend……..would be……..oh, Paul!"

Paul slid closer to Mary Ellen as she turned to him.

"That's the important thing, Mare! We *got through this*! We *all* got through this! It doesn't matter how. The only thing that matters is everyone survived and I still think you're the most beautiful woman on this planet."

Mary Ellen watched as Paul's mouth spread into his famous grin. She leaned forward and kissed him fervently. It was more than enough to arouse Paul.

"Let's go back in the house and call Marilyn. We'll tell her that we're going to be a little late…….."

"Uh-uh! Your doctor said absolutely no sex until he clears you."

"First thing tomorrow, I'm going to fire his ass!"

Laughing, Mary Ellen started the car and said; "Someone is waiting for us."

The couple arrived at Marilyn's apartment on the south side of the city at eight thirty-seven. Paul struggled to get out of the small car, his left arm encased in a cast, with a sling to support the weight. Marilyn greeted them at the door of the first floor unit where she had lived for almost fifteen years. She was thin and tired looking. Across her forehead, the heavily stitched gash had helped to disfigure the pretty face that Mary Ellen remembered. Her eyes still weren't right, as one drooped slightly, thanks to damage to the socket, damage that would, hopefully, be repaired with later surgery. Mary Ellen wondered why the hospital had allowed her to go home, in this condition. Although hidden from view, Paul and Mary Ellen were aware of the multiple bandages across Marilyn's back and the painful skin grafting she had endured and would, again. Her skin had literally been torn from her back as her kidnapper had dragged her for more than eighty feet down his asphalt driveway. Still, this determined survivor flashed a bright smile, as her face lit up at the sight of her two friends.

"I thought you guys forgot about me."

Paul smiled and said; "We could *never* forget you, sweetheart."

Marilyn shrugged her shoulders and said; "Well, let's *go*, then."

Paul reached out with his right arm and steadied Marilyn as she reached back to pull her door closed. Mary Ellen, worried that her husband might lose his balance, quickly rushed between the two of them, grabbing Paul's right arm and Marilyn's left and escorted both of them to her waiting car.

Once they were all seated, Paul in the front passenger seat and Marilyn behind him, Mary Ellen steered the car in the direction of Crater Street in Sheridan. As they drove, the three chatted about the Red Sox playoff chances, the beautiful morning and the presidential race, but spoke not one word of the events of the evening of August 19th.

Soon, Mary Ellen turned onto the dirt road off Crater Street, which led down to the old burying ground. She stopped the car after driving only a few feet.

"What's wrong, Mare?" Paul asked.

Mary Ellen seemed nervous and replied; "Paul, this road is very rough looking. Are you sure it's safe to drive on?"

"It's perfectly safe, as long as you stay out of the ruts and go slow. Don't worry. If there's a problem, help is only a phone call away." Paul said this, while holding up his cell phone.

Despite her husband's reassurance, Mary Ellen was still unconvinced that the rut-filled road was navigable and proceeded, at a snail's pace, keeping the left set of wheels on the center part of the road and the right set dangerously close to the edge of the road, where one slip would send the vehicle into a two-foot drop to the swampy ditch. Paul provided encouragement to his wife as they plodded along and before long, the party found themselves pulling up to the entrance of the cemetery. Mary Ellen turned off the engine and waited. Paul turned in his seat, half-facing Marilyn and asked; "Are you sure you want to do this? Because, if you're not, we can turn around and go home and there's no harm done."

Marilyn's response was unwavering.

"I'm sure Paul. I need to see that place. For me, it represents a........ turning point, I guess, in my life and I want to see where it occurred."

Paul winked and said; "All right, then; let's do it!"

The three got out of the car, the married couple on each side of Marilyn, supporting her, as they slowly processed into the tiny enclosure. Paul could feel Marilyn's body stiffen slightly, as they neared the dug-out depression in the ground, not yet filled in by the caretaker, who no doubt awaited clearance from the police department.

Scattered leaves from the first-to-drop-them swamp maples gathered in the corners of the small pit, while a lone yellow streamer proclaiming its ominous message 'WARNING: POLICE CRIME SCENE: DO NOT CROSS!' fluttered about in the gentle morning breeze, one end still wrapped and tied around a tall headstone nearby.

As they reached the shallow hole in the ground, Paul gripped Marilyn's left arm tighter, both as an added means of support and as a gesture of comfort. In turn, Marilyn wrapped her left arm around Paul's waist and her right arm around Mary Ellen's shoulders. Silently, they stood there, three friends, brought here separately at different stages of their lives, two nearly losing theirs almost fifty years apart, at this very spot. Words were not needed; only an occasional squeeze when one would sob, involuntarily. Teardrops rolled softly down the cheeks of all three, until, for Marilyn, the emotional impact of her tribulation culminated in an unstoppable torrent of tears and she bent forward, raising both hands to her face, as she cried in loud, coughing gasps. Paul and Mary Ellen immediately encircled her, embracing her tightly.

Mary Ellen whispered to her friend; "Let it all out, sweetheart, let it all out! I understand now, why you needed to come here. We love you so much!"

Marilyn continued to convulse, her shoulders rising and falling in spasms, as her body performed its cleansing action. Her friends held on tightly, sobbing along with her, until, raising her head, she yelled out, at the top of her lungs; "YOU DIDN'T BEAT ME, YOU BASTARD! WHO'S THE LOSER NOW?"

She then lowered her head and launched into one last volley of tears, until Paul, freeing his left arm from the sling, raised the encased limb to her face, along with his right hand and cradled her face close to his.

"Honey, whatever that guy told you is bullshit! You're a beautiful person and Mare and I want you to be a big part of our lives. I want you to always remember what Bill Fenton said to you, because it's true and something that we've known all along. *You are one hell of a woman!*"

Marilyn smiled, then burst out in laughter, mixed with the still-running tears and said; "I love you guys so much!"

Paul gently started to turn her toward the entrance, as he said; "Come on, girls! Breakfast is on me."

As he turned, Paul's eyes caught something that made him hesitate. He let go of Marilyn's arm, staring at a headstone to the left of the hole.

"What is it, Paul?" Marilyn questioned.

Without answering, Paul began to move in the direction of the stone, the same stone that Larry's body had broken; the same stone that grinning man had fallen against and, in front of. which, his torment of the woman he had tried to kill, had ended.

When he had reached the stone, Paul knelt down in front of it and ran his right hand along the worn lettering. The same hole in the forest canopy that had allowed a beam of moonlight to illuminate the lettering, now made way for a bright ray of morning sunshine, emblazoning the decedent's name and highlighting the grayish-green lichen that grew so feverishly, in its attempt to conceal the letters and numbers.

Paul's mouth moved silently, as he tried to make out the rest of the name on the marker. The last time he knelt here was on that fateful night, but he remembered reading a different name. He saw now, how the pale light from the moon hadn't allowed him to see all the letters, some of which were covered in the lichen growth.

Reaching into his pants pocket, Paul pulled out a small knife, opened it and began scraping the lichen from the letters which had been covered. Mary Ellen called out to him, in alarm.

"Paul. What are you doing?"

Marilyn had begun to inch closer to where Paul was kneeling, busily scraping the crusty formation. The look of curiosity was evidenced by her turned in eyebrows.

Finally, Paul spoke.

"When I came here that night……..I had no idea *why* I was here. I just knew I *had* to *be* here. But, something……..something drew me to look at this headstone…….."

Mary Ellen, standing a short distance in back of Paul, broke in at this point.

"Paul, that's the stone that Larry was…….."

"I know, Mare. That's part of what makes this so weird. Our old baseball, the same one we used the night that Larry was killed……..it was lying on the ground……..right there."

Paul pointed to the right of the stone. Mary Ellen was confused.

"Paul, how could that have happened?"

"I'm not sure, Mare. It must have gotten kicked aside the night of Larry's murder and been covered over for all those years. It probably got uncovered when that guy was digging the hole. He wouldn't have paid any attention to it. He had more important things on his mind."

Nodding her head in understanding, Mary Ellen remarked; "It's strange that the police never found it. I would think that would have been an important piece of evidence."

Paul thought about that and said; "I guess they didn't really look all that well, did they? Anyway, I knelt down and picked up the ball and held it up to make sure it was the same ball. When I realized it was, I just stared at it for a long time, until, all of a sudden, Marilyn's hand grabbed my wrist and almost scared the life out of me. I pulled free from her hand and fell on my ass. I just sat there screaming, but as I looked around, trying to see if anything else from my dreams was going to get me, this stone……..I know this sounds crazy, but……..it was like this headstone had some sort of calming effect on me. I wanted to run away at first, but I looked at the stone again, then something caught my eye. Well, it was Marilyn's bracelet and when I saw that, I knew it was a woman that needed my help, not some kind of dream-monster out to get me. The thing is, when we started to leave just now, I got this strange feeling again, which made me look at the headstone."

Paul motioned to the two women.

"Come over here and look closer, girls."

The two women moved in behind the kneeling man, staring in curiosity at the old, battered stone. Paul reached down and picked up a handful of leaves, holding them up over some of the lettering.

"This is what I saw that night, two weeks ago, when the moonlight played a trick on me. With these leaves covering these letters, like the lichen was that night, it appears to read; 'Martha Lynden', but, when I removed the lichen, or the leaves, you can clearly see that the name of the person was Marie Therese Lynden. No big deal, right?"

Both women looked at Paul. Mary Ellen shrugged her shoulders, but Marilyn turned her eyes back to the lettering and said; "I don't understand, Paul."

"Marilyn, when my friend had his body thrown against this stone way back in 1957, the impact broke the stone into pieces. It's a thin stone and broke fairly easily. When I first looked at it, I thought it had only broken in two pieces, but look, you can see two more small cracks here, four in all, to be exact."

Paul's fingers traced their way to the origin of the first large crack, halfway up the stone to the right of center.

"Look at how this large crack runs uphill, slanting to the left side of the stone. It splits her last name, which was centered below her first and middle name, in two, leaving the L, the Y and the N on one side, then continues on up through the first name, slicing cleanly between the I and the E, which leaves seven letters on the first large broken piece, M-A-R-I-L-Y-N."

Her eyes widening in surprise, Marilyn said; "Oh, Paul; that *is* weird."

Paul turned and looked straight at Marilyn.

"It gets weirder. Look at this."

Shaping the thumb and index finger on his right hand into a v-shape over a similar crack on the stone, Paul traced the outline of the crack so the women could follow it.

"See how this crack starts at the same spot as the first, about halfway up and just right of center, but it runs almost straight uphill. It removes the D-E-N in Lynden, the E in Marie and the T in Therese. This piece of stone had broken off completely, because the crack goes all the way through and you can see the bits of masonry repair cement, which was used to literally glue it back together. Next, you can see that the third crack also ran through a section that had broken off, see the cement filler. This section contained the letters S and E at the end of her middle name, Therese. Finally, the fourth crack doesn't involve any lettering, but ran from the lower part of the third crack, where it formed a point, inward, to the middle of the stone, where it petered out. The point, or arrow, if you will, aims to the right."

Paul arose and took a step back, where he stood between the two women.

"What you're left with is a bunch of letters; the only ones left on the main part of the headstone, the only part that remained intact on the night that Larry was murdered. I'll show you what it must have looked like."

Paul reached down on the ground and picked up a handful of the moist, dark soil. He rubbed it over the two sections of the stone that had completely broken off, which effectively obliterated the letters on those pieces. He then resumed his position between the women. Marilyn and Mary Ellen read the message aloud, in unison.

"M-A-R-I-L-Y-N ……..H-E-R-E".

Both women raised their hands to their mouths, attempting, unsuccessfully, to stifle their gasps, as they saw that the arrow pointed directly at the center of the makeshift grave. Marilyn glanced over at Mary Ellen and neither said a word. It was Mary Ellen who finally said to Marilyn; "This is either an amazing co-incidence or something we couldn't possibly expect to understand; how this message was visible forty seven years ago."

Marilyn responded; "I'm going to go with the first theory, Hon; the second one is just too much for me."

Now, they looked up at Paul, standing between them, who shrugged and said; "I told you it was weird."

The three friends turned simultaneously, as Paul flipped his sling over his shoulder, raised his encased left arm up and around Marilyn's shoulder and his right around Mary Ellen's and looked up at the cloudless blue sky. He took a deep breath of the cool September air and announced; "It *really is* good to be alive!"

Then they walked away. As they did, Marilyn looked over her shoulder one last time, as the others held up.

"Do you need more time?" Paul asked.

Marilyn's response was quick and to the point, as she shook her head negatively.

"I'm dying for a good cup of coffee."

THE END

About the Author

Known in his locality as a free-lance writer, Jim has had several of his articles published in local magazines and newspapers. Additionally, a moving article he wrote of his thoughts on the 9-11 disaster was widely circulated throughout America. This is his first attempt at a novel.

Jim lives with his wife, in a small New England town.